High Country

OTHER BOOKS AND AUDIO BOOKS
BY JENNIE HANSEN:

Abandoned

All I Hold Dear

Beyond Summer Dreams

The Bracelet

The Emerald

The Topaz

The Ruby

Breaking Point

Chance Encounter

Code Red

Coming Home

High Stakes

Macady

Some Sweet Day

Wild Card

High Country

a novel

JENNIE HANSEN

Covenant Communications, Inc.

Cover image: "Herd of Horses and Cowboys" © www.alamy.com

Cover design copyrighted 2009 by Covenant Communications, Inc.

Published by Covenant Communications, Inc.
American Fork, Utah

This is a work of fiction. The characters, names, incidents, places, and dialogue are products of the
author's imagination, and are not to be construed as real.

Printed in Canada
First Printing: January 2009

15 14 13 12 11 10 09   10 9 8 7 6 5 4 3 2 1

ISBN 10: 1-59811-589-8
ISBN 13: 978-1-59811-589-5

This book is dedicated to my best friend,
my husband, Boyd Hansen.

one

LAURA SAT ON the floor in the midst of stacks of carefully sorted papers and boxes. *Aunt Alice definitely could have been classified as a pack rat,* she thought. It had only been a week since her great-aunt's death, but she and her cousin, Bruce, were both anxious to clear the house of Aunt Alice's personal effects so they could sell them and get on with their lives. As the only heirs named in the will, Bruce and Laura were responsible for their aunt's possessions, but the task was proving more daunting than they had expected.

"Hey, look at this!" Bruce dashed into the room, a box under one arm and a sheaf of papers in his other hand. He dropped the box to the floor, and Laura's neat piles scattered. Ignoring her grimace, Bruce waved some papers under her nose. A broad grin was plastered across his face. "It seems there are a few things I never knew about my dear cousin—like your ranch . . . and your *husband*."

"What?" Laura looked at him with bewildered disapproval. "What are you talking about? You know perfectly well I'm not married, and I don't own anything but a half share in this house, which, if you remember, is why we're cleaning it. C'mon, Bruce. Considering I had to take time off work for this, we don't have time for your lame jokes. We need to finish this and get the key to the realtor. I barely have enough money to pay next month's utility bills until we sell this place. And we can't sell it until we've cleaned out all of Aunt Alice's stuff."

Simply saying Aunt Alice's name out loud brought a shimmer of tears to Laura's eyes. Aunt Alice was technically their great-aunt, but they'd never called her that. She had raised Laura's mother as well as Bruce's father briefly. Then later, after Laura's mom's marriage had gone bad, Aunt Alice had taken her and Laura in. Laura had little memory of any other home. Selling it was actually painful for her, but she didn't see an alternative.

"This is no joke." Bruce crouched down to Laura's level and laid two of the documents he carried in front of her. "This is a will, and this is a marriage certificate with your name on it. Here, look at this." With one finger, he jabbed at the first document. "This paper is the last will and testament of Jacob Warren Hendrickson. Your father, right?"

Laura started to murmur her affirmative answer, but Bruce went on without waiting for her response. "It says right here that your father owned a house as well as fifty percent of the High Country Ranch in Idaho, and that he left his share—including land, stock, machinery, buildings, mineral rights, and water rights—to his only child, Laura Hendrickson. That's you," he pointed out unnecessarily.

"Let me see that!" She didn't remember much about her father, but she was certain he hadn't left any property to her. Jake Hendrickson had died eight years ago, and neither Aunt Alice nor her attorney had mentioned a will, property, or even what had become of his meager belongings. It had never occurred to her to ask.

Jerking the paper out of her reach, Bruce pointed at the second document. "This is a marriage certificate for Laura Hendrickson and Paul MacPherson Burgoyne. Who is Paul MacPherson Burgoyne?"

"I don't know. Give that to me!" There was a buzzing in her ears as her mind swirled in confusion.

Bruce released a shrill whistle through his teeth as his fingers jabbed the paper without surrendering it to Laura.

"Look at this date! Talk about a child bride. You must have been only fifteen years old when you married this Burgoyne guy. And he was twenty!"

"Bruce, for the last time, I am not married to anyone. You know that. There's been some mistake. Now, who do these documents really belong to?" She wished Bruce wouldn't tease her at a time like this. She'd never appreciated practical jokes—even in the best of times.

"I'm not kidding, Laura. I think these really are yours—that or really good fakes. But at least some of the information lines up with what we know is true. Here's your birth certificate and your father's death certificate." Bruce stacked the documents on top of the pile he was making. "Based on these dates, you got married just a day before your father died. This last paper is a copy of the deed to the High Country Ranch. And see here . . ." He pressed his finger to a spot on the paper. "This will lists Jacob Warren Hendrickson and Paul Harold Burgoyne as equal owners of the High Country Ranch in southern Idaho and specifies that in the event of either partner's death, that partner's share goes to his only child. Your name and the Burgoyne heir's name are listed here. Hey, the Burgoyne heir is the same guy you're supposedly married to. This just gets weirder and weirder."

Laura moved so she could look over Bruce's shoulder to read the paper he was scrutinizing. She began a tentative perusal, looking for signs that would prove the document to be a fake. *Should either child die before producing children of his or her own, his or her portion reverts to that child's spouse or designated heir.* The more she stared at the papers the more certain she was that Bruce hadn't just concocted them as a joke. And yet she couldn't see how they could be legitimate either.

"Where did you find these?"

"I almost missed them." There was excitement in Bruce's voice. "This box is smaller than the others, and it was hidden behind a pile of newspapers and a bunch of junk on the top shelf of Aunt Alice's armoire. It was like she didn't want anyone to find it."

"Well, some of this stuff may be the real thing, but the rest just can't be. And even if this will is authentic, I don't see how it matters now. Aunt Alice said Daddy was nearly broke, that he didn't even have insurance to help with my medical bills. She said that she had to pay for Mom's medical care and burial, then my care, and that Daddy's partner took his body back to Idaho for burial after the accident because she couldn't afford another burial expense."

"You were in that accident too, but you never talk about it. Weren't you on your way to live with your dad when it happened?"

"Yes." She didn't elaborate. She had trained herself a long time ago not to think about the summer of her fifteenth birthday. Losing both parents and enduring an accident that led to years of physical therapy had left her with no desire to revisit the events of that long ago summer. Like a soldier with traumatic brain injury, she had almost no memory of the accident or the events surrounding it. She hadn't needed Aunt Alice's admonition that she try not to recall any part of that painful time.

"Why didn't I ever meet your father?" Bruce leaned back and watched her with obvious curiosity.

"I was so young when my parents separated; *I* barely remember my father. He didn't make many visits here after the divorce, and mother wouldn't allow me to travel to Idaho alone. It was like meeting a stranger when he showed up to take me home with him a few weeks after Mom died. He didn't want to stick around here, so we left the same day."

"I'm surprised Aunt Alice let you go."

"She didn't let me go willingly. She objected, but it didn't do any good. My father had papers giving him custody of me.

The two of them had a big fight, then my dad packed a suitcase for me, and I left with him, his partner, and another man who had come with him, though I don't recall either of them. Aunt Alice said she had a bad feeling about me going with my father. It seems her premonition was right. We were driving through Nevada when the driver of a semitruck fell asleep. His truck crossed the centerline, hitting the back of our car where my father and I were sitting. As you know, Dad died at the scene. I was taken to a little clinic in Elko, and later I was flown to Primary Children's Medical Center in Salt Lake City. I stayed there almost a month. Then, when I was released from the hospital, Aunt Alice brought me back here. The whole experience is hazy in my mind. The doctor Aunt Alice took me to for follow-up care said I may never remember much about the accident, but familiar places and objects could help me recall a lot of the events in my life before the accident happened. You know what I was like—for a while the most common words from my mouth were, 'Sorry, I don't remember.'"

"This marriage license was issued in Nevada. You must have married this Burgoyne guy before the accident. Maybe y—"

"I don't think I would forget something like a husband! All of this is too far-fetched for me. How about we get back to work and deal with the fictional documents later?"

"Uh, there's more." Bruce looked apologetic. He removed the lid from the box and set it in front of her. She felt reluctant to look, but when she finally mustered the courage to glance down, she was surprised to see a ring box, a journal, and more papers. With shaking fingers she reached for the small box and carefully lifted the lid. She recognized the rings at once. They were her mother's, and she hadn't seen them for years. With them was a man's ring that matched her mother's wedding band exactly.

Laura couldn't recall much about those years when her mother was still alive, but she remembered that her Mom had continued to wear her rings until the day she died, even though she'd been separated from her husband a long time. The fact that her dad's ring had wound up in Aunt Alice's possession suggested he had been wearing it at the time of the accident. She wondered why Aunt Alice hadn't sold the rings to help pay medical bills.

She picked up the journal and opened it to the first page where she read, *This book belongs to April Wilson. I am ten years old.* She hadn't known her mother kept a journal. She hugged the book to her chest, thinking how little she really knew about her mother and how sketchy her few memories were. What a wonderful opportunity the journal would give her to learn more about her mother.

"When I opened the box, this fell out." Bruce interrupted her thoughts to hand her two pieces of paper. She looked at them and read the same words at the top of each one. Scanning the page, she read, *The Church of Jesus Christ of Latter-day Saints, Baptism and Confirmation.* The top certificate had her mother's name on it and a date several years earlier than the one with her own name on it. She smiled as the words on the page brought back a distant memory.

"When I was little, Mom sometimes took me to church. Just now I remembered the day she took me to be baptized. It was right after I turned eight. She bought me a white dress, and she made me promise not to tell Aunt Alice. I think it was the only secret we ever managed to keep from her, though it seems she found out eventually, since she had this in her box."

"I can see why your mother didn't want Aunt Alice to find out." Bruce rocked backward, laughing as though he were enjoying a great joke. "It's pretty funny, really," he spluttered. "You're a Mormon! And you've kept it a secret for almost sixteen years, even from me."

"A Mormon? No, see right here. It says *The Church of Jesus Christ of Latter-day Saints.* Mom used to talk to me about Jesus, and she said it was important for me to be baptized into His church."

"I always knew Aunt Alice sheltered you from the real world, but haven't you ever heard that this church you joined not only has an official name but also a nickname more people recognize? The Church of Jesus Christ of Latter-day Saints and the Mormon Church are the same thing."

"No, that can't be. Why would Mom be a Mormon? Why would she want me to be a Mormon?" Laura couldn't help feeling betrayed. Aunt Alice had hated Mormons. She said they weren't Christians and that they did secret, evil things. She had devoted much of her life to writing anti-Mormon pamphlets and films. Laura's mom had refused to take part in any of Aunt Alice's ventures, but she had never explained to Laura that they themselves were Mormons. Surely Mormons couldn't be as bad as Aunt Alice claimed if her mother had become one. She wondered, though, why her mother had stopped taking her to church. Did she discover she had been tricked into joining? Somehow Laura doubted that.

"I wonder if my dad knows you're a Mormon," Bruce said, a wide grin creeping across his face.

"I don't know who knows or why it even matters. Obviously even I didn't know."

"It matters because a long time ago our ancestors left Norway to become Mormons in Utah. Those old immigrants crossed the plains in covered wagons and did the whole pioneer bit. Aunt Alice lived in Salt Lake City when she was young and was even baptized. But then her father got in a big fight with one of the leaders over a piece of property Great-Grandpa sold for the Church. He had invested the money he received for it and made a fortune. It seems his leader—apparently called a 'bishop'—thought the money belonged to the Church while Great-Grandpa said only the fair market value of the land belonged to the Church. He became angry and left the Church because he thought the bishop was trying to cheat him out of money he earned through his own ingenuity and investing skills.

"Great-Grandpa forbade his wife and children to have anything to do with the Mormon Church. When Aunt Alice sided with her father, her fiancé broke their engagement because he didn't want to marry someone who wasn't in good standing with the Church. As time went by, Great-Grandpa and Aunt Alice got angrier and began devoting their time and the fortune he had amassed to denounce the Church. Eventually, they left Utah and moved here to San Francisco. Alice's brother—our grandfather—didn't get involved in their campaign against the Mormons, but he never had anything good to say about them either. As you know, he and his wife died young, leaving your mother and my dad orphans to be raised by Aunt Alice."

"How do you know all this, but no one ever mentioned any of it to me?" Laura's resentment of her quiet upbringing rose to the surface. Her mother and Aunt Alice had home-schooled her, and she'd had little contact with children her own age other than her cousin, Bruce, as she'd grown up. As a child, she'd both loved and resented Bruce. He was only a year older, but he'd always seemed to know things she didn't. Still, without him, she would have been without any playmates, and without him and his parents now, she'd have no place to live. Sometimes his protectiveness and teasing annoyed her, and sometimes she was grateful that he seemed to like her even though she wasn't like his other friends.

"Mother told me as much as she knew about Dad's family in spite of Aunt Alice's desire to keep us both in the dark," Bruce admitted. "Mom believed it was wrong to shelter you so much. She thinks—and I agree—that going to college was the best thing in the world for you. It helped you come out of your shell and broadened your viewpoints."

"Does Uncle Alec feel the same way your mother does, or did he side with Aunt Alice?"

"Dad doesn't have any use for religion, but he refused to go along with his aunt's views on education or anything else. He said that when he and your mother lived with Aunt Alice was the most miserable time of his life. He was glad he was only there for a couple months; he just wishes he could've taken April with him when he left. Dad always referred to his aunt as 'dingy' and—forgive me for repeating this—said your mother must have been too, or she wouldn't have gone back to live with Aunt Alice when she left your father. He said even if her marriage didn't work out, it would have been better for the both of you if she'd gotten her own place."

"I don't think she could have afforded to rent an apartment. To stay close to me she refused to travel, so her concert schedule was limited, which, in turn, reduced her income. She and Aunt Alice always insisted on nice clothing and excellent music teachers for me, but otherwise, I always got the feeling money was tight."

"Dad offered to pay your tuition at the school I attended and to buy your uniforms, but Aunt Alice wouldn't hear of it."

Laura had certainly never heard about that, but there was no sense in worrying about it now. She took a deep breath. "So, are you going to hate me for being a Mormon?"

"No. It doesn't matter to me." He paused, then asked, "I suppose you know your father was a Mormon? That was one of the reasons Aunt Alice hated him. He was most likely the reason your mom became a Mormon and why she wanted you to be one."

"Are you sure?" She could tell from the pitying look in his eyes that he wasn't teasing, and she felt a sudden surge of anger. "It isn't fair that everyone kept so many secrets from me." Hearing her own whining voice, she decided she sounded like a petulant child and immediately scolded herself. It was important to her that Bruce see her as mature and ready to be on her own, even though she'd accepted his parents' offer of a home after Aunt Alice's death. The thought of living alone frightened her, but she wasn't a helpless child—even if Aunt Alice had always treated her like one. She had a bachelor's degree in business but had been working only part-time for a nonprofit performing arts foundation so that she could take care of her aunt. She hoped that someday soon she'd be able to support herself and get an apartment of her own.

"I'll read this later," she said as she returned the journal to the box. Perhaps it would give her some of the answers she needed to the questions she had about her past.

"I don't think so." Bruce reached past her to pull the journal from the box once more. He flipped through the pages, revealing that more than half of them had been torn from the book.

Laura was shocked and disappointed by the mutilation of the book. "Why do you think Mother removed all those pages?" she asked.

"Your mother might not have been the one who tore them out." Bruce watched her, appearing uncertain what reaction to expect from her.

Admittedly, she hadn't been entirely happy living with Aunt Alice, but a sense of loyalty had her flying to her great-aunt's defense each time Bruce made a negative comment about her. She bit her tongue to hold back a protest.

Laura's head felt as though it were about to explode, and her legs were cramped from sitting on the floor so long. She might have to quit sorting for today; she could hardly read the papers any longer

Bruce lowered his voice, speaking gently as though cushioning his words. "I think we need to make an appointment with Wayne Sylvester, Aunt Alice's old attorney. It seems to me that you need a lot more answers than I can give you."

"Aunt Alice's attorney isn't named Wayne Sylvester."

"I know he's not the current attorney, but he was Aunt Alice's attorney for most of her life, and he drew up her will. I think he'll have far more answers than we'll get from the lawyer we've been meeting with. He started representing her when she sued the trucking company responsible for your accident. But I have a feeling we should talk to Mr. Sylvester."

two

"I'M SORRY, MAC. It would mean my job to cash your check."
The bank teller looked apologetic.

Mac's eyes narrowed. He didn't know when he had ever
been so angry. Every check he'd written in the past week had
bounced, and now a teller he'd known since they were kids was
refusing to cash his check. Whatever was going on had to stop.
He had a ranch to run, and he couldn't do it without operating funds, and he wasn't going to allow some computer
glitch to interfere with what he needed to do. He needed to
get his grain harvested. Now!

"I-I'm sorry. There's nothing I can do. Your account has
been frozen by court order. If you would like to speak to the
manager, I'll direct you to his office."

"I would appreciate that, Karen. Thank you." He turned
away, stiff with embarrassment and anger, to follow the clerk's
directions to the manager's office. He squared his shoulders.
He'd straighten out the matter, then . . . No, he wouldn't lose
his temper. Someone had just made a mistake, pushed a wrong
button somewhere.

Ten minutes later, Mac slapped his hat on his head and
strode angrily out the door. The starter on his old pickup
truck scraped futilely for several seconds before the engine
roared to life. The gears growled their resistance as he tore
down Blue Lakes Boulevard. Unfortunately, the bank manager

hadn't had any more answers for him than the teller had. His only recourse was to pay a visit to his attorney. Mac had work to do, and he did not look forward to spending all afternoon in Twin Falls chatting with Mr. Cooper.

By the time Mac left his lawyer's office, he was not just angry but also confused. It seemed to be a case of identity theft. He'd heard of that but never thought it would happen to him. But he still couldn't understand why the state attorney general's office would order his bank account frozen. He paid his taxes, never hired illegals, and even though he hated bookkeeping, he kept meticulous books on his setup. He owned the ranch free and clear, and the only other person authorized to use his ranch account was his father, though with his heavy political schedule, Mac's dad hadn't involved himself with the business end of the ranch since deeding it over to Mac after his heart attack eight years ago.

There had been extensive fire damage that year, so the years since had been lean. He had mortgaged out of necessity, but with hard work and careful planning, he had paid off the loans and even taken a small profit last fall. He was headed for more lean years now if southern Idaho didn't get rain soon and a decent snowfall this winter. There was a little money in the bank, enough to see him through until his wheat was harvested. But he couldn't get his grain harvested if he couldn't pay the combine crew. He slammed a doubled-up fist against the steering wheel. Old Cooper's rambling explanation was sheer nonsense.

Three hours later the truck wove around hills, moving steadily toward the ranch. Mac's jaw tightened as he surveyed the dry land. There wasn't much grass this year. An unprecedented dry stretch was wreaking havoc in the area, causing ranchers to ruthlessly thin their herds to stave off buying hay so early and to keep their breeding stock healthy to face another year. Many of the ranchers were facing bankruptcy. Mac vowed his ranch would be among the survivors.

A glance at the gas gauge convinced him he ought to stop in Snowville. Flying J and Chevron were the only places to buy gas in town, and Flying J looked to be a shorter wait than Chevron. The pumps were all busy, so he pulled up to wait his turn.

As Mac waited, his irritation grew. Coop's story was just too fantastic. After all these years, someone was trying to claim Jake's share of the High Country! As soon as he got back to the ranch he would have his dad get in touch with a real attorney in Boise to stop this nonsense before it went any further. It was time to replace Coop. The old boy was better at playing cowboy than representing Mac's ranch.

Fuming, Mac drummed his fingers against the steering wheel. He turned his head. It might be faster to go next door. One look at the line of vehicles backed up at the pumps at Chevron convinced him otherwise.

Finally! The oversized truck in front of him inched away from the pump. Settling his cowboy hat more firmly on his head, Mac hunched forward and reached for the ignition key. Before the engine caught, a flashy little red Triumph sporting California plates zipped toward him and into the spot vacated by the truck.

"California driver! I might have known. But even he should have seen there's a lineup over here. Who does he think he is?" Mac struggled to control his anger. He didn't always have such a short fuse, but this day had been enough to try the patience of Job. His hand clenched the crown of his hat to tug it lower over his eyes. Beneath the brim, he glared at the young man stepping out of the little car. The driver's blond-tipped curls were windblown, and his pale blue, knit shirt and khaki walking shorts emphasized the smooth bronze of his sculpted muscles. He flashed a broad grin that showed plenty of gleaming white teeth. Mac quashed a sudden urge to knock out a few of those teeth.

Then Mac saw something that made him sit up straighter. The blond's companion stepped from her side of the car. He felt an urge to whistle like a seventeen-year-old kid. He seldom gave women more than a passing glance, but this one captured his attention. She didn't look as though she spent as much time in the sun as her friend. He couldn't help noticing that her body curved in all the right places, and he eyed her long, bare legs appreciatively. She wore white cotton shorts coupled with a bright red top and carried a large bag draped over one arm. Her face was framed by perfectly cut hair in a rich dark chocolate. He'd always been partial to that shade of hair color.

His eyes lingered on the woman's face. There was something about her. He shook his head as though clearing his vision. He couldn't see her eyes. They were covered by an oversized pair of dark glasses, but her face was oval with well-defined cheekbones and an impishly upturned nose. For just a moment she stirred some vague half-memory.

The woman wandered inside the store while the young man took his time washing his windshield. Mac glanced at his watch, checked the other vehicles—which seemed no closer to departing—then climbed out of his truck. He might as well get a drink to cool both his parched throat and his temper while he waited.

Inside the convenience store, his eyes sought and found the dark-haired young woman. She was standing at the back of the store filling two oversized drink cups. Chiding himself for acting like a schoolboy when he had more important matters to be thinking about, he drifted back to the drink machines. He picked up a cup, filled it with ice, and then shoved it under the soft drink dispenser without taking his eyes off the woman.

He liked the way her hair gave a little bounce as she ducked her head. She had nice hands, too, small and graceful. Her fingernails were nicely groomed with a hint of pale polish. He was glad she didn't go for weird colors or long red daggers like some women he knew. And no ring! *What is the matter with me? Why should I care! She's a beautiful woman, sure, but just a tourist passing through!*

Suddenly, she reached for straws and her bag jostled his arm. Mac jerked his hand back. Foaming soda dripped from his hand and ran down the sides of his cup, splashing to the floor.

"Oh! I'm sorry. Here." The woman, who had so thoroughly distracted him, reached for a stack of paper napkins. She shoved them toward him before turning to walk away. Mac took a step after her. His foot slid a little in the puddle made by his overfilled cup, sloshing more soda onto the floor. He dropped the napkins to the floor and with one foot moved them back and forth across the puddle before topping off his drink again. All the way to the cash register one boot left sticky tracks. Each step sounded like an old cow pulling a hoof out of mud. He winced and kept walking.

Emerging into the bright sunlight a few minutes later, he watched the blond man hold open the car door for the brunette, giving her shoulder an affectionate pat before squeezing past the gas pumps on the driver's side to return to his seat. Mac's eyes narrowed. Seeing the guy's hand on the woman irritated him. He knew he was overreacting. *She doesn't mind.*

Returning to his truck, he waited impatiently for the car to move. Instead of leaving immediately, however, the couple took their time. The woman pulled out a map, which they pored over while nibbling on sandwiches and sipping from the oversized paper cups. Their heads were close together, too close together. *What's the matter with me? Why should I care?* Mac thought again.

"Enough is enough!" Mac jerked open the truck door and stalked toward the sports car. Placing both hands on the passenger side door, he leaned forward. A faint whiff of the woman's perfume reached his senses, making him almost dizzy. For some reason this made him feel angrier.

"Get this car moving!" he roared. "Or do you plan to block this pump all day?"

* * *

"What . . ." Laura spun around when she heard the man shouting at them. Her drink went flying. She watched in horror as ice cubes and a wet stain spread down the man's blue denim work shirt. Her eyes made contact with heavily muscled arms, tanned a deep bronze, leaning against the door inches from her head. Raising her eyes, she looked aghast into stormy gray eyes. He was the same cowboy she had jostled inside the store a few minutes ago, but he no longer looked as pleasant as she had previously thought.

"You . . . I . . ." What could she say?

"It was an accident," Bruce cut in, while with one arm he pulled Laura closer in a protective gesture. "Your shouting startled her."

"I—I'm sorry," Laura stammered. "I didn't mean to . . ." She lifted her eyes apologetically, but he just glared back. The struggle to control his temper contorted his features. She dropped her eyes to see his fists clenched tightly against the side of the car. He seemed to exert great control as he opened his hands and stepped back.

"You obviously have nothing better to do with your time than waste it, but I have work to do. Get out of my way before I make you wish you had!"

"All right! Don't get bent out of shape." Bruce leaned forward to start his engine. "Neanderthal," he muttered under his breath as the engine purred into life, but Laura heard him, and she suspected the cowboy did too. Bruce gunned the engine, sending the little car flying from the station.

three

"ARE YOU OKAY?" Bruce asked a few minutes later.

"I'm fine." She smiled, attempting to appear composed. "You worry about me too much."

Laura kept replaying the awful moment when the entire contents of her drink had drenched the front of the cowboy. But not even shock had kept her from noticing how well his lean muscles fit into faded blue denim.

Suddenly she giggled. "Actually, Bruce, I'd met that man before." In response to Bruce's questioning glance, she explained about already dumping Coke on the cowboy inside the store a few minutes earlier. "I can't believe I did that twice. My nervousness has turned me into a klutz."

"Next time you feel like flinging ice cold soda pop on someone, pick on someone your own size. That cowboy looked like he might shoot first and ask questions later." Bruce broke into a chuckle. "I truly understand the meaning of icy rage now. Did you see that cowboy's face when you hit him with your Coke?"

Laura's mind could not, in fact, forget the face in question—sharply chiseled features; dark, highly arched eyebrows; a firm chin; a straight nose with just a little hump at its bridge; and a wide, straight mouth. Laura was annoyed just how easily she recalled every little detail. Here was a man who probably got more than his fair share of feminine attention.

"A man who is obviously accustomed to calling the shots and thinking only of himself," Laura thought aloud. *Like Daddy*, she added silently, remembering all the letters her father hadn't answered and the birthdays and holidays that had come and gone without any contact. She found herself becoming angry. "Arrogant, macho cowboys—I can do without them!" She knew her anger was out of proportion to the situation at hand. Her sense of fairness reminded her that she and Bruce had been at fault by inconsiderately sitting at the pump so long. But this wasn't just about the gas station incident anymore.

"What does this Burgoyne have against me anyway?" Laura asked abruptly.

"Take it easy, Laura. We promised your lawyer we would sit down calmly with your father's partner and give him a chance to explain his side of things. Mr. Sylvester has already taken steps to ensure that the guy can't hide the ranch's assets."

"I know, but I get upset every time I think about what that guy nearly got away with."

"Remember, we're only going to talk with him and make arrangements to meet with his attorney. After that, we'll let Mr. Sylvester know when to fly in to meet with all of us. It's simple really."

"It sounds simple, but I can't help feeling nervous. Mr. Burgoyne is going to be angry when he discovers he isn't going to get away with claiming Dad's half of the ranch."

"Do you remember anything about what this Burgoyne fellow is like? You met him when he came with your father to get you after your mother died, didn't you?"

"Yes. He and his son did come with Daddy, but I don't remember any of it clearly, except how upset Aunt Alice was. She said my father was a rough, arrogant cowboy with no concept of a young girl's needs and that if he had any regard for me he would leave me with her. She reminded me of how insensitive he was to mother's need for music and how he wouldn't buy her a piano so she could practice. Can you imagine a concert pianist without a piano?"

"She should have taken her own piano with her when she got married."

"Do you think she even knew that the piano in Aunt Alice's house was hers?" Laura shook her head, still feeling confusion and uncertainty from her recent talk with Mr. Sylvester. "I'm sure she thought what I did, that the piano belonged to Aunt Alice. Aunt Alice must have believed it was hers too, since it first belonged to her father and she'd played it since she was a young girl." She stared out the window of the swiftly moving little car until she felt she could speak calmly.

"Bruce, I still don't understand all of this. Mr. Sylvester said Aunt Alice paid off all of those medical bills, both mine and mother's, with large checks, and there was still a considerable amount of money left in her account. And why didn't I know that my father paid child support all those years? For some reason Mom never spent any of it. It's all there in an account with my name on it, tens of thousands of dollars. And there's a trust fund in my name with a stipend withdrawn monthly. There was no need for us to live so frugally. I always thought Mom and I were dependent on Aunt Alice's money, but it seems to have been the other way around. It's just so strange. Aunt Alice said there was no money for me to go away to college, and she grumbled about my expenses at the university in the city."

"I have no idea why the money situation was so messed up. I asked Mom what she knew about it, and she's as confused as we are. She had always assumed that when our grandfather died, my father was named as the only heir, with April getting nothing. But now we know that the court placed his fortune in a trust for each of his children that they couldn't touch until they were twenty-five years old or married. Your mother seems to have passed the trust fund on to you with a similar stipulation, as far as the age goes at least. Mom said, too, that your mother received compensation for the concerts she performed before her illness became too advanced, so I guess some of the money came from those."

"Why wasn't I told my father was part owner of a large ranch and that he left his share to me?"

"I asked my mother about that, too. She said when your mother first took you to Aunt Alice's you cried a lot and threw temper tantrums, demanding to go back to the ranch. Your mother probably thought you would adjust faster if the ranch was never mentioned again. Aunt Alice was probably too worried about you to speak of your inheritance after the accident, and in time it just slipped her mind. She was getting pretty old. Now, tell me about the Burgoynes, junior and senior."

"The only thing I remember about them is that they were taller and thinner than my father. Other than that, all I know is their names."

"That's not much to know about your husband." Bruce grinned. "Wow! Do you think that marriage certificate means you can access all of that money now instead of waiting until you're twenty-five?"

"That marriage certificate is phony, and you know it!" Laura snapped. The joke was wearing thin.

"You were with them two whole days before the accident happened, and you weren't a little kid. You should remember more than that," Bruce continued with single-minded determination.

"I was fifteen, but you know it's not that easy."

"I know it's hard for you to remember things, but I know you have avoided even thinking about the accident. Try to remember everything you can. It might be important." Bruce took his eyes off the road for just a moment to meet her eyes.

"All right." She sighed. She'd learned a long time ago not to argue with Bruce when he got stuck on an idea he wished to pursue. She closed her eyes for a moment and was surprised to realize she actually did recall some details. "I think traveling may be jogging my memory," she said. "I remember traveling for hours and being hot and tired. We stopped for the night at a motel with a swimming pool. I went swimming, and there was a guy a few years older than me already in the pool. His wet hair kept getting in his eyes, and he shoved it back with his hand. We talked some—about horses, I think. And before you ask, I don't know if he was Paul Burgoyne's son or not, but I think he might have been."

"You're doing fine. Keep talking." Bruce smiled, offering her encouragement.

"It was still dark when we left the next morning. I fell asleep, leaning against my father's shoulder. The accident itself is pretty fuzzy. Neither Daddy nor I were wearing seat belts, and I first knew something terrible had happened when I woke up enough to be aware that I was lying on the ground. Someone, my father I think, kept saying an ambulance was on its way and he would look after me."

"I thought your father was killed instantly."

"No . . . Aunt Alice always said he died immediately," Laura said slowly. "But I remember him in the ambulance and again at the hospital. We were in the same room; it might have been the emergency room. My eyes were bandaged, but he held my hand, and he kept asking me if I was all right. Over and over I said yes. Then he didn't come anymore, but someone else sat with me until I was transferred to the children's hospital in Salt Lake City. I don't know whether I knew this person or not. Maybe he was a doctor or nurse. He told me Daddy had died, but I could live if I would just make up my mind that I wanted to live. He promised he would help me to be happy again."

"You did receive good medical care, so whoever he was he must've done his best," Bruce said.

"I suppose so," Laura agreed. "Hey, here's our turnoff."

Bruce swung the steering wheel, and with a lurch the little car left the pavement to continue on its way along a rough, graded road. Dust billowed in their wake, leaving Laura with a lingering sense of sadness for her tiny, dainty mother who had apparently hated this barren, dry landscape. Laura wasn't sure what had attracted her mother and father to each other in the first place. They had met in college, and it was love at first sight for both of them. Laura had to agree with Aunt Alice: love wasn't all it was cracked up to be.

The April Hendrickson Laura recalled had been shy and vague, seemingly aware of little except her music. She wore simple pastel dresses at home and a long black skirt with a white silk blouse when she performed. Her pale hair was kept piled on top of her head. Laura seldom saw it down, she recalled. She remembered, too, her mother's long, elegant fingers on the keyboard, as well as the long silence when she no longer left her bed even for her beloved music. It was hard to imagine her mother in this harsh land, feeling hot and sticky with clouds of dust settling on her damp face and arms.

It was equally hard to imagine the large sum of money Laura had recently learned was in several accounts in a San Francisco bank in her name. Aunt Alice, as her guardian, had made a number of withdrawals from one account during the years after the accident to pay for Laura's physical therapy, to pay for the college education Laura had received, and to fund Aunt Alice's anti-Mormon cause. Mr. Sylvester said the money had come from a settlement with the company that owned the truck that had hit them. Regular amounts had been added to that account each month from Laura's trust fund. The withdrawals from the trust fund had ceased going to Aunt Alice on Laura's eighteenth birthday and had gone instead to a checking account set up by April for Laura. She'd learned she was to receive the balance of the trust fund outright on her twenty-fifth birthday.

Until Mr. Sylvester had gotten involved in trying to sort out Aunt Alice's estate, no one at Aunt Alice's more recent law firm had told Laura about any inheritance other than Aunt Alice's house. Between Aunt Alice's changing lawyers eight years ago, an inexperienced attorney, and some filing system changes, a lot of important information had fallen through the cracks.

Laura now understood that minimal Social Security checks and an allowance from April had been Aunt Alice's only sources of income until the insurance company's settlement for Laura's injuries and her father's life had greatly swollen the old woman's bank account. Laura couldn't help wondering why Aunt Alice had insisted on living an almost impoverished existence. There had been plenty of money to go around if someone had bothered to access it. According to her mother's will, Laura would be receiving the more than ten years of child support payments her father had sent once all the legal red tape was settled. She laughed at the irony of her situation, and Bruce turned a questioning eye her way.

"In a short time, I'll have more money than I ever imagined I would see in my lifetime," she said. "But right now, I'm so poor I couldn't afford this trip without your help."

"Not for long." Bruce laughed. "I can't believe I forgot to tell you! While you were inside at the gas station, our agent called my mobile. She got a preapproved offer on Aunt Alice's house this morning. The buyer is ready to close on Monday! Since we gave my dad limited power of attorney, he can sign all the documents for us. On Tuesday we'll both have a tidy sum to do with as we please—no strings attached."

Bruce pulled off on a small side road and followed it to a cluster of trees in a hollow. There he found a feeble patch of shade where they could finish eating their lunch and examine the map again. Laura tried to swallow a bit of her sandwich but found swallowing difficult. She stared off into the distance, watching a plume of dust draw closer then disappear behind a hill. In a short time she would confront the man who was once her father's partner. She couldn't help wondering what kind of man would steal a young woman's inheritance while she lay in a hospital critically injured. She shuddered, remembering the bitter animosity in Aunt Alice's voice on the rare occasions she'd mentioned the man who had been driving when the accident occurred. Would he chase them off with a shotgun? Did modern ranchers in isolated areas take the law into their own hands the way ranchers often did in the old western movies she'd watched?

Bruce folded up the paper wrapper from his sandwich and reached for his cell phone. "I promised Mom I'd let her know when we arrived," he said as he punched buttons on the tiny instrument. "No service," he muttered after a moment. He flipped the phone closed and started the car. "Ready?"

"Yes," she forced herself to say.

"According to Sylvester's directions, we should spot the ranch buildings soon," Bruce said as he turned back onto the gravel road.

A short time later they rattled across a cattle guard, crested a hill, and caught their first glimpse of the High Country Ranch. A vast wheat field stretched from the top of the hill they were descending, crossed a small valley, and swept partway up the mountain on the opposite side. Black rocky outcroppings covered with brush stood out like islands in the golden wheat. Where the grain stopped, a heavy stand of squat trees began with what appeared to be an endless vista of gray sagebrush.

Nestled into the side of the mountain and surrounded by the twisted trees was a long, two-story house built out of wood and stone. They glimpsed several other buildings and a large pole corral behind the house. They could see beyond the corral a number of shapes that appeared to be cattle or horses; it was difficult to be certain from so far away.

"Wow!" Laura breathed. "This is more impressive than I expected." An inner voice reminded her she had seen it before. She'd lived here as a small child. Her head turned slowly, taking in the vast openness.

Bruce whistled appreciatively as they approached the residence. "The house isn't bad either."

Bruce parked his car on a wide graveled strip in front of the house, but they didn't make a move to leave it for several moments. Gradually the dust stirred up by the car settled, and they looked around. Two other vehicles were parked nearby, assuring them someone was around in spite of the stillness. Twenty feet of shaggy, yellowing grass separated the gravel strip from the house. To one side was a scruffy row of unpruned bushes that must have once been a rose garden. A trail of flat stones imbedded in the grass led to the front door.

The house was far more inviting than Laura had expected. Built of natural black lava rock and cedar with a wide shaded veranda, massive wood beams, and large generous windows, it seemed to belong in the rugged setting. Several immense boulders and a variety of trees and shrubs were placed around the house, hinting at flower beds and landscaping that must have once been quite extensive but now showed signs of neglect. She felt a moment's curiosity about the man who had built this house for his bride, and she wondered if her mother had once cared for the flowers and shrubs.

"It's show time, babe." Bruce grinned at her. Taking a deep breath, she reached for the car door handle. She walked around the front of the red Triumph, and together she and Bruce made their way toward the house. Just as Bruce placed one foot on the veranda, a large black-and-white collie rose from a shaded corner with teeth bared. An ominous low growl served as a warning to come no farther.

Laura nearly tripped as Bruce hastily withdrew his foot. The dog came no closer, but they had no trouble understanding they shouldn't advance either. It looked like a standoff.

Nervously, Bruce cleared his throat before calling out, "Anyone home?"

"Mr. Burgoyne, call off your dog. I need to talk to you," Laura added.

The summer day seemed ominously quiet. The sun beat down relentlessly, and from the corner of her eye, Laura saw a dust devil swirl across the dry corral.

"Perhaps we ought to back slowly toward the car," Bruce whispered.

Laura glanced toward the car, then back at the dog, measuring their chances.

four

"MR. BURGOYNE!" SHE called again, then jumped as the screen door opened and she found herself facing a tall, silver-haired man. She could see that even without the high-heeled western boots he topped six feet. He was obviously a man accustomed to wielding authority. A little shiver slid down her spine as she met his sharp gray eyes. At a slight motion of his hand, the dog went to him, and the man rested his hand on top of the animal's head. The dog's tail thumped stiffly against the back of the man's pant legs.

"Are you Paul Harold Burgoyne?" Bruce asked, straightening to his full height but keeping Laura's arm tucked against his side.

"I am." The severe expression on the still handsome face never wavered.

"Was Jacob Warren Hendrickson your partner?" Laura struggled to control the instinct that made her want to turn and run to the safety of Bruce's car.

"How does that concern you?" A second voice emerged from the blackness behind the open door.

The accumulation of tension and insecurity that had been building for weeks burst. The anonymity of the voice emerging from the shadows was one uncertainty too many. *What right do you have to question me? This was my father's land and house. This was supposed to be my home! You stole it from me. Why are you living here in my house?* For a moment she thought she'd shouted the words aloud. When she gratefully realized that she hadn't, she concentrated on trying to appear poised and calm. She said, "My name is Laura Hendrickson, and I just recently discovered that half of this ranch is mine."

The older man's gray eyes bored into hers without flinching, and only silence came from the doorway.

Funny! She had expected a reaction: alarm, denial, something. She glanced toward the shadowy interior behind the man blocking the doorway. Her deep brown eyes met familiar steel gray. With a jolt, she realized the second man was no longer hidden by shadows and was now joining the older man on the porch. He wasn't just any man, either, but the angry cowboy she and Bruce had left thirty or more miles down the road, dressed now in fresh clothes. Either he knew a shorter route or he must have passed them when they stopped to check the map and eat their lunch.

Laura felt a frisson of shock streak down her spine as their eyes locked. No emotion showed on the man's face, nor did he speak. He seemed to be studying her, sizing her up. Against all reason, she felt a connection to this man. Why couldn't they have met under different circumstances?

Bruce's voice sounded far away. She forced herself to listen as he addressed the older man.

"Mr. Burgoyne, I am Bruce Wilson, Ms. Hendrickson's cousin. I have been asked by Ms. Hendrickson and her attorney, Wayne Sylvester, to deliver some papers to you and to set up a meeting between your attorney and Mr. Sylvester. He believes you are a reasonable man and that you should have a chance to meet Laura and discuss the property privately before entering into a legal battle."

The two men in the doorway exchanged almost imperceptible glances.

"Come inside." The stern figure held the door wide. With stately courtesy he motioned for Laura and Bruce to enter the house. A silent gesture sent the dog back to a shadowy corner beside a porch swing.

Laura couldn't resist scanning the large Spartan room as she stepped from the dimly lit entry hall. She blinked in the sudden bright light. The room was beautiful with one whole wall of windows facing south, providing a spectacular view of the rolling wheat fields and gray, cedar-covered mountains reflecting silver and gold in the brilliant sunlight. Exposed beams and wide windows seemed to extend the vast panorama indoors. A mammoth lava-rock fireplace dominated one wall, with a scattering of overstuffed chairs, sofas, and a low, round table gathered in front of it. The opposite end of the room was completely bare, leaving the room with an unfinished look. There was no doubt in her mind that her mother's grand piano was meant to occupy that end of the room. She couldn't help wondering why there was a space there now, so many years later. The room was clean and uncluttered—too neat, in fact. It lacked life, as though the house's inhabitants seldom used it.

Laura stood in the center of the room. Vainly her eyes sought something, anything, that might be familiar. She knew she had lived in this house the first four years of her life, but nothing struck a chord of remembrance. All she felt was the barest familiarity with the shimmery golden light filling the space.

"Have a seat." The older man indicated the grouping in front of the fireplace.

Gingerly Laura sat on the edge of a leather sofa, and Bruce joined her there. Not bothering to sit, the cowboy leaned against the stone fireplace. Laura wished he would go away. Something about him made her uneasy. As though sensing the turmoil of feelings surging through her, Bruce picked up her hand, holding it reassuringly in his. She thought she saw the cowboy frown, then decided she was mistaken.

"Now, young lady, suppose you tell me what this is all about." There wasn't a glimmer of warmth in Mr. Burgoyne's voice.

Laura sensed he was not a man to take lightly. He would be a dangerous enemy. As she met his eyes a shiver of déjà vu crossed her mind. She had seen those eyes before. A flash of memory told her he had once looked just that way at Aunt Alice. Pulling herself together, she leaned forward.

"Mr. Burgoyne, my great-aunt, Alice Wilson, recently passed away. In clearing her house and settling her estate, Bruce and I discovered my father's will and documents indicating he owned this house and half of the High Country Ranch. The will indicated that he intended for me to inherit both. We took the papers to our family attorney, Wayne Sylvester in San Francisco, who verified their legitimacy. Bruce kindly volunteered to deliver some papers to you, but my reason for coming is simpler. I wanted to see the land that was more important to my father than either my mother or I was."

"Very touching." Sarcasm tinged the younger man's voice as he leaned forward for emphasis. "But for your information, nothing was more important to Jake Hendrickson than his wife and daughter. And you're forgetting one crucial point. Laura Hendrickson is dead."

"Now just a minute." Bruce's arm slid around Laura's shoulders. Gently he pulled her to her feet. "If you are doubting Laura's identity, believe me, we can provide definitive documentation. If you're making some oblique threat, you're making a big mistake." He started to guide her toward the door, keeping himself between Laura and the mocking man who appeared completely at ease in her father's house.

"Leaving is a smart move. Next time pick a more gullible patsy."

Laura's spine stiffened. Pulling herself free of Bruce's protective arms, she whirled to face the stony figure. "This is none of your business," she snapped at the cowboy. Turning, she spoke directly to Mr. Burgoyne, who was standing now too.

"Aunt Alice told me little about you or this ranch, only that my mother was unhappy here, and I can understand why if she received the kind of welcome you gave me. She believed that you and my father kept my mother a prisoner here, depriving her of her music and family because the god you both worshipped was this miserable ranch. She blamed you along with my father for Mother's early death. She blamed you, too, for my injuries in that car wreck eight years ago in which you were the driver." At this point Laura swept back her hair to reveal scars along her hairline. "There are others that wouldn't be appropriate for me to show."

"Just a minute!" The cowboy tried to cut in, but Laura refused to back down. "Mr. Sylvester said I should judge for myself what kind of man you are after I had a chance to get to know you. The accident stole most of my memories of anything prior to it, including any recollection I might have had of you. But I can't forget I spent months in a hospital and years in physical therapy while you stole my father's property. I was a minor when my parents died, and you let me grow up believing my father made no provision for my future. You profited from the accident while I lost my second parent and had to rely on my aunt's charity! You sit here saying nothing while your hired hand questions my identity. I'm pretty sure you know exactly who I am."

She suddenly tore the thick envelope Bruce carried from his grasp. Tossing it at Mr. Burgoyne, she watched in dismay as it dropped to the floor, spewing its contents across the deep gold carpet. She felt a sense of horror to see her entire life spread so blatantly across the floor.

Along with photographs of herself as an infant and as a toddler playing in front of this very house, there was a photograph of her with her father taken during a visit he made to San Francisco when she was five or six. There were snapshots of her on crutches at sixteen learning to walk again, her college graduation portrait, and copies of her birth certificate, her parents' marriage certificate, and numerous letters and documents, including both of her parents' wills.

She couldn't move. Like in a slow-motion movie, she watched the cowboy stoop to pick up a piece of paper. She wanted to scream, *Don't touch my papers! Don't touch my life!* But the words wouldn't come.

For a minute that felt like an hour, he held the paper in his hand. The color slowly drained from his face as he read it. Sightlessly, he stared into space. He seemed lost in thought. Laura didn't understand the haunted expression on his face. It was only the release form her aunt had signed the day she took Laura home from the hospital in Salt Lake that he held in his hand. Finally, he folded the paper, making precise creases with his fingers, before tucking it inside his shirt pocket. Laura wanted to tell him to give the paper back but was still dumbstruck.

When Mr. Burgoyne stooped to begin gathering the scattered papers, Bruce knelt to help him. Over Bruce's and Mr. Burgoyne's heads Laura's eyes locked with those of the cowboy, catching a glimpse of pain before he turned away. What was his problem? None of this even concerned him.

Occasionally the older man held a paper or photo in his hands for several seconds, studying it carefully. When the papers were back in the envelope, both men straightened. Laura stood rooted to the spot. It wasn't like her to lose her temper and go on a rant like that, but then she wasn't accustomed to having her word and her identity questioned either. She wasn't quite sure what to do next. This was all new territory for her.

"If you will come with me, I think there is something you should see." Laura jumped when she realized Mr. Burgoyne's deep voice was speaking to her in a kindly tone.

Laura and Bruce exchanged glances. Bruce shrugged his shoulders before taking Laura's hand. Together they followed the older man down a short hall with a now silent cowboy following behind. They entered a room where bookcases lined two walls. A large oak desk with a roomy, black leather chair sat facing glass patio doors. Behind the desk, two maroon wing-back chairs sitting before a small stone fireplace proclaimed the room a man's retreat.

No one spoke while Mr. Burgoyne opened the deep bottom drawer of the desk to reveal a neat row of hanging file folders. Unerringly, he withdrew a stained and smudged envelope. Placing it in Laura's hand, he gruffly commanded, "Read this."

Turning the envelope over in her hands, she allowed herself to be guided to one of the wingback chairs. She recognized Aunt Alice's handwriting on the envelope and felt a sudden reluctance to view the contents. During the past two weeks she had begun to wonder if she had ever really known her aunt.

Taking a fortifying breath, she slid the single sheet of paper from the envelope. After reading the short, cryptic note, she carefully reread it. *Laura died two days ago. I have opted for cremation and a small private funeral, which is scheduled for tomorrow. The furniture she inherited from her mother should be sent to me immediately. Both her funeral expenses and Jacob's are being paid by the trucking company's insurance, so there is no need for any further correspondence between us.* It was signed *Alice Wilson.* Laura continued to stare at the paper, though she no longer saw it.

On some level, she was aware of the soft hum of an air conditioner, Bruce tapping his fingers on the edge of the desk, and the distant sound of a heavy motor; otherwise, the room was still. The back of her neck prickled. She glanced toward Bruce, as if seeking help.

"Well, it seems Alice didn't get the furniture she asked for, since this is obviously Grandfather's desk," Bruce remarked into the silence as he ran the palm of his hand across the rich wood. "It fits the description in your mother's list of furniture left to her by her parents and matches a number of pieces in Mom and Dad's home."

Why was Bruce talking about furniture? Didn't he understand there was much more involved here than furniture?

"Why did Aunt Alice tell you I was dead?" Laura scarcely recognized her own voice. She blinked back the tears she refused to let fall. *Lies! So many lies! Was nothing the way she'd believed it to be?*

The cowboy's eyes narrowed. His mouth was a straight white line, but he didn't respond.

"I don't know." Mr. Burgoyne's long, slender fingers formed a steeple beneath his chin. "Alice objected to everything about Jake. When he died, I suppose she assumed you were her responsibility. She was probably just making certain we wouldn't take you from her."

"She was protecting me!" Laura latched onto his words. Her thoughts were a jumble of memories of her aunt's words concerning this man who had claimed her father's estate and who had been driving when the accident occurred. She had difficulty believing he was an innocent party in all this.

"You do know I'm Laura Hendrickson, don't you?"

"Under the circumstances, I'm not going to answer that question," Mr. Burgoyne said. "On the surface your claim looks strong, and I don't deny you share some of Jake and April's physical attributes, but I will want to verify these documents. There's a great deal at stake here."

Something about the cowboy reclaimed her attention. He stared bleakly past the people in the room to the golden field beyond the window. He seemed so alone. She stifled an urge to rise, to go to him. His eyes turned to meet hers and seemed to hold a challenge. *Mr. Burgoyne knows who I am, but he'll fight my claim anyway.* Laura's shoulders slumped with weariness. Bruce rushed over to place a hand on her shoulder as he addressed the older man. "Mr. Sylvester instructed us not attempt to reach any kind of agreement about the property until he joins us to meet with your lawyer, Mr. Burgoyne."

Laura shook off Bruce's hand as she stood up. She hadn't understood before why she'd insisted on coming. Now she knew. She had been looking for a place she could call home, but these people would never accept her claim. They had too much to lose, this beautiful house and thousands of acres of ranch land. Even if she won the legal battle that was sure to ensue, she'd never feel the love she had once known here. It wasn't the home she had secretly yearned for. A fresh wave of grief swept over her as she acknowledged that Aunt Alice, her own flesh and blood, had been the one to throw away her right to claim it years ago.

Laura nodded at Mr. Burgoyne. "I think we should leave now. We can get rooms in Snowville or drive back to Burley."

"That won't be necessary," Mr. Burgoyne said. "There's plenty of room here. There's more involved than property here, and you and I are not the only people whose lives will be affected if your claim is valid." Surprised, Laura followed his glance to the cowboy who had become strangely quiet. "If you are Laura, this is your home. You have a right to stay."

"I-I don't know."

"Come; let me show you the house." Mr. Burgoyne extended his hand. "You'll want to see all of your mother's furniture." He glanced toward Bruce. The cowboy remained behind as she and Bruce followed Mr. Burgoyne from the room.

From the library Mr. Burgoyne led them to a large room which he explained had once been a playroom but was now unused. A formal dining room also appeared neglected. The kitchen was the heart of the house, obviously doubling as a family room. Upstairs, he led her first to the master bedroom, a spacious room that seemed to welcome her. She was surprised to see soft minty greens contrasting with deep forest greens, her mother's favorite colors. It seemed the room hadn't been repainted since the house was built. Less surprisingly, various masculine articles were scattered about. A leather belt lay across the foot of the bed, a pair of boots rested beside a chair, and a long-sleeved, white shirt hung from a doorknob.

They glanced briefly at three more bedrooms before the tour ended with Mr. Burgoyne ushering Laura into a smaller bedroom across the hall from the master bedroom. She looked around at the narrow white bed, the small matching toy chest, and a miniature rocking chair. In the corner was a bouncy horse. She knew without being told—this room had once been hers. She tried to imagine how the room must have looked to a little girl. Closing her eyes, she discovered it was easier than she had supposed to see her old panda bear on the bed, a line of dolls on a chest by the window, and a pair of red boots in the center of the rug. A sense of warmth and belonging crept over her.

"Would you like to lie down for awhile?" Mr. Burgoyne asked. "There's a bathroom next to this room if you'd like to shower before dinner." She nodded her acceptance. Quietly, he withdrew.

"Are you sure you want to stay?" Bruce moved reluctantly toward the door. When she nodded her head, he added, "I'll get your bag, then we can talk."

"I don't need my bag now." She wanted him to go. She had to think. Alone. Slowly she sat down on the narrow bed.

"Are you sure?" When she nodded her head, he left the room, closing the door quietly behind him.

Sitting on the edge of the bed, Laura slipped off her sandals. Idly, she trailed her fingers across the spread. Her life had turned upside down the moment she learned about the ranch, but nothing had prepared her for the events of the past few hours. Would reclaiming her inheritance prove as difficult as the years of physical therapy she had endured to be able to walk again? She shuddered, remembering how the cowboy's cold gray eyes had bored into hers and watched her every move. She had never before been so aware of any man. Who was he? What part did he play in all this? She curled into a ball. The room felt safe and comfortable to her, like pleasant memories hovering at the edge of her mind. She'd like to stay for a few days. *He doesn't want me to stay,* she thought. *But he has no right to interfere between Daddy's partner and me.* It wouldn't be the first time she found herself fighting a tough fight. Her eyes closed. Suddenly, they flew open. She sat straight up. Could the cowboy be Mr. Burgoyne's son? He looked to be the right age for that—maybe twenty-nine or thirty. Was he Paul MacPherson Burgoyne, the man whose name appeared on that phony marriage certificate? With a groan of dismay, she lay back down. Immediately, she forced her mind to focus on happier thoughts, and soon she fell asleep.

The sun was low in the west when Laura awoke to a tap on her door. Mr. Burgoyne invited her and Bruce to supper later on the patio, which she accepted. Deciding to withhold judgment where her father's former partner was concerned, she acknowledged he had been kind, even courtly, since her outburst in the sitting room. It might be just an act to disarm her, but since she wanted to stay, she would accept his hospitality at face value. For the present anyway. She didn't trust him entirely. There was an undercurrent between him and the cowboy that told her they were withholding something important from her. She chose not to think about the cowboy.

Refreshed by the short nap and a shower, Laura was ready to join her host for dinner. Some instinct or buried memory carried Laura from her room to a landing overlooking the entryway. Her feet moved down the stairs unerringly to the dining room. From there, double doors led to a covered patio. The late afternoon sun sent long shadows dancing across the wide, smooth planks beneath her feet. Both Mr. Burgoyne and Bruce were reclining on cushioned redwood seats gathered around a matching table. The cowboy was nowhere in sight. She relaxed until she saw that the table was set for four.

"Mr. Burgoyne?"

"Evidently, we'll be seeing quite a bit of each other in the future." Mr. Burgoyne rose to his feet to hand her a glass. He indicated she should sit in the chair next to his. "I think you should call me Hal. Jake always did, and so did his little girl, though April didn't approve."

"Why not?" Laura sat at the table, sniffing appreciatively as a perfectly grilled steak found its way to the plate before her.

"April wanted her daughter to be everything proper and feminine. She dressed her in ruffles and lace and insisted the child address adults formally." He chuckled. "The Laura I knew made a habit of escaping her mother. She was a stubborn little minx who preferred overalls and boots to dresses and ruffles. She kept Mac in hot water by copying everything he did or said."

His warm laughter surprised her. Until now, she hadn't seen him so much as crack a smile.

"Who is Mac?" she asked.

A sharp bark of laughter drew her attention to the doorway. The cowboy's familiar figure stood with one denim-clad hip leaning against the door frame. He braced one hand above his head against the opposite doorjamb. His free hand held his hat by its brim against his knee.

"Who is Mac?" He mocked her question. "I'm sure you could answer that question yourself, if you tried. Since I don't want to be thought rude, Laura, let me introduce myself. I am Paul MacPherson Burgoyne, better known as Mac. And I'm your husband, if you really are Laura."

five

"I DON'T HAVE a husband!" Laura bristled.

"If you are Laura Hendrickson Burgoyne, you do! Imagine my delight when my lawyer called yours a little while ago and I discovered that my child bride is not only alive but has taken legal action to shut down my livelihood until I produce fifty percent of the ranch's profits from the past eight years, pay her for my house and furniture, and buy out her half of the ranch."

"You actually believe I'm married to you?" Laura stood, aghast. He couldn't be serious!

"That's right. All nice and legal. When my attorney told me about you this afternoon, I didn't take him seriously. I was expecting a clever little impersonator, a con artist, not my dearly departed wife in person."

"You're crazy! I've never been married." Laura's fingers bit into the arms of the chair she clung to for support. She took a faltering step toward Bruce and felt his arm settle around her tense shoulders. It was true she'd forgotten a lot of things, but there was no way she could have forgotten being married to that cowboy!

"Come on, Laura," Bruce said. "You don't have to stay here and put up with this nonsense. We'll let Mr. Sylvester handle everything."

"Sorry, Cousin Bruce. You can get in your little toy car and go anywhere you want, but my wife is staying right here. She and I have some talking to do."

"I'm not your wife!" Laura stepped closer to Bruce as though seeking protection.

"What are you trying to pull? Leave Laura alone. She's no more your wife than mine." Bruce took a protective stance.

"Well, darling, I'm glad you aren't guilty of bigamy."

"That's enough!" Hal Burgoyne spoke with an edge of steel. "We clearly need to sort through some things, and I suggest we behave like the reasonable adults we all are. Now, everybody take a seat."

"Under the circumstances, we really can't stay here!" Bruce protested. "I think it'd best if—"

"Butt out, Wilson! Laura and I need to talk."

"Go easy, Mac." Hal's voice was soft, but it held a hint of warning.

"We're leaving!" Laura insisted as she reached for Bruce's arm.

"Have a seat, Laura." Mac's voice was softer, but he ended up sounding more condescending than courteous. "There are facts you are unaware of about this situation. Timing is essential in running a ranch, and if you walk out of here without resolving certain issues, there will be no ranch left to fight over."

Reluctantly Laura sat on the edge of her chair. Bruce hesitated, then resumed his seat. Mac sat on the rail encircling the deck.

Laura resented being spoken to like a naughty child. Most of all she resented the strong reactions this cowboy stirred in her. Fighting back or arguing just weren't things she did. She kept picturing that crazy marriage license Bruce had found. Was she really married to Mac? She'd been certain it was just one of those mock certificates people get at amusement parks when they have their pictures taken in silly old clothes, but now she was beginning to fear it might be real. Mr. Sylvester had told her it had checked out in his initial inquiries, but he had promised to look into it further. There was no way it could be real, she reminded herself. Her eyes went to Mac. She hadn't expected him to turn over half of his ranch to her without a fight, but she was unprepared for the emotion emanating from him. She glanced away when he answered her appraising stare with one of his own. Bruce noticed the look and pointedly slid his chair closer to hers.

"On second thought, maybe we should try a more comfortable setting, Laura. Come with me. We'll go to the library, where the two of us can carry on a civilized conversation." Mac stood, pushing away from the rail and moving to Laura's side. He placed his hand on her arm to escort her inside the house, but she flinched slightly at his touch, and he immediately released her arm.

Straightening her shoulders, Laura preceded him to the library. She was no coward, even if she did avoid confrontational situations as a rule. Anyway, she might as well get this over with.

* * *

Mac led the woman he instinctively knew really was Laura to one of the wingback chairs before claiming the desk chair for himself. He watched in annoyance as Hal took the other chair and Bruce settled on the hearthstone at Laura's feet. He wished the other two men had stayed on the deck as he'd expected they would; he wanted to talk to Laura alone. No matter. Whether alone or with the others, he didn't know where to begin.

Today had been full of surprises, mostly bad ones. And the one that should have been good—Laura's being alive—had not been turning out well at all. He felt like he had been trampled by a raging bull. Mac's eyes followed Laura's long legs as she crossed them. This couldn't be real. He shook his head as though trying to clear a picture from his mind. How could this stunning, sophisticated woman be his Laura? Deep in his gut he knew she was, but he much preferred the rambunctious child who had once dogged his footsteps or even the hesitant but sweet teenager her father had placed in his care. He'd had little experience with women in his life, and nothing had prepared him for the perfectly groomed, exquisite one seated across the desk from him wearing an expression of distrust and determination.

Hal broke the silence. "Mac, are you convinced this young lady is Jake's girl, Laura?"

"There's no question. The scars she showed us match too perfectly the gashes I held towels against while we waited for help to arrive. Obviously, she's older, and her hair is shorter, but she's the same girl. Coop tried to tell me, but I didn't believe him. Laura's stubborn, interfering old aunt lied to us." He patted the pocket holding Laura's hospital release form.

"Yes, it seems she did." Hal seemed thoughtful, then turned to Laura. "Laura, what do you remember of the accident when your father was killed?"

Laura tensed as though reluctant to answer, then shrugged her shoulders before responding to the question. "Not much. I only have hazy memories of the weeks before and after the accident. I didn't even remember my mother's death until months later when Aunt Alice prompted me about it."

"Don't you remember when Jake came to get you?"

"Only in a vague way. I've been told there were two days between when I left Aunt Alice's home and the accident, but I don't remember much about those days. As I was traveling today, I thought I remembered a swimming pool from that trip, though I'm not certain whether it was a dream or a memory. And I think Daddy was holding my hand in that little clinic near where the accident happened before the air ambulance took me to the hospital in Salt Lake. During the months I was recuperating, I sometimes had horrible brief flashes of events filled with blood and lights. There were confusing pictures of people running around, then Daddy holding my head and insisting I answer some questions."

Mac maintained a calm exterior at this explanation, but inside he felt betrayed. How could she have forgotten? He only had to close his eyes to remember the blood and confusion, Jake insisting with his dying breath that the two of them marry, and Laura's head lying in his lap while he pleaded with her to stay awake, to stay alive. Jake had known he was dying, and the paramedics had held out little hope that Laura would survive either. It had been his hand, not Jake's, she had clung to during that nightmare ride to the clinic and during their brief ceremony. Hal had stayed at Jake's side while his partner stubbornly held on to life long enough to see his daughter and the ranch placed in Mac's keeping. Surely, the woman remembered these details.

"I have to say, this seems a convenient memory loss," Mac said.

Hal sent Mac a quelling glance before urging Laura to continue. "Do you remember the questions you were asked?"

"No." Laura shook her head. "The neurosurgeon at the hospital told me fear and confusion with loss of memory of the actual trauma are common side effects for accident victims."

"Maybe you could bring us a note from your doctor," Mac said snidely.

"Mac, confine your remarks to something constructive," Hal reprimanded.

"Dad, this is no poor little orphan. Our Laura is a full grown woman, bent on destroying us and everything we've worked for."

"I'm not trying to destroy anyone. I only want what my dad wanted me to have. What does the accident have to do with the ranch anyway?"

She couldn't possibly be as unaware of the situation as she pretended. Of course, he might be the one who didn't know the facts. She, with the help of that conniving aunt of hers, might have had the marriage annulled years ago. If that turned out to be the case, he would lose everything for sure. The only thing he could do was play along, spell it all out for her. One thing was for sure, the woman who called herself Laura was no longer the girl he'd married.

"You and I are married, Laura. That's a fact." Mac spoke with precise bluntness. "I married you because Dad and Jake convinced me it was the only way to protect you from growing up under your aunt's thumb if you survived or to keep the ranch out of her grasping hands if both you and your father died. When we were hit by that truck, it didn't look like either you or Jake was going to make it. We had to wait at a clinic in some little town for what seemed like hours until an air ambulance arrived. Even though he was in a lot of pain, Jake got to worrying about you and the ranch. His will left everything to you, and he believed that if he died, guardianship would go to Alice Wilson, a woman he despised. If you and Jake both died, your aunt would get everything he had ever worked for and bankrupt Dad by forcing a sale of the ranch. Jake didn't want that to happen. He knew she'd sell your share of the ranch and give the money to that hateful bunch of religious bigots she supported. It was his idea for us to marry, so that I would get your share of the ranch if you died and so you could come here, beyond that woman's reach, if you lived.

He ignored Laura's gasp and continued. "We were in one of those little towns with a clinic but no staff doctor. It didn't take long to round up a preacher; Jake signed the consent forms, and we were married before the doctor arrived.

"How could my dad do that to me? How could you?" Laura's eyes were round with shock. "No one can get married while unconscious or without consenting, can they?"

"You weren't unconscious, and you didn't object."

"I can't be married to you."

Her words sounded hoarse, and there was a look of panic on her face. Being married to him was apparently one of those fates worse than death. Hurt, he struck back. "Look, I'm not exactly thrilled about the situation either. Dad gave me his share of the ranch not long after I inherited the other half from my supposedly deceased wife. While I worked sixteen hours a day on what should have been our ranch, you lived in the lap of luxury, never giving a thought to the cost of keeping your father's ranch together through fire, drought, staggering feed costs, and low beef prices. And then you come waltzing in here out of nowhere and expect me to hand over half of everything I've worked for all these years."

"My life hasn't been the bed of roses you seem to think it has been. Among other things, my own blood relative hid things from me and essentially stole from me for years. I've had it with all the secrets and lies, and no one is going to steal my share of this ranch."

"No one calls me a thief!"

"Enough!" Hal's roar stopped Mac. "Anger and accusations are getting us nowhere. Mac, you're only confusing Laura. Let's stick to the most pressing issues here."

Bruce looked up at Laura from his seat on the hearth. "Don't worry, Laura," he said in a reassuring voice. "I'm sure Mr. Sylvester can get the marriage annulled, if it ever was a real marriage."

"It's real all right, but I'll do everything in my power to prevent an annulment. You see, an annulment would award all the cookies to you, dear Laura. I had a little talk with my attorney this afternoon. He tells me if the marriage is annulled, then it's as though it never existed and I had no right to Jake's half of this ranch. I would have to turn it over to you along with compensation for its use and face possible criminal charges for withholding it from your aunt. A divorce would cut deep, but I would probably lose less. A judge would have to take into consideration all I've put into the ranch along with your absence and neglect."

He glanced at his dad, who looked thunderous, then back to Laura, who looked frightened. This discussion was going no better than the previous ones. "Of course, I'd fight the divorce, too. According to my attorney, staying married is the next best option to your staying dead. That way, I continue to run things my way, and I only have to provide a home and some reasonable amenities for my little wife."

Suddenly, Bruce laughed. "You're a piece of work, man. I can hardly wait until Mr. Sylvester gets hold of you. I think you're in for a rude awakening to the twenty-first century. You're going to find Laura has rights you never even heard of!"

Quoting old Coop had been a mistake. It was clear Bruce had not understood that Mac was being facetious with that last bit. Mac wished the guy would just back off. He tried to maintain a calm and even tone as he said, "You know, Mr. Wilson, you're starting to get on my nerves. None of this is even any of your business."

Bruce stood and rested a hand on Laura's shoulder. "You're mistaken. I've looked out for Laura for a long time. If you are her husband like you claim, where were you when she needed someone to hold her hand when she faced surgery for the sixth time or someone to lean on when she learned to walk all over again? I've always been there for her. Her concerns will always be mine." Mac rose from his chair, jaw clenched, but Bruce didn't back down. "You, on the other hand, don't care one bit about Laura. You don't deserve to be called her husband."

"You have no idea what you're talking about." Bruce's speech cut Mac deeply and raised pictures like wounds in his mind. "Now, Laura, I need to talk to you—alone." Mac took a step closer. With one arm he pushed Bruce aside, catching Laura with the other. Taken by surprise, Bruce staggered against a chair, toppling it over on its side. Unable to halt the momentum quickly enough, he stumbled over the chair and sprawled across the carpet.

Mac didn't wait for him to regain his feet. He picked Laura up and carried her through the door. He dashed down the hall with Laura kicking and screaming, trying to break his hold.

Laura made a grab for the door frame, and he swung her over one shoulder. Gravel crunched beneath his feet, and she gasped for breath.

"Put me down!" She fought him every way she knew how, but before she could free herself, she found herself sliding across the front seat of his truck. Before she could gather her wits about her, Mac climbed in and started the engine. He shoved it into gear and tromped on the gas.

* * *

Laura gasped at the sudden acceleration, then as she began to reach for her seat belt, she asked, "Where are you taking me?"

"I thought it would help if we could talk alone, and up the mountain we've got a little cabin."

"What?" She panicked at the implications of going to a cabin together and let the unlatched seat belt slip from her grasp. This man kept insisting they were married. What if he . . . She shuddered. This couldn't be happening. Frantically, she reached for the door handle. Mac pulled her to his side just as she felt the latch release. The unlatched door swung erratically as the truck bounced and swerved until a particularly hard jolt brought it slamming shut.

"Don't be stupid," Mac shouted. "You can't jump from a moving vehicle without killing yourself."

"I know that! Stop this truck and let me out!" She tried to sound authoritative but suspected she looked and sounded as frightened as she felt. When Mac didn't slow down, she stopped her struggle and huddled on the seat.

* * *

Mac felt an urge to comfort her but knew he'd blown any chance of her accepting comfort from him. He hadn't meant to hurt or scare her and was confused by his own behavior. Couldn't she see they weren't getting anywhere with Dad and her overly protective cousin interfering? He didn't know what to make of her, but he intended to get to the bottom of this whole mess. Once they got to the cabin he could find out how much she really knew and what she wanted. If there was any of the old Laura left, perhaps they could work out a compromise. The sooner they got there, the better. His foot gradually increased the pressure on the gas pedal, and the truck leaped forward.

A glance her direction showed him that Laura's face was taut with anxiety and that she was holding her arms around her body protectively. Guilt slammed into him. This whole day had been one shock after another, and he was in danger of blowing everything he had ever dreamed of. There was just so much at stake!

"Mac! Look out!"

Mac jerked his eyes back to the road. A huge buck stood silhouetted in the truck's headlights.

"Duck!" he yelled as he tried to keep from hitting the animal. Grimly he fought to control the speeding vehicle. *Not again! Please, Father, don't let her die when I've just found her!* He pumped the brakes futilely as the truck shot from the road then plunged down a steep incline. He struggled to avoid smashing into rocks and to keep from rolling, but there was little he could do to control the truck's movements at this point.

His arm shot in front of Laura as he realized he couldn't avoid the tree looming in front of them. He tried to press her back against the seat and take the brunt of the collision himself, but the truck's momentum carried her forward. Mac threw his body between her and flying shards of glass from the splintering windshield. The truck jerked to a stop with its nose buried against the tree. Mac's head slammed against the dash.

* * *

Laura had clutched the edge of the seat, feeling the vehicle plunging wildly through the sagebrush and rocks scraping its sides. She closed her eyes, expecting the truck to tip or crash into a boulder. Memories of that other accident had flashed through her mind as a weight suddenly knocked the breath from her lungs.

Slowly regaining her senses now, Laura became aware of two things. Her head throbbed and her chest ached, as though she were struggling to breathe from under a great weight. She tried to shift her shoulders. She couldn't move. Panic gave rise to a scream, and then a creeping awareness told her she wasn't paralyzed. She really was trapped under a heavy weight, and that weight was the man who claimed to be her husband. Mac's head lay against her shoulder; his left arm trailed off the side of the seat.

Was he alive? He lay so still. She wondered if she could free herself when just breathing was an ordeal. She wondered, too, if moving him might cause further damage if he was seriously injured. She tried to summon her meager knowledge of first aid. If he was alive, perhaps she could wake him and get him to move.

"Mac," she called softly, then louder. "Mac!" There was no response.

six

LAURA INHALED AS far as possible and held every muscle still for a moment, focusing all her faculties. Mac's breath, like a slight breeze, blew against the damp skin of her throat. She exhaled loudly in relief. He was alive!

Deciding she must do something, she began trying to get out from under his crushing weight. Pausing at frequent intervals to catch her breath and to shore up her small reserve of strength, she eased her way forward a little bit at a time until her shoulders touched the door and she could draw a full breath. She lay there for a long time filling her aching lungs; then, grasping the door handle, she used it to lever herself into a sitting position with Mac's head on her lap.

Pain lanced through her left hip and upper thigh. She closed her eyes and compressed her lips. It was the old pain. It would go away, she told herself. She couldn't bring herself to consider that she might have reinjured her hip. As soon as she felt a little more rested, she'd free her lower body from its cramped position.

When she opened her eyes again, it was to discover that night's darkness was now illuminated by a full moon. She had no idea where she was or how far she and Mac had traveled from the ranch—or even in which direction she should go to find help.

Through the broken windshield she could see the twisted, snarled branches of a juniper tree in the bright moonlight.

Turning her head, she looked through first one side window, then the other. A desolate desert of lava rocks and sand, interspersed with the dark shapes of sagebrush and shadowy junipers, disappeared into ominous shadows. She wondered if she should start walking. But she didn't know which direction to go, and she didn't dare leave an unconscious man alone. She wished Mac would wake up.

Long ago her mother had taught her to pray, but she hadn't prayed for years. Now she found herself praying not just for help for herself, but for the stranger who lay deathly still inside the battered truck. She was a little surprised to discover that praying restored her sense of equilibrium and filled her with determination to do something about their situation.

A faint breeze chased through the silent truck cab, leaving her shivering in her sweat-dampened clothes. She clasped her arms against the chill, then glanced down at the still face resting in her lap. Mac's face was eerily pale. He needed to be kept warm, and she needed to discover the extent of his injuries.

She noticed now his high cheekbones and the way his long, thick eyelashes lay closed in smooth half-moons against them. Her fingers moved to brush the tendrils of damp hair off his forehead, and she recognized something boyishly familiar in his still features that awakened tenderness in her heart.

Why didn't he wake up? She didn't see any bumps or cuts on his head. Her eyes drifted lower until she noticed her white shorts were covered with dark stains. Blood! Her legs were numb from the weight that pressed against them, but she was certain she couldn't have lost that amount of blood and be unaware of it.

That meant Mac was bleeding. But where was the wound? Accident victims shouldn't be moved, she remembered, but how else could she find his injury? Fearing he had internal injuries or that his spine was broken, she tried to think what was the best course of action to take. He was bleeding, and that had to be her first priority. She would have to turn him over to locate the source of the blood.

She eased the door open to enlarge her working space, then lowered Mac's head to rest against the seat before working her way out of the truck to stand beside it. While clinging to the open door, she placed her weight on one foot, then the other. She trembled, but her hip held.

Turning back to Mac, she knelt beside him, grasped his belt and his shoulder, and strained to turn his limp body. When she succeeded in rolling him to his side, she slipped back inside the truck, scrunching herself into the narrow leg space on the passenger side. She brushed her hair out of her eyes and swallowed deeply, managing to dredge up enough courage to look for Mac's wound.

Blood thoroughly smeared her clothes, and she could feel sticky wetness where she knelt, but she couldn't find a wound on his back. While she debated her next step, she felt a wet droplet strike her bare leg. Her eyes went to the arm dangling over the side of the seat, the one he had flung across her body to save her from flying glass. It oozed blood from several places, but one gash appeared deeper than the others, and it bled steadily. If she didn't do something quickly, he would bleed to death.

She grasped the unconscious man's shirt where it already sported several rips and tore the fabric into pieces she could use to stanch the flow of blood. Forming a pad by folding the cloth, she pressed it against the wound. Long minutes passed before she felt reasonably certain the bleeding had stopped. She tied the pad in place with longer strips from Mac's shirt, then she settled down to wait.

He groaned several times but didn't awaken, which caused her to worry that he might be bleeding internally. Perhaps he had a concussion. She didn't think his head was bleeding, but she could see dried specks on his face that had probably come from scratches left by flying chips of glass. She wondered if head injuries always showed on the outside. She wished she could better remember a first aid class she'd been required to take during her first year at college.

Mac's continued unconscious state worried her. She lifted his eyelids, but she didn't know what she was supposed to look for. It was something she'd seen someone do in a movie.

She worked her fingers through his thick, straight hair until she discovered a small thumbnail-size lump above his left ear. It wasn't bleeding, but she wondered if it could account for his unconscious state.

She jumped when he suddenly moaned and rolled toward her. One hand snaked upward to capture hers, pressing it against the spot where his heart thumped. Breathless, she waited for him to move again or say something, but he seemed to be unconscious again. When she gently tugged her hand free, he released it without a struggle. She wished . . . No, it did no good to wish she could remember a younger, gentler Mac who might have been her friend.

Wearily, Laura climbed out of the truck again. Brushing the back of her hand across her forehead, she looked around hoping to see some sign of habitation. No lights of any kind met her eyes. She considered climbing back up to the road, but she knew that even if she reached it, she wouldn't know which way to go. She had been so wrapped up in her struggle with Mac that she now had no idea in which direction the ranch house lay or even how far they might have gone.

A sudden shiver shook her body. She recalled that at high altitudes, the nights can be cold even if the day was warm. A sound from the truck caught her attention, and she looked back at her patient. His shirt had been reduced to almost nothing. She feared he would freeze in the cold night air. His wounds needed to be washed and cared for properly. She had no idea where a water source might be, but at least, she decided, she could check the back of the truck for something to cover him.

With more determination than strength, Laura pulled herself inside the back of the pickup truck. There wasn't much there—a couple of bales of hay, a saddle, a horse blanket, a canvas tarp, an ax, and a small toolbox were all she found. Perhaps she could use the dusty horse blanket to cover Mac. It was better than nothing. Taking it with her, she climbed back down. Weariness slowed her steps as she returned to Mac, and she rubbed her aching hip as she walked.

Back inside the truck cab, she checked Mac's wounds once more. There didn't seem to be any fresh bleeding, and he looked as though he were simply sleeping.

"Mac," she whispered. "Wake up, Mac." He groaned and mumbled something unintelligible.

She spread the horse blanket over him, then eased his feet back inside the cramped cab so she could close the door. Before it shut, she noticed a familiar large soft-drink cup wedged behind the seat. Hoping it wasn't empty, she pried the cup free, removed the lid, and found several inches of water inside. It must be the melted ice from after his drink was finished earlier that day.

She took a sip and then, using the straw, she trickled a few drops of the melted ice past Mac's lips. He swallowed, then drew his lips together as though seeking more. Carefully she dribbled a little more into his mouth.

Cold compresses! That's what he needed. She'd read many times of placing a damp cloth over a lump left from an injury. Remembering a paper tissue in her pocket, she saturated it and held it against the lump on Mac's head, then wiped away as much of the dried blood on his face and arms as she could with the corner of her blouse.

Convinced she had done all she could to make Mac comfortable, Laura withdrew from the cramped truck to a nearby rock. She sank down beside it, resting her arms against its still warm surface. Was there anything else she could do? She tried to think, but she was so tired. She tried to keep her eyes open. She had to watch the road for headlights. Her head lowered of its own volition to rest against her arms. She fought to stay awake, but it was a useless battle. Her eyes closed.

* * *

Mac groaned. Instead of opening his eyes, he ground them more tightly shut. He hurt, really hurt. He lay still, trying to pull himself together. He hadn't hurt this badly since . . . Well, he'd never felt so much pain before.

He groaned again. This time he slowly opened one eye. He could see stars through the windshield. Windshield? What was he doing sleeping in his truck? What happened to cause all this pain? Slowly, he tried to sit up. His head hurt like it was caught in a blacksmith's vise, and his right arm felt like it had recently connected with a meat grinder. Every muscle in his body screamed as he pulled himself to a sitting position. He sat still for some time with his eyes tightly closed.

When he opened his eyes again, he found himself staring straight into a tree, one of the scraggly cedars some folks called junipers. Its rough aromatic branches intruded where his windshield should have been. Then something clicked in his brain, and he began to frantically look around.

Laura! She had been with him before . . . He remembered the accident in excruciating detail. Had she been thrown from the truck? Neither of them had been wearing a seat belt. He recalled her struggle to break free from his hold, and he groaned, remembering how he'd feared she might jump from the truck as it careened down the road. He'd been irrationally angry, and she'd been scared of him. She could be dead, or she might have taken off running to escape him.

"Laura!" His voice came out in a hoarse croak. Again he called. Again there was no answer.

He threw off the blanket. It hurt to move, but he struggled until he succeeded in getting out of the truck. His feet touched the ground, and his knees buckled. Desperately, he clutched for the door. His legs were like rubber, and a swirling blackness threatened to obliterate the starry night.

Slowly, his head cleared. His thinking sharpened. Laura had survived the crash! His arm was bandaged, and someone had draped a horse blanket over him. That someone had to be Laura, but where was she now? Surely she wouldn't try to make her own way back to the ranch at night across rugged, unfamiliar territory. Hand over hand, grasping the sides of the battered truck, he made his way around the wreck until he spotted her.

She was curled in a shivering ball against a rock, looking like the little girl he'd known a long time ago. He walked toward her, moving to her side as rapidly as his battered body would permit. Kneeling beside her, he breathed a sigh of relief. She wasn't unconscious; she was sleeping. A soft whimper reached his ears. Tears formed a mist before his eyes, and an ache formed in his chest as he remembered that soft cry from the first accident eight years ago.

Crouching on his heels, he gently shook her shoulder. She didn't awaken, and her skin was icy under his fingers. He felt for her pulse and found it steady and even.

It might be exhaustion making her sleep so soundly, or it might be hypothermia. He needed to get her warm. He noticed the dark splotches of color on her shorts that looked like dried blood. His worry increased that she may have been injured. He was going to have to get her back to the truck where he could check. His first priority, however, was to get her warm. Her shorts and lightweight blouse were no protection from a night in the High Country.

Intent on looking after her, he hurried back to the truck. Not daring to place any strain on his injured arm, he moved to the rear of his truck to drop the tailgate with his left hand. He picked up the ax he kept in the back of his truck and swung it to break up the bales of hay he'd planned to take up to the cabin. It took only minutes to scatter the hay. Then he covered the fragrant mounds with the tarp to protect Laura from the sharp dried stems of the hay before climbing out of the truck bed.

He stood leaning against the cold metal for several seconds. His breathing sounded harsh in his own ears, and his head pounded with each jarring movement. His arm ached, and he was beginning to feel dizzy. But he couldn't rest yet. He returned to the cab of the truck, retrieved the blanket and flashlight, and shut off the wavering headlights. The strong beam of the flashlight revealed the blood-drenched remnants of his shirt and the dried blood on the seat and on his pants. He headed back to Laura.

Mac knelt on the ground to slip his good arm under her shoulders and placed the other under her knees. He ground his teeth together as pain lanced through the arm Laura had bandaged. As soon as he was in a position to do so, he'd have to find out the extent of the injury to that arm. He felt so weak he wasn't even certain whether he would be able to regain a standing position.

Silently, he prayed he'd be able to get Laura to the bed he had prepared in the back of the truck. She was slender and probably didn't weigh much, but even a bucket of oats would feel like it weighed a ton right now. She stirred, then snuggled like a kitten against his chest. Suddenly, he felt stronger.

He rose to his feet with her, swaying momentarily. He stood still until he regained his balance, then walked toward the truck. Perspiration stood out on his forehead, and his arms shook. At last he leaned across the lowered tailgate, and his trembling arms released their burden none too gently onto the bed he'd prepared for her. He held his breath, waiting for her eyes to open. When they did, she looked at him vacantly, then closed them again. He dropped the horse blanket over her.

He fell twice before he managed to pull himself onto the truck bed. Moving on automatic pilot, he secured the tailgate before falling onto the canvas beside Laura, breathing heavily.

This day had been one long nightmare—from the shock of learning the bank wouldn't cash the check he'd written to secure a grain combine and crew, to finding out all of his assets were frozen pending a hearing to determine legal ownership of his ranch, to discovering the claimant against his ranch was Jake's daughter, a girl he had believed was dead for eight years. His wife!

"She-e-z!" His head hurt, as did his arm and almost every other piece of his anatomy he could name. He was bone tired. And thirsty. If only he hadn't acted like an adolescent fool from the moment he learned the woman trying to steal his ranch was the same one who had dumped her drink down his neck earlier. Something about her had gotten under his skin from the first moment he saw her. Her friend had called him a Neanderthal back at the gas station, and honesty forced him to admit that he'd certainly acted like one. After his temper had gotten him in a few fights back in high school, he'd worked hard to achieve self-mastery over a fault he considered an unacceptable weakness.

For a long time now, he'd prided himself on the reputation he had earned for his good judgment and the calm, sure way he faced every crisis. He'd become a leader in the local stock growers association and a Young Men's leader in his ward in Snowville. Well, he'd blown it this time.

seven

A LONG, DRAWN-OUT howl floated in the air, awakening Laura from exhausted slumber. She clawed a coarse blanket away from her face. What was that sound? More importantly, where was she? She seemed to be looking directly through a large open window. A diamond-sprinkled, black canopy of night-time sky spread beyond the window, and she stared wide-eyed at the grandeur before her, almost forgetting the sound that had awakened her. She'd never before spent a night outdoors away from city lights. The sky looked like an illustration from a book, with its blackness without end, broken only by glittering chips of ice casting a brilliance beyond anything she had ever seen before.

Mac! It all came crashing back. Was he alive? How could she have fallen asleep! She didn't remember climbing in the back of the truck, but she knew that was where she was lying. Her heart pounding, she struggled to sit up. She had to find Mac!

She turned her head. There was Mac's sleeping face, inches from her own. A flood of relief washed through her as she listened to his heavy breathing. She knew she couldn't have moved him, so he must have awakened on his own. He must have moved her to the truck as well, though that much concern for her welfare seemed unlikely.

She considered awakening him to check his wounds, then decided against it. She wasn't in any hurry to confront a conscious Mac Burgoyne again. She shuddered, recalling where they had been headed. What was he planning to do with her?

I've got to get out of here! Knowing Mac had regained consciousness, and that she wouldn't be abandoning a helpless man if she left, she resolved to get away from him. She felt certain she could find her way back to the road. She could follow it even if it led all the way back to the High Country. If she found another ranch house first, she could report the accident and call Bruce.

Mac mumbled something, and her eyes flew to his face. He didn't look frightening right now. In fact, there was something boyishly appealing about him with his face relaxed in sleep and a thick lock of hair plastered across his forehead.

But awake he resembles a madman more than a little boy. I'd better leave before he wakes up again. She began to inch her way toward the tailgate. Each time the hay rustled, he groaned, but little by little, she made her way toward the end of the truck bed. Reaching her goal, she paused to listen but could no longer hear him. Had he lapsed back into unconsciousness? She considered that possibility. *No, he's just asleep.*

The cold night air brought shivers to her stiff body as she left the blanket behind and prepared to climb down from the truck. Drawing her legs beneath her, she hoped her hip wouldn't suddenly give out when she shifted her weight. Ever since the accident, her hip had ached when she was cold or remained in one position too long.

Suddenly, the night air was split by a haunting coyote chorus. Laura froze. She glanced about in alarm. A long vice-like arm pulled her back down to the straw.

"No!" Laura struggled to free herself.

Mac merely wrapped the blanket around her, holding it in place and thus preventing her from escaping.

"Go back to sleep."

"No! Let me go!"

"You're staying right here. Use some sense, Laura. You don't know the way back to the ranch. Stumbling around out there in the dark on this mountain would be suicidal."

The coyotes howled again, and Laura shivered. She knew Mac was right, but she was more afraid of him than of the coyotes. A long, eerie cry rent the night air. *Well, maybe not.* Were coyotes as ferocious as wolves? Aunt Alice hadn't devoted much of Laura's schooling to studying wildlife.

Uneasily, she recalled Mac's refusal to consider an annulment. The way he held her now made her nervous. Panic lent her strength, allowing her to twist away. Before she could gain her feet, Mac grabbed her ankle, and she landed abruptly back on the straw. He leaned over her, and she jabbed at his face with a doubled-up fist.

Gathering her flailing fists in one hand, he warned, "Listen, you little cat, you're not leaving this truck tonight. Now get that through your head and stop fighting me!"

She screamed, tossing her head and twisting her body in a futile attempt to escape despite his order.

"Hold still! I'm not going to hurt you!" he shouted. The volume of his voice seemed at odds with his words but shocked her into stillness.

* * *

Dark shadows hid Laura's eyes, which he knew were an unusually dark shade of brown. They appeared shiny black in the moonlight now. Brushing his thumb across her cheek he discovered the shine came from tears. He didn't like the idea of tears in her eyes. Unbidden, he remembered another time when he had helplessly held her while tears spilled from her eyes. What was he thinking, scaring her half to death! Tenderness for the old Laura assailed him, and his arms tightened about her.

She bit him! Mac jerked back.

"Are you crazy? Anyone would think I . . ." Mac stopped. A chill swept through him. That's exactly what she thought! It had probably been worrying her ever since he told her where they were going earlier. And he couldn't say he blamed her after the way he'd treated her.

Neither one moved. The moon bathed the mountain in light, allowing Mac to see the fear and confusion in Laura's eyes.

"Don't look at me like that." Mac's voice was gruff. "I'm not going to . . . um . . . take advantage of you. I know I haven't given you much reason to trust me, but please believe I would never intentionally hurt you—in any way. You're quite safe with me." When she neither moved away nor resumed screaming, he continued speaking. "My head aches, and my arm feels like it's on fire. You must have injuries that need attention, too. Neither one of us is in any kind of shape for a long hike. When it gets light, we can appraise our situation better." He wouldn't make it two miles, and even if her injuries were slight, he'd be irresponsible to let her wander around in the dark in rough terrain at this altitude.

They both needed sleep. He couldn't stay awake all night to make sure she didn't try to leave. What was he supposed to do, tie her up? Taking a deep breath, he tried again to reassure her.

"It's really not safe for either of us to be out here alone. Besides, you're shaking with cold. If I promise to keep my hands off you, will you lie back down and try to sleep until morning?"

* * *

What he said made sense, but could she trust him? Laura nodded her head warily. Without taking her eyes from his face, she lay back down on the canvas. She tried not to flinch when Mac covered her with the horse blanket. For what seemed like hours, she lay on her back, shivering as she watched the night sky. With all that had happened, should she trust Mac to keep his word? Strangely, she did. With that realization, she relaxed to drift into sleep.

* * *

Mac awoke before daylight. Far above him the stars shone bright and brittle. Watching Laura sleep, he smiled wryly. She might not remember him, but he remembered her. He'd been six years old when Jacob swept him up to peer over the side of her bassinet. One look from her wide brown eyes, and he was a goner. He recalled the way he had nearly burst with pride and how all the ranch hands had laughed when she'd elude her mother to follow him around the ranch, mimicking his every action. Then April took her away when he was only ten. He closed his eyes against remembering the lost, lonely days that had followed. He had been bereft without her. He'd missed April, too. She was the closest to a mother he'd ever known.

He thought of seeing Laura in San Francisco, a fifteen-year-old girl wearing a summery lace dress, her long dark curls tumbling to her waist from some kind of clip covered with pearls and pink flowers. He still had that clip; he'd kept it after it fell to the ground when the paramedics slid her onto a gurney.

He'd been tongue-tied when he'd seen her for the first time after more than ten years apart. He was freshly home from a mission and planning to return to college in the fall—he was embarrassed to think he had a crush on a young high school girl, no matter how cute she was. Of course, *cute* wasn't quite the right word to describe her. Even at barely fifteen, *beautiful* or *gorgeous* was more fitting.

Given her age, he couldn't consider pursuing her, but he had followed her with his eyes the way she'd once followed him in her tiny red boots. She had been so oblivious to him; she had barely said two words to him until the night in the motel pool when she'd shyly flirted with him and they had laughed together over inconsequential little things. That night he'd begun to hope that after she grew up he might have a chance to win her. And when Jake asked him to marry her to protect her if she lived and to keep the ranch intact if father and daughter both died, he'd done so willingly, even though in his youthful infatuation he feared he would die, too, if Laura did.

Bitterness returned as Mac considered how she had re-entered his life only to bring him financial ruin. That it was Laura doing this to him hurt most of all. He closed his eyes tightly in a vain attempt to block out the thoughts and memories that kept him awake until the sun sent its light spreading across the mountainside.

eight

LAURA AWOKE TO the sun streaming into her eyes. For a few minutes, she thought she was alone; then she heard a clanging, followed by angry, muffled words she couldn't quite make out. Raising her head, she looked around and then stood. *Oh-h!* She was stiff! Gingerly, she rubbed her hip before making her way over the tailgate of the truck. It seemed an awfully long drop to the ground.

When she straightened, she saw Mac bent over the front end of the truck. The hood lay crumpled on the ground, and his toolbox sat in the dirt near his feet. She approached him with care.

"Can you fix it?"

"Not a chance!" He didn't look up. "At least not here. Once I get it back to the shop, I can probably get it going again."

Laura looked at the twisted metal wrapped around the tree, the shattered windshield, then the heap of metal on the ground. Unless the impact had popped the hood open, she couldn't see how he had managed to remove it. She knew little about engines, but what she could see didn't look encouraging. Loose wires, bent metal, and dripping hoses looked pretty hopeless to her.

* * *

It didn't surprise Mac when Laura stood on a rock and bent her head to look inside the engine compartment of his truck. Little Laura had always stuck her nose in everything he did. One corner of his mouth lifted in a faint smile as he remembered.

Slowly, he straightened, wiping greasy smears down the sides of his pants before turning to look at her. He watched her run her fingers through her short sleek hair, prompting it to fall into a semblance of order. He suppressed the urge to reach out and tousle the silky strands himself. He remembered how his fingers itched to touch her hair that long-ago summer. He'd only touched it once, and the occasion had fallen far short of romance. His eyes darkened, recalling her head lying in his lap while he struggled to stop the gash on her head from bleeding.

Dark shadows hovered under Laura's eyes in the early morning light. Her face was pale and streaked with dirt. A bruise showed on her collarbone above the rounded neckline of her torn shirt. Several smaller bruises disappeared beneath the fabric, and a matching set decorated the top of her right arm. The knuckles of her right hand were scraped, and her stained shorts brought a gasp of fear to his throat.

"You better sit down." He reached to help her.

"I'm all right." She shrugged off his hand.

"You look like you've lost a lot of blood." He hustled her back toward the cab of the truck. His hands settled at her waist to boost her to the seat. She sat with her feet dangling out of the open door, watching him warily. He moved his hands towards the button fastener of her shorts, then paused, ignoring her hands slapping his.

"I'm not sure what to do," he said. "The blood has dried; taking off your shorts might start it bleeding again."

She stopped hitting him, and her eyes darted to the bandage on his arm. His eyes followed.

"It's your blood," she said.

"Mine?" His eyes widened. "Are you sure? There's a lot more blood on your clothes than mine."

"You fell across me. You were knocked out by the impact and cut when the windows shattered." He looked at her assessingly, trying to decide whether or not she was telling him the truth. After a long pause, he nodded and stepped back. "Okay. That makes sense. I'm sorry if I scared you, but I was really worried."

She smiled a wobbly smile, the first she'd smiled since she'd bumped into him at the gas station.

The early morning sun was beginning to warm the air. It wouldn't be long until it turned hot. He ran his hand across the black stubble on his chin. His head didn't hurt so much now. They were closer to the house than the cabin. He could walk back to the ranch, but what about Laura?

"Laura, we're only a few miles from the ranch. Do you think you can walk that far? It's a steep climb up the hill to the road."

"Won't someone be looking for us? Wouldn't it be better to stay with the truck?"

"If we were lost, but we're not. I know where we are, and since Dad won't be worried, he won't send anyone looking for us."

"Bruce will be worried."

"Dad will have smoothed everything over by now."

She gave him a dubious look.

He met her dubious stare with a look she couldn't decipher. "Can you walk?" he repeated.

"Yes." She struggled to her feet, finding herself uncomfortably close to Mac. Taking a hasty step back, she bumped into the truck's tailgate. Rosy color climbed her cheeks. She hated that she blushed so easily! Bruce had always liked to tease her just to make it happen. In business classes, she'd gotten used to speaking in front of a group, but in personal situations she still blushed at the slightest provocation. She attempted to turn away, but Mac reached out to take her hand.

"Just a minute," she stammered, freeing her hand. "There's a little water left. Maybe we should take it with us."

Mac was surprised to see her reach for the soft drink cup he had forgotten about and then extend it toward him. He had a vague memory of dreaming he was lost in the desert. He'd been dying of thirst when a tiny trickle of rain fell from the sky. He shook his head to clear away the image, then winced at the stab of pain that followed.

"We're going to need both hands to climb, but it would be a good idea to drink this before we start." Lifting off the lid, he held the cup out to her. She took a swallow then passed it back. He drained the cup of the tiny amount left in it.

Climbing back up the hillside to the road wasn't easy. He wanted to take her hand and guide her over the roughest spots, but he feared she'd turn tail and run if he even looked like he might touch her. He kept moving up the steep slope, and Laura followed.

"Ouch!" She stubbed her toe. Walking was harder than Laura had expected. She had so many sore muscles and bruises that she didn't know where she hurt most. Sandals left a lot to be desired as hiking shoes. By the time she reached the road, several toes were bruised and bleeding, her hip throbbed, and she thought she would die of thirst. Standing at the top of the ravine, she turned slowly, taking in a panoramic view of a valley that seemed to go on forever. Her toe struck something sharp as she turned, causing her to lose her balance.

She screamed as she began sliding backward. Mac grasped her arm, pulling her forward to stand beside him on the road. As soon as she was steady on her feet again, he released her, at which point she promptly sat down in the dust and picked up her foot to examine it.

"Stupid cactus!" She pulled three long spikes from her toes.

Once the needles were out, Mac urged her to her feet, and they began walking. At first it wasn't so bad, but as the morning grew warmer and her feet grew more bruised, she became irritated.

"Watch where you're stepping." Mac seized her arm, jerking her back before she could walk too close to a pile of rocks. "There are rattlers out here." Mac's admonition to watch out for snakes didn't do much to endear her to the rugged landscape. She resented becoming personally acquainted with every prickly cactus, rock, and shrub on the mountain. And she resented Mac for driving her out here in the first place.

Standing on the narrow dirt road panting from the exertion of a painful hike that seemed to have no end, Laura glanced at her companion. His skin looked gray, and a deep double furrow drew his eyes closer together. In spite of her anger with the man, she felt a twinge of sympathy.

"Your head hurts."

"I'm okay. Let's get moving." He shrugged away her concern.

She shrugged as well. *All right*, she thought. *Suit yourself.*

Their pace was slow, and they didn't speak much as they walked. Occasionally, Laura glanced at Mac. He seemed to be concentrating on where he placed each foot, and she suspected he was experiencing more pain than he let on. She looked away and out over a brush-covered valley. Outcroppings of lava rock appeared at irregular intervals, providing a black contrast to the silvery sagebrush. The sky was an incredible shade of blue she hadn't seen since her Crayola days. A few stout, twisted junipers dotted the mountainside. She felt something wild and free clutch at her heart, and she knew that she'd once loved this land of stark contrasts.

What was she thinking! She certainly couldn't be attracted to this wild, empty land any more than she could feel any attraction for the enigmatic man walking a few steps ahead of her. She needed to keep her attention on moving forward.

An animal suddenly leaped from under the brush beside the narrow dirt road. Laura's heart pounded, and, without thinking, she clutched at Mac's arm.

"Jackrabbit."

Feeling foolish, Laura dropped her hand to her side while, wide-eyed, she watched until the rabbit disappeared in a blur of black and gray into the brush. That was no soft, cuddly bunny, she decided. It was all muscle and sinews. She couldn't help seeing some similarities between the lean grace of the animal and the man beside her. Obviously, neither one carried a spare ounce of fat, and they each moved with a grace that left her breathless.

Of course, comparing Mac to a rabbit was ridiculous! She rolled her eyes. It would be more accurate to compare him to some snarling creature with fangs and claws. She wondered if she was in an early stage of sunstroke.

At one point, their steps carried them up a long incline. As they climbed, Laura found breathing increasingly difficult. Her side hurt. The pain urged her to stop while bleeding toes and blistered heels exaggerated her slight limp. She tried to ignore the pain but couldn't. Would Mac stop to let her rest if she asked? She wouldn't ask; instead, she trudged on.

The road, nothing more than a couple of dusty ruts cutting across the side of the mountain, curved under a steep outcropping of black rock at its highest point, providing a brief respite from the searing heat of the sun. With or without Mac's approval, she meant to take advantage of the meager patch of shade.

Limply, she slid to the ground, easing her back against the rocks behind her. Little spots danced before her eyes as a blinding pain built inside her head. "I can't go on," she gasped, swallowing her pride.

"We'll rest a few minutes." Mac kicked the brush beside the road several times. His eyes took their time scanning the nearby rocks before he leaned his shoulder against the side of a boulder taller than him. He stood silent and motionless, his eyes focused on something in the distance.

Laura glanced up at the figure standing a few feet away. Her head pounded, and her vision was distorted. Her skin felt hot and dry. Mac appeared to be a wavering black shadow. She was going to be sick. Nausea made her clutch her stomach.

Clasping her arms around her bare legs, she bowed her head, resting it against her knees. After a few minutes, she slowly opened her eyes. Her vision seemed to have almost returned to normal, and her head felt much better. Her eyes drifted across the valley spread before her, and she recognized the dots in the distance as cattle.

"We better get moving." Mac's voice cut into her thoughts.

"I'm not sure I can walk," Laura said as she slowly pulled herself to a standing position, wincing as her sandal straps cut into her blistered heels.

"No one with a lick of sense would wear shoes like that in the mountains." Mac looked disdainfully at the thin straps crisscrossing her feet.

"I didn't plan to hike in them," she shot back. Only an awareness of how painful such an action would be on her bare toes kept her from kicking the unfeeling cowboy's shin. She rubbed her hand across her aching hip. He'd probably just think she was making a bid for sympathy if she told him about the three long surgical steel pins holding her hip together.

Biting her lip against the pain, she moved forward onto the road, mocking her own stubbornness. *At least my headache is taking my mind off my hip!*

Soon they crested another hill, and before them spread acres and acres of golden wheat. Just beyond the grain stood the ranch house and behind it miles of unbroken sage and juniper trees. Laura stared at the dazzling view. There was so much land and sky! Where had she gotten the idea this land was ugly? It was beautiful, so wild and free. She felt a moment's sadness for the little girl who had left all of this to live in a crowded city.

"Mac, this will sound like a stupid question to you, but can you tell me how you plant the wheat so it grows halfway up the mountainside and why little islands of lava rock and brush are left scattered through the fields?"

He looked startled by the question, then relaxed as he explained the basics of farming the rugged terrain. He gestured broadly with his good arm for emphasis as he talked about the land he clearly loved. As he was about to expound on the harvest season, he stopped abruptly and walked on in silence for several seconds.

"Don't stop now, Mac. I'm really interested in learning about the ranch. What else can you tell me?" She hoped Mac would keep talking, if for no other reason than to distract her from her increasing discomfort.

Mac did speak but with unexpected bitterness. "We're both going to lose it, thanks to your greed!"

Laura was stunned at the pain and anger behind his words. "Why should we? I have no intention of taking anything of yours. I only want my share. You're the greedy one. You're trying to keep me from my inheritance."

"Do you see that wheat?" His voice dripped with sarcasm.

Little black dots were dancing before her eyes again, but she nodded her head in spite of the pain. "Of course I see it."

"That field of grain is worth thousands of dollars if it is harvested this week, but it's going to sit there until it rots because I can't harvest it."

"Why can't you? Why blame me because you can't do something with it?" The field swirled around in circles like a gigantic whirlpool.

"Because—" his voice sounded like a roar in her aching head— "it takes money to hire equipment and crews, and you, my dear, sweet wife, have frozen my bank account. I own a ranch valued in seven figures, but thanks to you, I can't lay my hands on a measly couple of thousand to harvest that grain. I can't buy a scythe, let alone hire a combine and trucks."

She tried to make sense of what he was saying, but the ground wouldn't hold still, and she knew she was going to be sick. She swayed forward, and he caught her upper arms.

"Are you all right?"

She decided she must be imagining the concern in his voice.

"I really didn't think I was injured too badly," she murmured, "but either I was hurt more than I thought or I have the flu."

"Headache?" he queried.

She nodded her head, sending lightning strikes of pain shooting through her skull.

His palms touched her cheeks and forehead. Her eyelids drooped. She was too tired to object to his scrutiny. She should push his hands away, but she couldn't remember why. His touch felt cool and soothing. Besides, it would take more energy than she had to push him away.

"It's the altitude."

His words made no more sense to her than the unexpectedly gentle tone in his voice.

"What does the altitude have to do with a headache?" She managed to get the words out but wasn't certain she cared whether he answered or not.

"We're pretty high here—over six thousand feet. Physical exertion at high altitudes, when you're not used to it, can make a person sick. I'm not sure we're high enough for true high altitude sickness—your nose isn't bleeding, and the nausea appears mild—but trauma added to altitude can bring on a form of the illness."

"Your head aches too, but you don't seem to be sick."

"Different cause. I took a little bump on the head, and I lost some blood. A good meal and a few hours sleep in a cool room and I'll be fine. You're not accustomed to this altitude. I am."

She could feel herself sliding toward the ground. Then she was cradled in his arms. The cowboy was shouting at her, then Bruce was shouting, too. Someone gave her something to drink. It was vile tasting. She wished everyone would just go away and let her sleep. Something wet and cool brushed her skin. It lingered and soothed. Obediently, she swallowed when she was told to, then she was blessedly free to drift into a soothing darkness where there was no heat or pain.

nine

"HI! IT'S ABOUT time you woke up."

Laura stared with unfocused eyes at Bruce.

"Does your head still hurt?"

"Yes, but not so much." Her words sounded mumbled and slurred to her own ears. She pinched the indentation between her eyes and slowly surveyed the room. For just a moment when she first awoke, she'd thought she was back in the hospital where she'd spent so much time as a teenager.

In actuality, the room bore no resemblance to a hospital room. Even in the dim light she recognized the room Hal Burgoyne had pointed out to her as the master bedroom. The heavy brocaded green and white drapes were closed, but she remembered the lacy sheers behind them and recognized the rich cherrywood of the bedroom set she suspected was her parents' and that should now belong to her. It still seemed strange to think she owned a whole house full of beautiful furniture, half a ranch, and would soon inherit a small fortune from a trust fund she hadn't known existed. Until a month ago, her aunt's shabby home was all she knew.

Yesterday, when she saw the room where she now lay, a number of masculine items were in evidence. They were nowhere to be seen now. She wondered which room the occupant had moved his things into. She assumed Hal had claimed this room after her father's death. She wondered again why the

Burgoynes lived in her family's house and why they didn't have one of their own.

She let her fingers trace a tiny square in the quilted bedspread. She had no recollection of returning to the house or being tucked into bed. Keeping her eyes lowered, she asked, "How did I get here?"

Bruce shifted uneasily in the chair beside her bed. He opened his mouth a couple of times, but no words came out.

"Bruce?"

"Umm, you and Mac were in an accident. You weren't hurt seriously, but the long hike back caused you some problems. You're going to be all right," he hastened to assure her. "You're just going to have a headache for a few days, and you might feel dizzy and nauseated if you get up too quickly."

"I remember the accident, Bruce, and the hike back. What I don't recall is how I got *here*." She emphasized her point by patting the quilt.

"Uh, you passed out. Mac carried you back to the house."

Glancing down at herself, Laura didn't recognize the shirt she wore as one she had packed in her suitcase before leaving Aunt Amy's house. It wasn't even her shirt, and it didn't look like one of Bruce's either. In fact, it looked suspiciously like a man's white dress shirt. She remembered the shirt hanging on the doorknob earlier. Slowly, she lifted her hand to touch her face, then her hair. There was no blood or dust on her arms, and her hair felt clean. A blush rose from the deep V of the shirt and spread to the roots of her hair.

"Bruce, who cleaned me up and put this shirt on me?" She couldn't meet his eyes as she held her breath waiting for an answer.

Bruce released a hiss of breath he had been holding too long. "Look, I know it seems humiliating, Laura, but we had to make certain you were okay."

"Please don't tell me you . . . that Mac . . ." Her eyes shot to Bruce's face. He flinched from her shock and anger.

"Laura, there was absolutely no way I could prevent him from taking care of you. When I saw him coming up the road with you, I jumped into my car and went to meet you. You were both covered with dry blood, and Mac looked like he was hurting nearly as badly as you were. He climbed in the car with you in his arms, and when we reached the house, he stepped out of the car, still carrying you, and walked right up the stairs and into this room. Before I could get to you, he locked the door."

Turning her face to the wall, Laura found herself wishing she could pull the covers over her head and never have to face any of the men in this house. She felt Bruce pick up her hand. Gently, he rubbed the back of it with the knuckles of his other hand.

"Laura, I don't think it was quite what you imagined. When we heard water running, Hal went downstairs to get a key to open the door, but by the time he found it and got back, Mac just opened the door and walked out. You'll never know how tempted I was to take a swing at him, but he looked like someone already had, and I just wanted to make certain you were safe. While I was trying to see how badly you were hurt, I heard Mac tell his father he had wrecked the pickup and that you were only bruised and suffering from a touch of altitude sickness. He said he'd only washed away the blood and grime from your face and limbs and that you'd probably want to undress completely and shower after you woke up."

"Oh, Bruce, I wish we hadn't come." Tears streamed down her cheeks. Seating himself on the side of her bed, Bruce gathered her into his arms. "It'll be all right," he whispered. "Hal called a doctor in Burley who assured him you only need to rest and get plenty of fluids."

"My, what a touching scene."

Laura looked up to see Mac leaning negligently against the door frame. One quick look revealed a story of deep fatigue. Just when she thought she was too angry and embarrassed to ever face him again, he stepped into the room and she found herself wanting to comfort him! It was unsettling to see glimpses of a lonely little boy where she expected to see only a hard, ruthless adult.

After lowering Laura back against the pillows, Bruce stood and slowly turned to face Mac. From beneath lowered lashes, Laura watched the two men face each other. The nearly palpable tension between these two made little sense to Laura. Mac was possibly an inch shorter than Bruce's six foot two, but his high-heeled western boots made him appear taller. His lean frame was considerably lighter, but there was something about Mac's corded muscles that spoke of tightly compressed power. No one would be foolish enough to consider Mac the smaller man. She hoped neither one was going to pick a fight right now. She wasn't sure she could handle any more drama.

"I'm glad you're here," Bruce said, though he sounded anything but glad. "I wanted to tell you that we're leaving here as soon as Laura can get dressed. She came here in good faith to find answers. From the moment she set foot in this house— her house—she has been insulted and abused. You've admitted you intend to steal her property, dragged her off for who knows what purpose, and nearly killed her. From now on, you can talk to her attorney or the sheriff."

"Laura isn't going anywhere. She's a sick woman right now and shouldn't be moved until she recovers. You're welcome to go, of course. I'm her husband, something you'll never be, no matter how much you might want to. I won't let her leave."

Bruce's right fist connected with Mac's left eye. Laura's eyes widened. She couldn't believe it. Easygoing Bruce, her cousin who never lost his temper, who always laughed and talked his way out of every tight spot, had struck Mac. Hard. Mac didn't even try to defend himself; he staggered backward until he crashed into the door frame. Bruce held his position with the balls of his feet pressing lightly on the deep plush carpet, his arms hanging loosely at his sides, ready to assume a defensive position.

Laura sat forward, holding her breath as Mac steadied himself. The cold, opaque glitter in his eyes sent a tremor of fear rushing through her. She opened her mouth to scream as Mac took a step toward her cousin. His words stopped her.

"Okay, Wilson, I deserved that. Consider it on the house. But don't try a second one."

Neither man backed down. They faced each other with a scant three feet of carpet separating them. Laura struggled to free herself from the confining quilt. She had to reach them, stop them from hurting each other. The room began to spin, telling her she was going to be too late. Perhaps if she sat back down. Slowly, she sank to the floor beside the bed, her head dipped between her knees as she fought the blackness and nausea.

"Mac! Bruce! What are you two doing?" Hal's voice cut the tension like steel. "You're supposed to be in bed, Mac. Doc said twenty-four hours, and twenty-four hours it's going to be. And you, Bruce, go on down to the study. We've got some talking to do."

"I'm not leaving Laura alone . . ." Bruce started to speak, then turned to see her on the floor. Mac knelt beside her. Gently, he lifted her into his arms and then placed her back on the bed. He pulled the sheet up to her shoulders. Turning away, he abruptly stepped into the bathroom en suite to return moments later with two small tablets and a glass of water.

Bruce didn't interfere when Mac lifted Laura's shoulders and urged her to accept the tablets. She swallowed them without resistance before he lowered her back to the pillow and pulled the sheet up to her chin. He briefly reached out a finger to brush her cheek before he spun on his heel and headed for the door.

Bruce stepped to Laura's bedside, and Mac paused, uncertain what to do. He didn't want the overprotective, so-called cousin to whisk Laura away before they'd had a chance to sort things out.

"Laura, are you all right?" Bruce knelt beside the bed, lifting her hand in his. "Don't worry. I'll get you out of here."

Mac's hands balled into fists.

"Wilson." Laura heard Mac's harsh voice as though it came from a long distance away. He sounded tired, drained of his previous anger. "I spoke with a doctor by phone a few minutes ago. He said Laura needs to stay in bed for a few days. She shouldn't be moved."

"I'll take her to a hospital," Bruce argued.

"The closest hospital is a couple of hours away. Getting there involves some pretty rough roads. Go on downstairs. Call your own doctor and see what he advises."

"I don't know . . ." Bruce's voice trailed off.

Hal shook his head signaling his annoyance with the two younger men. "I'll stay with her until she falls asleep." His voice turned dry as he added to Bruce, "Mac isn't going to hurt her. He's got a king-size headache of his own, his arm is sore, and I don't suppose his eye is feeling up to par either. You go on down to the study and wait for me. And you . . ." He turned to his son. His voice sounded slightly amused. "Go to bed. She'll be safe with me."

Sensing, rather than hearing, both Mac and Bruce leave the room, Laura kept her eyes closed. A slight sound near the bed brought her eyes open moments later. Hal stood beside the bed, holding the back of a rocking chair. The chair creaked as he sat on it. She felt his gaze on her face.

"Would you like a cold drink?" he asked.

The drink must have been sitting on the nightstand because before she could answer, she felt his hands behind her shoulders, and he was holding a glass to her lips. Too late she realized the glass held something other than water. It tasted like lemon and honey, with a bitter, spicy aftertaste.

"You'll feel better when you wake up." Hal smoothed the light covering over her shoulders before settling in the rocker. He picked up a book that was lying on the bedside table and began to read.

When next she awoke it was to discover Mac sleeping in a different chair beside her bed. His arm had been rebandaged, but his face still looked fatigued. Her head felt much better, and she wondered if she could make her way to the adjoining bathroom without waking him. She decided not to risk moving too quickly. Instead, she eased her way to a sitting position. That seemed all right, so she swung her feet off the side of the bed.

"Where do you think you're going?" Some slight sound must have awakened Mac. She blushed, recalling she was wearing very little, but in the dim light she hoped he couldn't see.

"To the bathroom." She hated to explain her private needs.

His arms scooped her from the bed, and in a few short strides, he deposited her in the bathroom. Before she could voice a protest at his presence, he backed out of the room, closing the door behind himself.

Laura's hands clasped her burning cheeks. The shirt she wore was woefully inadequate. How she hated feeling at a disadvantage with Mac. He had gotten her back to the house when she could go no farther, and he had allowed her a few minutes privacy in the bathroom, but those small points in his favor didn't offset all the pain he had caused her.

Awhile later, a light tap sounded on the door.

"Go away!"

"One more minute, then I'm coming in after you."

Laura didn't doubt he would carry out the threat. Lifting her chin at a defiant angle, she opened the door to walk on her own only to be swept off her feet before she could take a step toward the bed.

"Put me down!"

Ignoring her command as well as her feebly kicking heels and the fist she ineptly pounded against his chest, he carried her across the room. Instead of returning her to the bed, he settled himself—with her still in his arms—in the armchair he'd pulled up beside the bed.

"I'm going to scream," she warned.

"Don't wake the whole house," he admonished. "Neither Dad nor Bruce has slept for two nights. There's no reason to disturb them."

"Leave me alone," she whispered, hating to admit he was right but conceding the point. She tried to twist out of his arms.

Tightening his hold, he continued speaking. "We need to talk, and we need to do it without your boyfriend interrupting or Dad giving orders."

"Bruce isn't my boyfriend."

"Could have fooled me."

"Bruce is my cousin!"

"So you say. But there are lots of different kinds of cousins."

"Oh, for Pete's sake! He's my first cousin, Mac—my only cousin, in fact. His father, my Uncle Alec, is my mother's older brother."

Mac felt happier at this news than he had all day, though he knew it shouldn't matter to him. He tried not to let his improved spirits show. "Fine then, your cousin. Whatever he is, he has no part in this discussion. Now, are you going to listen or not?"

"Are you going to let me go?" She shot back.

Mac surged to his feet, and Laura found herself thrust back into bed with both pillows plumped behind her back. Perversely, she felt bereft when his arms released her. He returned to the chair, leaning back with his bare feet extended and his ankles crossed in front of him. *He should be less formidable wearing a bathrobe,* she thought resentfully. *But he still makes me nervous.*

Before the silence between them could become awkward, Mac broached the subject of the ranch again, hoping that this time they could have a productive discussion for once.

"This ranch has been my responsibility since I was twenty-one years old. Dad had a heart attack not long after we got home from that California trip. At that time, he turned his share of the ranch over to me. He'd dabbled in local politics before, and with the doctor's orders to avoid too much physical exertion, he decided to pursue his political interest more fully. He wanted me to completely take over running the ranch, and, in his generosity, he pretty much gave me everything, taking the role of a consultant."

Mac took a deep breath before continuing. "Jake's share became mine when Alice notified us of your death. As far as I understand it, you abandoned your claim to the ranch when you came of age and did nothing to stake a claim to it."

"I couldn't do anything. I didn't know Daddy left his share of the ranch to me, and I didn't know what Aunt Alice had told you."

"You keep saying that, but I find it hard to believe."

"Whether you believe me or not, it's the truth. I'd like to know how you managed to claim my inheritance, anyway. Where was my death certificate? Why weren't my attorney and family notified? Didn't anyone question the validity of that marriage certificate between a twenty-one year-old man and a fifteen-year-old girl who was practically on her deathbed?"

"I hear what you're saying, but I didn't steal anything from you. Jake and Dad wanted the ranch kept intact. Originally, they intended for us to someday become partners, but when it appeared you were going to die, Jake's first concern was to make certain the ranch wouldn't be broken up."

"Of course the ranch came first. It always came first." The words sounded bitter even to her own ears.

"Come on, Laura. Jake thought you were dying, and he knew he was. The ranch was his life's work; he had to do what was best for it. He tried to do what was best for you, too. He knew that if you lived, money wouldn't be a problem, but you were too young and inexperienced to run the ranch. He trusted my dad and me to take care of you. Besides, he wanted to give you a chance to escape that battle-ax, Mormon-hating aunt of yours."

"Don't criticize Aunt Alice! You didn't know her. She devoted her whole life to taking care of mother and me. And as for Daddy's will, it seems clear that he wanted me to have his share of the ranch with no strings attached. No matter what either of us believe his intention was, legally half this ranch is mine. There is no way you could have taken it over without lying and cheating, since there was no death certificate." Laura's head bounced for emphasis, sending a stab of pain down the back of her neck.

"I didn't lie, and there was no cheating involved on my part. Your aunt's letter said you were dead. I had our marriage certificate in my wallet. Together these satisfied the state. In my safe there's a deed showing I own this ranch free and clear."

"Mr. Sylvester believes otherwise. He had no trouble getting a court order to protect my claim."

"Oh yes, your court order." Mac took a deep breath, willing himself to remain calm and rational. "Let me explain a few facts to you. It takes a considerable amount of money to operate a ranch this size. I write checks to pay expenses, and your court order has frozen my checking account and closed my access to credit. I have exactly thirty-one dollars and fourteen cents cash in my pocket. That means I can't harvest my grain. Without that crop, there's no money for feed to get my cattle through the winter. We're in a drought here. The cattle can't survive on range grass that isn't there, and with that court order in place, I can't buy anything to feed them. So you see, there's an immediate cash-flow problem that in turn creates even more problems as time goes on. It's a domino effect."

He left the chair to pace across the floor. Laura followed his movements with a sense of bewilderment. She didn't want revenge or to penalize anyone, least of all helpless animals. She wasn't trying to shut down the ranch—she only wanted what was hers. Whether Mac would believe her or not, she knew what it meant to lack the money to meet everyday needs. Discovering she would soon be a wealthy woman had come so recently; she hadn't yet learned to accept what both Mr. Sylvester and Bruce insisted was reality. And anyway, she didn't have any money yet.

"I'll call Mr. Sylvester Monday morning and ask him to release your money," she offered.

"And what do you expect in return?"

"I don't expect anything from you, except what is rightfully mine. I'm willing to release your bank account, but I'm not dropping my claim."

"No, that would be too good to be true. What worries me most is that you'll never give up until you get your hands on everything I own."

"That's where you're wrong, Mac. I'll take what is mine and not one thing more. If you want my part of the ranch so badly, you can buy it; then I'll leave, and you'll never have to see me again."

"You're forgetting one important point, Laura." Mac was suddenly leaning over her with one hand on either side of her pillow. "You're my wife, and that gives our little problem a whole different twist."

It was difficult to breathe with Mac's face inches from hers. There was something in his eyes that brought goose bumps to her skin. Fighting to maintain control, she licked her bottom lip, then felt Mac's eyes zero in on her mouth as surely as if he had physically touched it.

"I'm not your wife," she said slowly and deliberately. "A marriage I can't remember can't be legal."

"Oh, you remember all right. You can't deny you knew we were married or that you conspired to make me believe you were dead."

"Why would I want to do such a thing? Of course I didn't know," Laura insisted.

"Don't deny it. Your aunt wrote demanding the return of April's furniture at the same time she told us you were dead. Why would she want furniture when her house was already fully furnished if it wasn't for you? Now, as it happens, Dad and I returned from that disastrous California trip to a raging range fire that wiped out half our grazing land plus our house with all of our furniture and belongings. We were forced to camp out in your house. I wrote back to your aunt, explaining about the fire and enclosing a copy of our marriage license, letting her know I intended to keep what my wife had inherited from her father, including the house and furniture. Amongst your dad's paperwork were details about the trust fund your mother had left you and other financial information that related to April and Alice. Knowing Alice had no income of her own, I told your aunt I wouldn't touch your personal fortune as long as she remained alive and needed to draw on the arrangement April had set up for her support. I never heard from either of you after that. I believe the court is going to consider that an abandonment of claim against your father's estate."

"No!" Laura barely breathed the denial. Her eyes were rounded with shock and her skin pale. She couldn't absorb the implications of all he was saying. "Aunt Alice couldn't have known. If she had received a letter from you, Bruce and I would have found it. She never threw anything away. She had a copy of the marriage certificate, but obviously, she thought it was as fake as I did when Bruce discovered it. Aunt Alice wanted me to marry the son of one of her friends . . . I dated him a few times . . . If she knew I was already married, she wouldn't have . . . But I'm not married!"

"Oh, you're married all right," he said softly.

She was having difficulty taking all of this in. She bit down on her bottom lip, then smoothed the slight indentation with her tongue.

Unable to resist, he smoothed her hair back from her face, savoring the sleek satin of her skin until he encountered scar tissue. Abruptly, he withdrew his hand. Scars! And the scars weren't all on the outside. Physical scars didn't matter; she was still beautiful. But the other scars did matter. This woman wasn't the grown-up Laura of his dreams. This Laura was set on a course of destruction. Her aunt had attempted to destroy Jake because she couldn't bear having her precious April married to a Mormon. He didn't doubt she'd passed on her bigoted views to her great-niece. And to think he'd been making plans to have his deceased wife sealed to him in the temple this fall.

What's the matter with me? How could he think for one minute this woman was his Laura? Like the old Laura, she touched something tender deep inside him, but this was a Laura he didn't know.

The door didn't slam as he left the room; he pulled it quietly closed behind him. She heard no footsteps down the carpeted hall, but the soft whisper of a closing door in the distance served to jolt her into an awareness that nothing had been resolved. Why did every discussion turn into arguments and recriminations? The long hours before dawn afforded her plenty of time to think. Self-pity alternated with anger as she thought of all the people who had hurt and betrayed her. It wasn't just Mac. Her whole life appeared to have been built on lies. If the things the Burgoyne men had told her about Aunt Alice were true—and she was beginning to suspect they were—that meant the person she had depended on all those years to love and care for her had lied to her. In fact, her whole life was filled with lies and deceit. Her own mother had lied by omission, letting her believe they were living off Aunt Alice's generosity when, in fact, it was the other way around. Her mother's money had supported Aunt Alice's household from the beginning.

Laura had always known money wasn't important to her mother. She'd often thought music was what mattered most in her mother's life, but Laura had always believed that both her mother and her aunt loved her, too, in their own ways. She'd believed her great-aunt had loved her enough to make great sacrifices for her, but now, with the new information she'd gained about her family, it seemed that holding on to the family resentment toward the Mormons was more important to Aunt Alice than anything else. She hadn't cared enough about Laura to bother mentioning she was married. She thought resentfully of Aunt Alice's efforts to get her to marry a man she'd never particularly liked. Apparently, bigamy was all right with Aunt Alice.

When Laura's thoughts turned to her father, she didn't feel any better. For years, she had resented the man who had placed his ranch before his wife and daughter. At first, Laura had felt comforted when she'd found out about the bank account that held the accumulated support checks from her father, but now, knowing his last act on earth was to use her to save his ranch . . . This information cut deeply, negating the softer feelings she had begun to entertain. Mac seemed to be cut from the same cloth as her father. He would go to any lengths to save the ranch; the land mattered more than she did.

Her mind became so jumbled with feelings and concerns that she thought she might scream. To take her mind off her family's betrayal and her own predicament, she reached for the book Hal had been reading earlier but had left behind. The leather binding was worn, but she could faintly make out the title: The Book of Mormon. She leafed through it, finding many lines and whole paragraphs highlighted. She read some of the highlighted passages and found them intriguing, not at all the sort of thing she'd expected after reading some of her aunt's pamphlets. She turned to the front of the book and was surprised to see her father's name written with bold strokes inside the cover. Her curiosity aroused, she turned to the beginning and began to read.

Dawn was painting the eastern sky with faint streaks of gold and pink when the dull ache low in her abdomen subsided. Slipping from the bed, she tested her hip. It felt fine. She walked on bare feet to the curtained window to pull the drape cord. Standing there, she watched as the first rays of sunlight touched the ripe wheat fields with a Midas touch, turning the grain to glittering gold. Beyond the wheat stretched endless miles of grazing land and distant mountain peaks. Already, she knew how cruel this land could be, yet it called to her. Was it perhaps her "promised land"? If she stayed, would it become her life as it had been her father's? She shivered when she realized she was actually contemplating staying on the ranch.

Whatever his reason, my father left this land to me, she reasoned. *Mac admitted Daddy intended for me to be a partner. I'm not naive enough to believe he meant a real partnership. My role was probably only meant to ensure financial support for the ranch. It seems Daddy and the Burgoynes knew about Mom's money.* She thought bitterly of the fortune that lay in a bank waiting for her to reach her twenty-fifth birthday and about which Mac seemed to know a great deal more than she did. Everyone knew more about her affairs than she did.

Lifting her chin at a stubborn angle, she whispered softly to the early morning breeze stirring the tops of the grain. "Maybe I don't have to wait until I'm twenty-five to inherit mother's money. I'll take the gift you gave me, Daddy, but you and Mac are in for a big surprise. You and this land are not going to use me. I'm through running a distant second behind your ranch, mother's music, and Aunt Alice's obsession. The money in mother's account and half of this ranch belong to me now. In a very short time, Mac is going to discover he has a real partner.

ten

"YES, THANK YOU. We'll be there by two o'clock on Tuesday . . . No, I'm fine . . . Really . . . How long will it take to get it here if you make the arrangements right now? . . . I appreciate your help more than you'll ever know . . . Yes, good-bye."

Slowly, Laura hung up the phone. Putting her plan into action hadn't turned out to be as complicated as she'd feared. She pursed her lips while twirling a pencil in her fingers. Suddenly, she bent forward to write with quick, sure strokes in the notebook lying on the desk that had once been her father's but had at some point been taken over by Mac. She'd taken great care to sequester herself in the office without any of the men in the house being aware she'd left her room.

When she finished her notes, she gathered up the papers scattered across the smooth oak surface and deposited them in an envelope that she carried with her. Once again taking care not to be seen, she left the office and hurried back up the stairs.

* * *

In the room where she had felt like a prisoner since Saturday, Laura took a shower and dressed in a pale yellow blouse and chocolate brown pants, an outfit she knew enhanced her dark hair. She applied her makeup as carefully as she ever had for an evening out. It was important she look her best. If she felt good about her appearance, Mac would find it more difficult to intimidate her, she reasoned.

An hour ago she'd removed her suitcase, travel case, and handbag from one of the large closets in the master bedroom, where she'd spent the past three days. They hadn't been unpacked since she'd merely pulled out items as she'd needed them. She tucked her father's Book of Mormon, which she had been reading each day since the accident, inside one of her bags. The fact that it had been her father's gave her the greater claim to it, she reasoned. Frowning, she glanced at the other closet, which held clothes she had finally realized belonged to Mac, not Hal. If she'd known the room was Mac's, she would have insisted on moving to another room sooner. Just the idea of sleeping in Mac's room made her uneasy.

Peering into the mirror, she applied a touch of lip gloss. She wanted to look strong and confident. Yesterday, Bruce and Hal had insisted on bringing all of her meals to her, but today she planned to join them—and Mac. She hadn't seen Mac since he left her room that first night, but she hadn't been able to put him out of her mind. She had come to realize he wasn't the monster she had at first assumed him to be, but she still wasn't sure how much she could trust him. She both looked forward to and dreaded seeing him again, and she was prepared to resist any effort he might make to keep her from changing rooms.

Taking a deep breath, she stepped back into the bedroom to return her makeup to her traveling case; then she carried her bags to a spot near the door. Right after explaining her decision to Mac, she intended to move back into the room Hal had first given her.

Glancing at her watch, she saw that it was seven o'clock, time to go downstairs to breakfast. *Stay cool and businesslike,* she told herself as she marched down the stairs.

"Good morning," she said as she entered the kitchen. Hal was flipping pancakes while Bruce lounged against the countertop, his long legs wrapped around his bar stool.

"Pull up a stool. Breakfast is ready." Hal smiled as he indicated an empty space next to Bruce. He didn't appear surprised to see her. He'd probably been aware of her trip downstairs to use the telephone, too.

She perched on a stool, feeling a little off balance. Aunt Alice's kitchen had little counter space and no bar stools. She suspected that even if her house had been larger, her aunt wouldn't have permitted anything so casual as sitting on a bar stool to eat a meal.

"Are you sure you should be up?" Bruce asked. He appraised her with narrowed eyes.

"I'm fine," she assured him. To prove she was fine, she reached for the platter of pancakes. She placed a couple on her plate and poured syrup over them. She was halfway through her second helping when the door opened to admit Mac, trailed by three men dressed in jeans, blue denim shirts, and boots.

Hal did the honors. "Laura, these three men are Chance, Andy, and Billy, the ranch's only full-time, year-round hands. Boys, this is Laura Burgoyne." Chance, who appeared to be in his late fifties, grinned broadly while the two younger men mumbled brief greetings. After accepting full plates from Hal, they made their way to the table.

Laura felt stunned by Hal's introduction. She didn't know how to respond without creating a scene. Mac didn't contradict his father when he introduced her as Laura Burgoyne, so she opted to say nothing. There would be time later to clarify everything. She started to relax. Then Mac picked up his plate and made his way to the stool on the opposite side of her from Bruce. The moment he sat down, her appetite left. Butterflies danced in her stomach, and she became painfully aware of the man beside her. Determined to appear poised and in charge, she picked up her fork and forced herself to eat.

Little was said during the meal. The men concentrated on eating, and Laura concentrated on appearing unconcerned by Mac's presence, especially since she suspected he'd sat next to her just to annoy her. The meal seemed to stretch on forever until one of the ranch hands stood to return to his chores.

"Glad you're back, Laura," the hand named Chance said as he picked up his hat. "Your pony's been gone a long time, but there's a little Appaloosa mare in the corral that should be about right for you."

"You know me?" Laura gasped.

"I took you for your first horseback ride," he said, grinning. "'Course it wasn't planned that way. Your ma didn't want you anywhere near the horses. You were just a little cuss then, with a big temper and them little brown braids a stickin' straight out from your head. Your ma told you to take a nap, but you sneaked out the back door and came lookin' for Mac here." He slapped a work-roughened hand on Mac's shoulder. "You didn't find him, and we were all pretty worried by the time we found you. I heard you before I seen you. You was down in a gully stompin' along and yellin' for Mac at the top of your lungs. I picked you up and set you in front of me on my horse for the ride back to the house." He chuckled and punched Mac on the shoulder before plunking his hat on his head and following the other two grinning hands out the door.

Laura quickly glanced at Mac. He wasn't laughing with the others but was reaching for his hat. Her eyes followed his back as he moved toward the door. She had to say something now, or the opportunity would be lost.

She cleared her throat and slid off her stool to follow him. She watched, unable to speak, as he picked up a pair of chaps, buckled them low on his hips, then bent forward to fasten the leg ties. *No man has a right to look that good in jeans.* She was allowing herself to be distracted. She frowned and pulled her attention back to her plan.

"Mac, I'd like to speak with you." Good. She got the words past her lips.

"Now?"

"Yes, it's important."

"All right, if you make it fast. We can go into the office." His reluctance was evident in the way he placed his hat on the counter and with stiff steps led the way.

"Laura . . ." Both Hal and Bruce began to speak, a question in their voices.

"I think it would be best if Mac and I spoke alone," Laura threw over her shoulder, pleased that her voice sounded calm. She didn't dare include Bruce in this discussion. Something about her cousin seemed to antagonize Mac, and she knew Mac wasn't going to like what she had to say. She didn't want this discussion to degenerate into a fight between Bruce and Mac.

Mac was elaborately courteous as he held the door for her to enter the office before him. Whether from habit or from an attempt to claim a position of authority, he seated himself at the desk and swiveled his chair to face the fireplace, waving a hand negligently toward the nearer wingback chair to indicate that Laura should be seated.

Ignoring the chair, Laura chose to come around the front of the desk to stand. "This won't take long," she began.

"I'd appreciate that, since I've got work to do."

It took considerable willpower to look directly into Mac's face, a face she was both chagrined and slightly pleased to see sported a narrow black crescent just below one eye.

"I called Mr. Sylvester at his home early this morning. I explained the situation here," she began bravely.

"Okay . . ." Mac looked wary.

Laura continued, "He will draw up the necessary papers and fax them to your attorney in Twin Falls this morning. We both need to be there to sign them at two this afternoon."

Mac raised an eyebrow at this, but Laura didn't slow down. "Half of the money currently in your account will be placed in a personal account for your private use. The remainder of the money in your account will be matched by an equal amount of my money from the sale of my aunt's house to form a joint business account for ranch expenses. The bank will require both of our signatures on all checks. Once the papers are signed, neither of us can draw on the ranch's assets without the other's approval. Keep in mind this is just a temporary solution. Profits will be deposited to the ranch account with the court to determine later how everything should be divided."

"Whoa!" Mac was on his feet, both hands spread on the desk, his elbows straight as he leaned forward to stop Laura's speech. "You're out of your mind! I don't answer to anyone when it comes to running this ranch!"

"You won't have to *answer* to me," she said evenly, hoping Mac wouldn't notice how nervous she really was. "You will only have to *share* decisions with me until a legal determination is made about what is yours and what is mine."

"I know what is mine! This ranch is mine!"

"The court will decide that!" Laura said, her exasperation with this man beginning to show. "You need to face reality, Mac. You're the one who pointed out to me that you have a crop to harvest and a payroll to meet. I'm giving you a way to do precisely that!"

"So long as I come, hat in hand, and beg nicely."

"I don't expect you to beg, but I won't either. I expect us to sit down like two civilized adults and make decisions together."

"What do you know about ranching?"

"Nothing! Absolutely nothing! But I think you'll find I know quite a bit about business administration. I assume this ranch is a business." She could have explained that she had attended an excellent business school in California for four years and that for the past two years she had managed the financial affairs of a major performing arts foundation in San Francisco, but she didn't think it would make any difference to this stubborn cowboy.

They glared at each other across the desk. Then something flickered in Mac's eyes, causing a tremor to slide down Laura's spine.

A smile creased Mac's face, but it wasn't a pleasant one. "You're still forgetting, dear little Laura, you're my wife."

Laura's tone was sugary sweet. "That's debatable! Mr. Sylvester is looking into that, too. In the meantime, he assured me that even if the marriage was legal, it has no bearing on my inheritance or our partnership."

"We don't have a partnership. You're my wife, not my business partner."

Laura slapped her hands on the desk and leaned forward, her face only inches from Mac's. She spoke quietly but firmly. "You have that backward. I'm your business partner, not your wife."

"We'll see about that." Mac's voice ended on a shivery whisper as he leaned closer still. She had the unsettling premonition he was going to kiss her.

For a moment, she wondered what it would be like to be kissed by Mac. Then she pulled away, disappointed that he would try that tactic—disappointed in herself, too, because she had almost allowed him to kiss her. They looked uncomfortably at each other, but before either one could say anything more, a loud knock sounded on the door.

"You might as well answer that," Mac said. He sat back down.

"You're as close to the door as I am."

"Fine!" He sent his chair flying as he lunged to his feet and strode to the door. He jerked it open, nearly toppling Bruce into the room. One look at Mac's face and Bruce headed straight for Laura.

"Are you all right?" Bruce gripped her arm.

"Of course she's all right," Mac snapped.

"It's Mac you should worry about." Laura lifted her chin, boosting her nose to an arrogant angle. "He's not too happy with the terms of our partnership."

"I can live with it, but can you?" Mac said. She suspected there was some hidden message behind Mac's sudden acquiescence.

"I'll handle it just fine," she assured him. "Oh, and since your truck hasn't been repaired, you're welcome to ride with Bruce and me to Twin Falls to sign the papers. It will be a tight squeeze, but we'll manage. We'll be leaving at noon." Not wanting to stick around for the snide remarks that were sure to follow, Laura turned to run out the door. Unfortunately, her hip gave a twinge and lurched more than dashed from the room.

"Laura!" Mac's voice thundered behind her.

Assuming he intended to continue their argument, she raced up the stairs. Rapid footsteps followed. Mere seconds passed before she slammed the bedroom door, but the door crashed open again almost immediately, slamming hard against the wall.

Laura whirled around to face Mac as he came charging toward her. What was this guy's problem? She stood her ground, refusing to retreat a step. His long strides carried him across the room. Clamping his hands around her upper arms, he nearly lifted her off her feet.

"What's wrong? I thought you said you weren't injured!" He nearly shouted.

Her brow furrowed in puzzlement. This was not what she'd expected. "Nothing's wrong. My headache is gone, and Band-Aids took care of my blisters."

"Then why are you limping?"

Before she could answer, Bruce responded from the doorway. "It's her hip. For a man who claims to be her husband, you don't know much about her. Her right hip has more plastic and steel than bone. Did you think she just walked away from that accident eight years ago?"

Mac looked shaken. "Why didn't you tell me?" he demanded of Laura.

"What difference does it make?" She shot Bruce an irritated glare. "It doesn't change anything. It doesn't even bother me, except when I'm tired or cold."

"Are you tired or cold now?" Mac's skepticism showed on his face.

"No. I just haven't been moving around much the past few days, and I'm a little stiff."

"You're seeing a doctor when we get to Twin Falls."

"I'm all right. Really."

"I'll meet you out front at noon." Abruptly, he left the room. Bruce glanced at Laura, shrugged his shoulders, and then he too left, leaving her alone to regain her poise.

eleven

WHEN LAURA CAME down the stairs at noon, she found Bruce and Hal standing beside an SUV. Mac sat behind the wheel. Hal told her he had decided to go with them, and he assured her they would all be more comfortable in his vehicle than in Bruce's car.

"It would be a waste of gas to take two cars," he suggested persuasively. He held the front passenger door open for her, but she ignored it to slide in beside Bruce in the back.

At first, the two-hour drive to Twin Falls passed mainly in silence. Laura spent the time reviewing her plan and the information her attorney had given her. None of the others seemed inclined toward conversation either. Mac seemed intent on driving, and Hal opened his briefcase and spent the time reading various papers.

Laura assumed Mac had filled his father in on the basic details of the agreement she and Mac were to sign, so she outlined the proposed agreement to Bruce, limiting her explanation to a few terse, softly spoken sentences. Mac's frequent glances in the rearview mirror were a reminder of his disapproval—of both the plan and Bruce.

Her head ached again, and it took a major effort not to yield to tears. Why, she asked herself, did she feel so compelled to claim her inheritance when doing so exposed her to Mac's erratic temper? Why had her slight limp upset him so much?

And why did his sudden concern for her old injury fill her with some kind of strange warmth? The man was dangerous. Not only was he claiming her inheritance without compunction, but he obviously suffered no qualms when it came to laying siege to her emotions.

According to his own admission, she reminded herself, Mac had married her to get her share of the ranch. Obviously, he had no intention of losing it now just because she had inconveniently remained alive. He was adamant about keeping her share of the ranch. She suspected he thought he could do that by making her stay married to him. She didn't want a marriage like her mother's, one where she felt like a prisoner. She wouldn't be a helpless pawn either. Almost everyone she'd once thought loved her had betrayed her with their lies and selfish obsessions. Perhaps she was a fool, but she expected more from life than being the means of fulfilling someone else's dreams. She certainly wanted more than that from the man with whom she would someday share her life.

* * *

Mac drove down the mountain and across the valley to the freeway, leaving a plume of dust behind them. He'd hoped Laura would sit beside him so he could point out property boundaries and perhaps ease the tension between them. She appeared reluctant to have any more to do with him than she considered absolutely necessary. He'd noticed she'd made a few brief statements to Bruce but seemed reluctant to do much talking. He watched her in his mirror and wondered what she saw as she stared out the window at the monotonous vista of dry, brush-covered mountains. She was probably counting the minutes until she could rush back to the city.

He felt like pounding his fists in frustration. He would have left her with the truck and gone for help alone if he'd known about her hip. Why hadn't he noticed? It seemed he was destined to forever let Laura down.

For years he had suspected he'd somehow let her down when her mother took her away. She had counted on him to look after her, just like a big brother, and he just let her leave. Sure, he'd been a ten-year-old kid, but there must have been something he could have done, he told himself irrationally. He'd let her down again when she lay injured in his arms alongside a Nevada highway and he couldn't prevent her pain. His instinct had been to stay with her in that tiny Nevada clinic, but the air ambulance arrived and the emergency crew had taken over. He'd let Dad convince him there was nothing he could do to help her and that he was needed at the ranch. Worst of all, he'd accepted that hate-filled old harridan's word concerning Laura's supposed death.

Now he'd done it again! When he should have been looking out for her after his pickup truck skidded down the mountain, he'd let her walk several miles back to the house with an injured hip. What kind of man was he, anyway, to have dragged her off without explanation that night? A fine bead of sweat broke out on his upper lip as he considered the possibility that she had sustained serious damage. It seemed when it came to Laura, he always managed to mess up.

Once, she glanced up to meet his eyes watching her in his mirror. When he winked at her, she tightened her jaw and moved closer to Bruce. Something needed to be done about Bruce. *You might think you have some kind of claim on Laura, but she's my wife, and I hope soon she can be my friend again,* Mac said silently to the man he considered his chief rival. Laura said Bruce was her cousin, and he had no reason to doubt that, but the guy had too much of a hold on Laura for Mac's comfort. He and Laura could work this out if they didn't have so much interference.

Once he'd gotten over his initial shock, Mac had realized Laura's proposal was a fair one. The more he'd thought about it, the more he believed she really wasn't trying to bankrupt him but was probably just as much a victim as he was of her aunt's unscrupulousness.

By the time the car pulled onto the freeway, Laura had fallen asleep with her cheek resting against Bruce's broad shoulder. Mac scowled when the other man lifted his arm to bring her more comfortably against his side. Mac knew he was acting like a jealous fool, but he couldn't seem to be able to help himself.

Once, Hal glanced over his shoulder to ask, "Is she all right?"

"I think she's just exhausted," Bruce answered quietly. "But it's not a bad idea for her to see a doctor while we're in town."

Mac caught Hal's sideways glance as he concurred. "Perhaps she and Mac both ought to."

"I don't need to see a doctor. I'm fine." Mac dismissed his injuries while renewing his plans to have Laura thoroughly checked by a medical professional.

One corner of Hal's mouth lifted slightly as he cast an assessing glance at his son. There was an unmistakable glint in Hal's eyes as he commented dryly, "I'm not too sure about that. Seems to me you've been acting as touchy as an old bull moose ever since you bumped your head."

Mac's hands tightened on the wheel, and his foot rode the gas pedal a little harder, but he made no response to his father's baiting comment.

Almost an hour later, in response to a suggestion from Hal, Mac pulled the car to a stop at a lookout point high above the Snake River canyon. Laura awoke, aware the car was no longer moving. Lifting her head, she saw the car was perched on a gravel strip surrounded by shrubs and boulders. Farther away she could see cultivated fields. There was no house or business near, and she wondered if they were experiencing car trouble.

Pulling herself to an upright position, she gasped as she caught her first glimpse of a slender bridge spanning a huge schism and picked out the black and gray of the opposing cliff. Far below was a slender ribbon of water.

"Come on, Laura." She hadn't even been aware of the door opening beside her. Mac stood there, his hand extended toward her. "This is a sight you shouldn't miss."

Bruce and Hal followed a short distance behind as Mac led her to the edge of the lookout point. It was incredible; the mighty Snake River she had read of in every history text of the great Northwest appeared as a tiny stream nearly five hundred feet below.

"One of the first bridges linking the north and south sides of the river was built across this narrow point of the canyon around the turn of the century," Hal explained as he joined them. "It was called the Hanson Bridge. Now that was a bridge! It was made out of wood and was just wide enough for one buggy or car. There was a network of wooden girders overhead. The whole thing shook and grumbled, scaring folks half to death when they crossed it."

Mac watched Laura's face as she listened to Hal tell her of the famous river and the thousands of springs that emerge from Idaho's great aquifer through the canyon wall to double the amount of water in the river.

"Everything is so dry and dusty; it's hard to believe a major river is so close," she said. He followed her eyes to view land that hadn't seen but a few drops of water in months, maybe years.

"This area is lucky if it sees ten inches of rainfall in a year. The past few years, we've gotten less than that." Mac placed his hand beside hers where it rested against a low rock barrier. He wanted to place his hand over hers but figured doing so would set off another confrontation, and he didn't want to fight with her anymore. "Farmers and ranchers in southern Idaho depend on the river and the vast underground reservoir that empties into it to supply water for crops and stock. If we counted on local rainfall, our land would have dried up and blown away a long time ago." Mac's voice conveyed a deep love for the harsh land, and he was neither arrogant nor defensive as he spoke of it.

"Look down there!" Excitement entered Laura's voice as she leaned across Mac to point to a movement far below. "Is that tiny yellow speck a raft?"

"Could be. Though it's too far away to be certain." Mac enjoyed the soft flutter of her hair across his arm and took pleasure in her excitement. He wished he'd thought to bring binoculars so she could see the raft close up.

They fell silent, watching a hawk glide effortlessly on the vagary of an air current in the canyon until a van of noisy tourists pulled into the space beside Hal's SUV. As the chattering group rushed to the barrier along the lookout point with cameras in their hands, Mac took Laura's arm to lead her back to the car. Her skin felt warm where his fingers touched, and he was glad she didn't pull away.

* * *

Laura's first impulse actually was to pull away, but in the interest of avoiding a scene, she didn't. Each step brought prickles of awareness, and as his hip brushed hers, she stumbled slightly. His grip tightened, and she clenched her teeth.

"Is your hip still bothering you?" He actually sounded concerned.

"No. The ground is rough, that's all." She breathed a sigh of relief when he released her arm, allowing her to slip inside the car where she leaned back against the headrest with a sigh. Mac started the car engine, sending a cool blast of air against her warm face.

Through half-closed eyes she watched long slender fingers close around the gear shift. Tiny gold hairs on the back of a sun-bronzed arm stood out as his grip tightened, then relaxed as the vehicle picked up speed. Suddenly, her eyes opened wide. She was sitting in the front seat beside Mac! She twisted about to see Bruce seated behind Mac. Catching her eye, he offered a faint shrug as if to say, *I don't know how it happened.*

Shortly before two o'clock, Mac stopped the car in front of what looked like a comfortable brick home. A black-and-white sign in the shape of a western saddle hung by short lengths of chain from the cross arm of a black metal post, proclaiming, in fancy script, *D. Derwent Cooper, Attorney-at-Law.*

Sidestepping Mac's move to take her arm, she reached for the small case of papers Bruce carried for her; then, being careful to keep Bruce between Mac and herself, she started toward the building. Bruce opened the door and she stepped briskly to the receptionist's desk to announce their arrival. Before Laura could speak, an inside door opened, and she found herself facing a heavyset, balding man who appeared to have been poured into the expensive-looking, gray western suit he wore. His shirt was white and shiny with black embroidery, and a black string tie was held in place by a huge chunk of silver and turquoise. Heavy turquoise rings weighted his stubby fingers, and the fanciest pair of high-heeled, western boots she had ever seen were on his feet. She'd seen dessert plates smaller than his belt buckle.

Ignoring her, the man stepped past her, his arm extended. Bemusement turned to trepidation as she heard the man's jovial greeting.

"Glad you could make it, Senator! We'll have this little problem all worked out in no time."

twelve

SENATOR? LAURA KNEW Hal had an interest in politics, but somehow she'd missed this specific detail. He couldn't be a national senator or she would have heard of him, so that must mean he was in the state senate. Her eyes narrowed as she watched the man shake Hal's hand with one hand and clasp his shoulder with the other. She felt sick. No wonder Mac was so sure he could get away with taking her land. He'd counted on his father's political connections to provide a ruling in his favor. Turning around, she watched Cooper thump Mac on the shoulder. Over the rotund attorney's head, Mac winked at Laura.

What's the meaning of that? Is he laughing at me? Laura fumed. Well, it wasn't going to be as easy as he thought. She wasn't the kind of person who gave up just because something was hard. She'd learned to walk again against stiff odds, and she'd claim her inheritance, too. Lifting her chin and squaring her shoulders, she stepped forward.

"Mr. Cooper, I believe we have business to conduct. My attorney informed me he has been in touch with you."

All his jovial bonhomie disappeared. With a swelling of his chest, he turned to face her. His nostrils flared slightly as he assumed a superior attitude. His first words were meant to intimidate.

"Take my advice, little girl, and drop this nonsense right now. Prison is no place for a girl as young and pretty as you are." He finished with an oily smile.

"You've got to be kidding!" Bruce exploded. "These people steal Laura's property, and you threaten her with prison?" He reached to take Laura's arm. "Wayne Sylvester will be in touch with you."

All Laura's frustration and hurt of the past week boiled to the surface. She had been goaded, lied to, and humiliated too many times. And she didn't need Bruce protecting her! Shaking off his hand, she stepped toward the pompous, small town lawyer.

"It won't be me going to prison." She spoke each word slowly and emphatically. "The shyster attorney who probated my father's estate is the one who will be in trouble. My father had a valid will, and I am his only relative. No search was made for me, and there was no death certificate presented. He handed my property over to Mac Burgoyne illegally. That just might be grounds for disbarment."

"Oh, you're an attorney now, too?" Cooper's voice held an insulting sneer, and there was no mistaking the enmity in his eyes.

"Since when do you conduct business out here, Coop?" Mac surprised Laura by taking her arm and steering her toward the open door of a large office.

The room they entered projected a mood as overbearing as its owner. It was filled with overstuffed leather furniture, a massive desk, and bookcases filled with dusty tomes and little statuettes of horses. Spurs and horseshoes hung on the wood paneling along with framed portraits of Teddy Roosevelt and John Wayne. The heavy aroma of cigar smoke brought tears to Laura's eyes. She felt a moment's gratitude when Mac shoved open a window, though the heavy, dry summer breeze did little to clear the air.

Cooper indicated that Hal should take the large overstuffed chair and steered the rest of them to straight chairs gathered in front of his desk. He then leaned back expansively in his well-padded swivel chair to address Hal.

"Well, Senator," the attorney drawled. "This is sad business. Let me assure you, I won't let some slick California lawyer cheat your boy."

Even as upset as she was, Laura almost laughed at the ridiculous reference to Mac as "boy"; neither did she fail to hear Bruce's derisive snort. Her eyes flew to Mac's face. It reflected nothing other than a hint of annoyance.

"Cut the bull, Coop. Just hand us the papers we need to sign." Mac held out his hand.

With a long-suffering look of reproach, the lawyer reached into a drawer of the big desk to withdraw a slim folder. With elaborate care, he extracted two sets of legal papers and two pens. He tossed one set of papers and a pen to Mac and began scratching *x*'s on the other set, indicating where Laura should sign.

Picking up the lengthy paper, Laura began to read. Her emotions were in so much turmoil that at first the legal jargon made little sense. When Cooper spoke to her in the tone of voice of an irritated adult speaking to a not-quite-bright child, reminding her he had already marked all the places where she should sign, her suspicion was aroused. Consequently, she slowed down to read the document carefully.

No! What was he trying to pull? Before she finished the first page, Laura recognized that the document was no simple financial agreement setting out terms to keep the ranch operating until a full legal settlement could be made. It was on the third page, near the bottom, that the words seemed to jump out at her. Signing the paper would virtually end her claim to the ranch and allow Mac access to the fortune her mother left her as well. He would have complete managerial and financial control of the ranch. His only obligation would be to support her in the manner he deemed reasonable and provide for any children of their marriage. It also stipulated that Mac would become her heir, but only a child fathered by Mac could inherit any part of the ranch in the event of her death. Should she seek a divorce, she would give up claim to the Idaho property, though Mac could claim a fifty percent community property settlement from what remained of her inheritance from her mother and aunt.

Laura struggled to keep her hands from shaking. It was absurd! How could anyone possibly think she would agree to such a piece of chauvinistic nonsense? This certainly wasn't the agreement she had discussed with Mr. Sylvester that morning. She carefully placed the papers back on the desk. What was Mac thinking, pulling a stunt like this? He must have called his despicable attorney right after their conversation this morning. Did he think that because his father was a state senator he could somehow force her to sign the agreement?

"I want to see the document Mr. Sylvester faxed to you this morning." Her voice didn't quaver as she stared straight into the smirking face across the desk.

"Now, missy, I don't know what you're suggesting!"

Glancing up from the paper in his hands, Mac observed the frown on Laura's face deepen. She looked mad enough to spit nails. She'd dictated the terms of the agreement, so why was she angry? Catching the smug expression on Cooper's face, Mac's jaw tightened, and his eyes dropped to the papers to begin a careful perusal. It didn't take long to see why Laura was upset. *The old fool! If his meddling costs me the funds to get my grain harvested, I'll start disbarment proceedings myself.*

"Do as the lady says!" Mac was on his feet leaning across the desk.

"But . . ." Cooper's surprise turned to indignation as he turned to the senator.

"I think you'd better do as *the boy* says." Hal leaned back in his chair, an enigmatic smile on his face.

Mac noticed that his father suddenly seemed to be enjoying himself. Out of the corner of his eye, he saw him pick up the papers Mac had dropped onto the desk. Hal carefully creased Mac's copy of the document and placed it inside his jacket pocket.

Displaying every indication of affronted dignity, the attorney extracted a crumpled ball of paper from his wastepaper basket. He left the room, calling instructions to his secretary to make copies. While they waited, Mac tried to catch Laura's eye, but she refused to look at him.

"Laura, this isn't the way it looks. I didn't—"

"Of course not." She cut him off, her voice dripping with sarcasm.

Cooper eventually returned with two new documents that Mac and Laura read silently and both signed.

Without waiting to ask permission, Laura, still holding herself under rigid control, picked up the telephone sitting on the desk. Her fingers quickly punched in a desired number. Two states away, Wayne Sylvester picked up his private line.

Laura informed her attorney that the papers had been signed and witnessed. She requested that he contact the banks involved immediately to arrange the accounts. Then, while Cooper made spluttering sounds in the background, she informed him she would send him a document the Burgoynes' attorney had tried to substitute for the one he had sent. She paused to listen a moment, then spoke firmly into the mouthpiece.

"Yes, I want to go ahead. Please include all of the important options. Yes, that too."

After hanging up the telephone, she picked up her briefcase, nodded curtly to Cooper, then spoke directly to Mac, her voice precise and businesslike. "The bank needs both of our signatures on file," was all she said before turning on her heel to exit the room.

Bruce caught up to her on the sidewalk. Gripping both of her shaking shoulders, he turned her to face him.

"What happened in there?"

The temptation to throw herself in Bruce's arms and let him comfort her was strong, but, suspecting she wouldn't be able to hold back the tears, Laura stayed the impulse. The time had come to stop leaning on Bruce. Though she appreciated his kindness and assistance since Aunt Alice's death, she would not allow herself to become as dependent on him as she'd been on Aunt Alice. Somewhere, almost lost inside her, was a remnant of the scrappy little girl the old cowboy had described that morning, and she meant to find that long forgotten part of herself. Besides, she didn't want to let Mac see how hurt she was by his duplicity. In terse, succinct sentences she explained the content of the first contract.

"That cheat!" Bruce growled. "How did he think he was going to get away with that?"

"Obviously, they thought that I would be too stupid to read the thing. They expected me to just sign where I was told to sign."

"That may be true of Mac and that sorry excuse for an attorney, but I can't see Hal having any part in anything like that. He's a stiff, authoritative old guy, but he seems pretty straight to me."

"Oh, Bruce, I don't know what to think. How can I trust either of them? Hal, not Mac, was Dad's partner at the time they took over my share of the ranch. He had to be part of the scheme."

"We can sort all this out later, or you can turn it all over to Mr. Sylvester. I don't think anyone puts much over on him. Let me take you to the airport. A town this size must have an airport." He looked around doubtfully. "You can still pursue your claim from San Francisco."

"No, I'm staying," she responded stubbornly. "I won't give Mac the satisfaction of running me off."

* * *

Mac stood on the wide front step of the lawyer's office breathing heavily in an attempt to get his anger under control. He hadn't ever faced so many aggravating things in so short a time as he had the past few days. He'd wanted to hurry after Laura when she left so he could explain things, but angry as she was, she probably wouldn't speak to him anyway. Instead, he'd opted to stay behind to share a few choice thoughts with Coop. Now Laura really had ammunition for slicing up his ranch and hightailing it back to the city.

Mac watched Laura speak to Bruce. There was no mistaking her angry stance. Undoubtedly she blamed him for the substitute papers, and he couldn't say that he blamed her. His father had given his legal business to Cooper as long as Mac could remember. The two had grown up in the same small town, and Mac supposed that explained the relationship, but he would be shopping for a new attorney as soon as possible. His dad could do as he pleased, but Mac had no intention of trusting his affairs to Cooper ever again.

Laura and Bruce stood close together at the end of the walk. He didn't like how cozy those two were. He frowned. *It should be me, not Bruce, Laura turns to.* That morning he had resolved to regain Laura's trust and rebuild their lost friendship. Of course, he didn't want her tagging him around like she did when they were kids, but he had to admit he didn't like seeing those big brown eyes that used to follow him reserving their trust for some blond west coast surfer!

Laura took a couple of steps, and Mac's eyes narrowed as he noted that her limp was more pronounced. He supposed Laura would fight him every step of the way now when he insisted she see a doctor. He straightened his shoulders and headed for the car. This was a fight he intended to win.

Laura adamantly refused to see a doctor all the way to St.

Luke's Hospital. There was nothing wrong with her hip, she insisted. Just an occasional minor twinge was all she would acknowledge. Mac ignored her protests. He didn't argue; he just drove. And both Bruce and Hal backed him, which was helpful yet strangely didn't lessen his irritation with Bruce. When the car stopped, Laura didn't move.

Mac turned to look at her. "You can walk inside, or I'll carry you. It's your choice."

Laura knew from experience it would be a waste of time to argue further. She walked stiffly up the steps, refusing either Mac's or Bruce's arm. She'd know if there was something new affecting her hip or if the injury had worsened, but it was quite obvious she couldn't convince the bullheaded men around her who seemed to think they knew more about her health than she did.

Inside the trauma center, a nurse led her away to be examined. After she'd provided a quick outline of her medical history, X-rays were taken. While waiting for them to be reviewed, she was sent back to an examination room to dress and wait for the doctor.

Laura was slipping on her shoes when the doctor stepped into the small room. Mac was right behind him. Laura gave him a venomous look. He wasn't really her husband. He had no right to just walk in. What if she hadn't finished dressing?

"Nothing to worry about, Mrs. Burgoyne." The young doctor's voice oozed the fake cheeriness endemic to medical personnel that she'd learned to dislike during her long rehabilitation and years of physical therapy. "There's a little bruising around one of the pins, but it's not serious. It won't even bother you after a day or two. You were fortunate to have a good orthopedic surgeon reconstruct your hip after that accident eight years ago."

Mac asked the doctor several questions while Laura gathered up her handbag. *He doesn't need to act like a concerned husband—especially when he made it quite clear with those documents that he doesn't really care anything about me.* She fumed inwardly even while thanking the doctor politely, if stiffly, and preparing to leave. She didn't want to spend any more time in a hospital than necessary. Hospitals made her nervous. She glared at Mac each time the doctor called her "Mrs. Burgoyne" and shrugged away Mac's hand when he attempted to take her arm. Acting unconcerned, he slipped his hands in his back pockets and followed her out the door.

After leaving the hospital, they made a stop at the bank where Mac had an account. Mac expected to sign account cards quickly and be on their way, but the manager invited them back to his office to take care of the paperwork. As they walked down a carpeted hall, Laura spotted a restroom and excused herself. Mac attempted to be crisp and businesslike in taking care of the required formalities, but he had to struggle to appear unconcerned when Laura didn't rejoin them as quickly as he thought she should.

In spite of the doctor's giving her a clean bill of health, he worried that the physician might have missed something. He was about to go in search of her when at last she entered the bank manager's office without a glance Mac's way. She appeared calm and completely at ease as she spoke with the manager and signed her name on each card beneath Mac's signature. When she finished, the bank manager walked beside her to the front of the bank where Hal and Bruce waited. Mac trailed behind, disguising the twinge of sadness he felt when Laura stepped to Bruce's side and continued to ignore him.

thirteen

BEFORE STARTING BACK to the ranch, Mac drove the car into a supermarket parking lot. He climbed out of the car, and, before either he or Bruce could reach Laura's door, Hal opened it. Hal then walked beside her and attempted to ease the stiffly polite atmosphere the three young people seemed determined to maintain.

"I plant a garden at the ranch every summer, but I'm not much of a gardener," Hal said amiably. "Being so far from grocery stores, I make a practice of picking up fresh produce and items we can't grow each time I go to town. Mac raises all the beef we need, but other meats have to come from the store. Of course, we usually shop in Burley or Tremonton, but since we're here I thought we might as well pick up a few things."

Once they entered the grocery store, Mac disappeared while Laura and Bruce followed Hal up and down the aisles. Laura made no suggestions or comments as Hal filled the shopping cart. Only when he picked up a couple of gallon buckets of ice cream did she even raise an eyebrow, but Hal noticed.

"There's an ice chest in the back of the SUV. We'll pack dry ice in it so the ice cream won't melt before we get back to the ranch." He shrugged his shoulders and looked a little sheepish as he added, "Mac and I both have a soft spot for ice cream."

Laura had a sudden memory of sitting on the front step of the ranch house trading licks of ice cream with a small cowboy. Taking the hem of his shirt, the boy had wiped away the spots on her dress after she'd bitten off the pointed end of her cone and the melting ice cream had dripped onto her clothes. She still liked to bite off the tips of her ice cream cones. Only now there was no one to share them with. The memory gave her a bittersweet feeling of nostalgia, and she found herself looking around for Mac, but he was nowhere to be seen.

Bruce wandered off to browse the magazine stand, and Hal took the opportunity to speak in a soft voice of the events of the early afternoon.

"Laura, neither Mac nor I had anything to do with the papers Derwent Cooper first gave you to sign. He was acting entirely on his own initiative."

"He must have had some reason to believe that was what you wanted, Senator."

"He's not being paid to make assumptions, and I intend to bring his actions to the attention of the state bar."

"Whatever you say, Senator."

"I thought we agreed you would call me Hal."

"Whatever you wish." Laura shrugged her shoulders and walked on. Hal sighed and followed her.

"Laura, I am a state senator, that's true. Perhaps I should have mentioned that to you earlier, but it didn't seem important. Whether you like it or not, I also happen to be your father-in-law. But as far as I can see, neither of those facts has any bearing on your dispute with Mac nor with what happened today. I promise you, I'll not use my position to influence your relationship with Mac or to affect the terms of whatever settlement is eventually reached between the two of you."

"I should believe a politician's promise?" Her voice was bland, but the words were meant to cut. Hal made no further attempt to speak to her. He quietly finished his shopping and paid for the groceries.

There was a quiet dignity to Hal's movements, but Laura noticed that his shoulders drooped and his face looked tired. She read a hint of sadness in his eyes. She felt ashamed of herself. She had no business being so rude to Hal. She owed him an apology. She told herself that when they got back to the ranch, she'd find an opportunity to talk to him privately.

Mac was waiting beside the car when they emerged from the store. He took over shifting the bags to the cargo space. While he was occupied, Laura climbed into the vehicle, making certain she shared the backseat with Bruce.

When she was seated, Mac handed her a paper bag. Puzzled, she peeked inside. Jeans! The bag contained two pairs of ladies' boot cut denim jeans. To her recollection she'd never owned a pair. Aunt Alice had considered them unladylike. She stared at the pants in amazement. They were her correct size. How did he know? Was this Mac's way of apologizing? As nice a gesture as it was, it would take a lot more than a couple of pairs of pants to make up for the fiasco at the lawyer's office. She didn't know whether to thank him or throw them at him. Manners and a secret childish longing to wear jeans like everyone else did won out. "Thank you." The words sounded warmer than she'd intended.

Mac touched his hat in silent acknowledgment then slipped a CD in the stereo, filling the air with a haunting country ballad. She found herself listening intently to the music. She admitted she'd never given country music much credit. Mother had played classical piano, and Aunt Alice had forbidden Laura to listen to "noise"—which meant any music that didn't have Aunt Alice's approval such as pop, rock, or country. She hadn't really cared for much of anything but classical anyway, but suddenly she realized how much she'd missed out on while growing up in the elderly woman's care.

* * *

No one appeared interested when Mac asked if they wanted to stop in Burley for dinner, so he drove on. After what Cooper tried to pull, he doubted Laura would ever speak more than polite monosyllables to him again. It frustrated him that she assumed he was behind that stinking stunt. The arrogant fool had no idea of the damage he'd caused. He'd actually thought Mac would be grateful he'd taken a chance on getting Laura to sign the absurd document he'd drawn up.

Mac knew the jeans weren't much in the way of an apology. He hadn't meant them that way anyway. She'd said she wanted to be a partner. Okay, if she was going to be a partner, she'd have to dress the part. Though not ready to admit as much out loud, the idea of Laura as his partner was growing on him. He was hoping she'd see the pants as his acceptance of their partnership agreement. It was a start. He didn't want to allow himself to start thinking she'd stay, but she hadn't thrown the Wranglers in his face. That was a good sign, wasn't it?

He sighed. The atmosphere in the car was glum. Left to his own thoughts, he mused on the current predicament. He found he was a lot angrier with himself than with Laura. If he hadn't acted like such a dolt all this time, he and Laura probably could have worked the whole thing out by now. He was more at fault than she was, he recognized, and he didn't understand what it was that made him mouth off and sabotage every attempt they made to have a real conversation.

Frankly, he didn't understand why he had been so filled with anger when he'd discovered Laura was alive. He had mourned when he thought she was dead, and he'd believed his dreams had died with her. His hands gripped the steering wheel, turning his knuckles white with pain as he recalled the agony that had engulfed him when he read the words Alice Wilson had written informing him and his father of Laura's death.

He'd walked up the mountain from where the fire had at last been contained after rampaging across the range for nearly two weeks. Half the herd was dead, and there wasn't enough grass left to keep the remaining half alive until Christmas, let alone through the winter. The house he had lived in all of his life was gone, telephone service was out, and he had no idea whether any of the horses had made it to safety. Dad had collapsed from smoke inhalation and then suffered a heart attack before being been transported to the little hospital in Tremonton, Utah. With the telephone lines down, he'd had no way of knowing if Dad was even alive.

Chance had pulled into the yard in a battered, old pickup truck. Mac had watched him park the near-useless heap close to where the barn had stood a short time earlier. His movements had appeared in slow motion as he pulled himself out of the truck and limped toward Mac.

"Sheriff hauled me to town—thought I busted my leg when I went over the ridge ahead of the fire," Chance reported. "Warn't busted, so I checked on your pa while I was there and picked up the mail. Your pa ain't doing too good. His old ticker couldn't take the smoke, but he might make it. Here's your mail, just one letter. You don't suppose Jacob would mind if I sacked out at his house, do you? Only thing left standing, you know. 'Course you got the say-so, being as how you're the boss for now."

Mac had slowly nodded his head, and the man who was old enough to be his father had staggered his way to Jake's front door. Mac's blistered fingers turned the letter one way, then the other, leaving black fingerprints on the already smeared envelope. He'd felt reluctant to open it but knew he couldn't just stand in the gathering dusk staring at the envelope. Holding his breath, he tore off one end of the envelope and shook the single sheet of paper free. Picking it up by two fingers, he had read the words that ripped apart his heart. Laura was dead.

Tears had cut rivulets down his smoke-blackened face from eyes burned red by the relentless fire. Before he knew what it was to be a husband, he was a widower. He had lost almost everything: Jake, his home, his horses, half of his herd, perhaps his father—and Laura. The little girl with her pigtails and freckles who had made him feel like a hero, filling a motherless little boy's empty days with love, the little girl who had gone away then suddenly reentered his life as a shy, sad, beautiful teenager was gone.

Fifteen-year-old Laura, who had just lost her mother, had found them all strangers. She had been painfully polite, and he had struggled to make her feel at ease. He couldn't begin to understand the fascination he felt for a fifteen-year-old kid. He just knew he didn't ever want her out of his sight again. None of the women he'd met at the university had drawn him the way little Laura had. It wasn't Jake's plea that persuaded him to marry Laura. He'd married his own private dream.

He had been twenty-one years old. He had reached the milestone that proclaimed him a man. Suddenly, he was a man with a load of responsibility and no dream. In a way, he realized now he'd been sleepwalking ever since that day. He'd made a vow to Laura's memory that he would make the ranch blossom, that he'd wisely use the land and other resources that otherwise would have been hers. He'd continued to live a seemingly normal life but without any kind of deep feeling for anything but the land which he and Laura should have shared. Laura's return had been like the bursting of a dam, setting free all the doubts, pain, resentment, fear—and yes, love—he'd kept bottled inside of him for so long. After clinging to his vow and burying himself in the ranch so long, it was frightening to face life again.

"Slow down, Mac. We'd like to get there alive." Hal interrupted his son's recollections.

"Sorry," Mac muttered as he eased off the gas.

What was the matter with him, daydreaming about the past when he had enough problems in the present?

Perversely, his mind returned to that painful day when he had stood there in all his grime, grieving for a wife and worrying for a father, shaking his fist at the blazing blue sky, demanding to know why he had to lose everything, even that one bit of softness and sweetness he had encountered so briefly.

Only once had he held her after the ambulance arrived, and that was as she lay crushed and bleeding in a small town clinic, struggling valiantly to repeat the vows her father pleaded with her to make while the throb of a helicopter warned she would soon be whisked away. She had lapsed into unconsciousness after the words were said. He had continued to hold her, feeling her pain, pleading with her to stay alive, to stay with him. He remembered the promises he'd made her. He would take care of her, give her a new horse, anything she wanted, if she would just live. He'd wait for her to grow up and get as much education as she wanted, then he'd take her home as his wife, and she wouldn't ever have to leave again.

The paramedics had been forced to pry his arms from around her before they could lift her aboard the air ambulance. She had opened her eyes just once, and in them he had read the fulfillment of all his dreams. He loved her then, and—he suddenly realized—he loved her now, fool that he was.

Wryly, he thought of the now very much grown-up Laura. She wasn't the adoring child or the sweet, shy teenager he remembered. She was an assertive, capable woman, and he wasn't sure he was ready to exchange his dream Laura for this real-life version. He could see now how foolish he had been to rest all his hopes and dreams on a young girl he barely knew. Not only had he missed opportunities to connect with other people over the last eight years, but he was now faced with the need to reconcile the girl he remembered with the woman she'd become. He didn't want her to be the mindless chattel Coop had in mind for her, but it was difficult to set aside his memories of a girl who needed and adored him. Merging memory with reality was more than he was prepared to do right now, especially when this reality not only didn't adore him but hated and distrusted him. And when it came right down to it, he didn't trust her either.

* * *

Once the car left the paved road, they moved more slowly. Shadows were getting long, and the farther into the mountains they traveled, the more the waning sunlight seemed to dim. Several times, Laura noticed small groups of cattle in the distance. She was surprised to notice that one of the herds was made up of deer, not cattle. She hadn't expected deer to be found on these dry, brush-covered slopes. Didn't deer live in the kind of mountains that were covered with pine and birch trees, where there was plenty of water and meadows of deep green grass? If things were different between herself and Mac, she could have asked him about the deer.

If things were different between Mac and me. But they weren't. She felt incredibly sad. For a moment her thoughts went back to the boy who had once shared her ice cream cone. With a shake of her head, she reminded herself she couldn't get sentimental about Mac. She would never place herself in the hopeless situation her mother had found herself in by falling in love with a man who was all wrong for her. Laura's parents had lived in separate worlds, and neither world had had enough room for her.

Just after they clattered across the cattle guard, Mac leaned his palm against the horn. The sudden blare startled her into an involuntary exclamation.

"Why did you do that?" she asked in irritation.

Mac raised one hand to point ahead. Bounding through the rippling grain were five sleek brown deer. Their hooves seemed to barely touch the ground as they flew in great graceful leaps across the field.

"How beautiful," she murmured. She forgot she wasn't speaking to Mac.

"They'll make good eating."

"Eating! You'd eat those graceful creatures?" Laura was horrified.

"Why not? They've been getting fat on my grain."

"They're too beautiful to eat," Laura argued.

"Cattle are beautiful, too, but I notice you eat steak and hamburgers."

"That's different," Laura argued.

"I don't see any difference, except beef tastes a little better. They both roam all over these hills, then fatten up on my grain."

His reasoning might make sense, but still it appalled her. Looking up, she caught Mac's eyes in the mirror. She felt a sudden suspicion he was deliberately baiting her.

As they pulled up in front of the house, Laura reached for the door handle but stopped short when Mac suddenly shouted, "What is that?"

Laura leaned around the seat in front of her to get a better view of the mammoth machine that rested in the middle of the yard. Suddenly, it was difficult to quell a childish giggle.

"I think it's a grain combine."

"I know it's a combine, but why is it here?"

"For heaven's sake! It's here to cut our grain—what did you think it was for?"

"Laura, who does it belong to, and where did it come from?" Suspicion filled Mac's voice.

"It belongs to me," Laura said smugly. "You said the grain had to be harvested this week and that the crew you planned to hire had taken another job, so I bought a combine. We can harvest the grain ourselves."

"Laura, you can't even drive a car. How are you going to drive that thing?" Bruce asked incredulously.

"You just picked up the phone and ordered a $130,000 combine like it was a pizza?" Mac shook his head. "What am I saying? You can't even order a pizza over the phone out here!" He released the catch on his door. Slowly, as if in a daze, he walked over to the huge piece of farm equipment. It sat like a great yellow beast left over from dinosaur days. Well above his head was a glassed-in box where the operator would sit sheltered from dust and flying chaff.

"I suppose it has air-conditioning, too."

"Well, of course it does." He hadn't heard Laura approach. "I told Mr. Sylvester about our problem. He ordered the combine for me. Naturally, I told him to include something as important as air-conditioning!"

"Naturally!" Mac's voice was tinged with sarcasm. "What about our agreement? What happened to your little speech about how we would share decisions? It looks to me like my so-called partner is making the decisions all by herself. It couldn't be that she plans to use her money to push me right out of the picture, could it?"

"Don't accuse me of reneging on our agreement. All I did was buy a combine you said we needed. It didn't cost you a dime, and I had the crazy idea you'd actually be happy to see it. Need I remind you that it was you who tried to trick me into signing away my share of the ranch and half of the inheritance left me by my mother?"

"That wasn't my idea, Laura. But speaking of your inheritance, I thought you couldn't get at your money until you turned twenty-five. How did you pay for this?"

"I had some money from the sale of property that wasn't included in the agreement." She didn't tell him it had taken the rest of her share of the money from the sale of Aunt Alice's house and part of the support money Jake had sent to April. If he knew that detail, he'd probably refuse the combine. "Look Mac, if you don't like the combine, send it back, but if you send it back, don't you dare begrudge those poor deer all the grain they can eat." She turned away from him, close to tears.

Mac watched in amazement as Laura fled to the house. He didn't understand women, especially this one. He'd grown up without a mother, sisters, or even the girlfriends other guys seemed to collect, so how was he ever going to figure out Laura?

Slowly, he walked around the massive piece of machinery. He knew exactly what it cost and where she had purchased it. Every time he'd made the trip to Tremonton during the summer, he had stopped at a particular farm equipment company to daydream a little, then returned home to rejuggle his accounts; if they got a couple of good rainfalls, if his calf crop was particularly good, if the price of beef . . . He always ended up shaking his head and saying, *Maybe next year*. What on earth had possessed Laura to go out and blow all that money on a grain combine? He shook his head slowly.

Chance joined Mac and gave the combine an approving nod. "She's a beaut, ain't she?"

"She sure is," Mac concurred, but he wasn't referring to the giant machine.

fourteen

"BRUCE, I WON'T change my mind. I'm staying."

"After what they tried to pull yesterday, how can you even think of staying?" Bruce stood before her with his hands on his hips.

"That's the reason I can't leave. I agreed to a temporary partnership, and I intend to keep my part of the bargain."

"But Laura, now that you've given him access to the money he needs to harvest his grain, he doesn't need you here. Come with me."

"No, I'm staying," she persisted.

"Then take my phone, so you can call me if you need help." He tried to press the small telephone into her hand.

"You said yourself, there's no service out here."

"I forgot. Middle of nowhere . . ." he muttered.

"I'll be all right. Now go, or you'll miss your flight." She gestured toward his car.

Mac stood a short distance away, apparently engrossed in conversation with one of the hands, though Laura didn't miss how often his eyes glanced their way.

"You'd better hurry. Your boss was adamant that you be there tomorrow morning." Laura encouraged Bruce to be on his way. Though she appreciated all of the help Bruce had given her, she needed to do this alone. She'd spent too much of her life passively obeying instructions instead of making her own decisions. Assertively assuming her right to a full partnership with Mac was something she needed to do.

"Look after my car for me." His sports car was his pride and joy.

"I will. Now don't worry. I'll be okay."

Bruce wrapped his arms around Laura to give her a farewell hug. She leaned against his shoulder long enough to assure him once more she would be fine, then stepped back to allow him room to open his car door. Chance climbed into the other bucket seat with a whistle of approval for the sleek little car. He'd made no secret of being pleased that Bruce had asked him to drive the car back to the ranch after Bruce caught a plane in Twin Falls. Uncertain when he'd be able to get away to return for Laura, Bruce had decided against leaving his car in long term parking at the airport.

Laura watched until the road curved, and she lost sight of the small car. For just a moment, she felt a sense of panic. Then she reminded herself that dealing with Mac and claiming her share of the ranch was her fight, not her cousin's. She continued watching the plume of dust the little car left behind until Mac spoke from behind her.

"Now that pretty boy is gone, do you think we might get down to work?"

Laura bristled at the question. Clamping back the impulse to retort in kind, she pasted a pleasant expression on her face and turned to face Mac. "Of course, I'll do whatever I can."

"You've got a lot to learn today. To begin with, go get that truck parked over there behind the toolshed, then follow me into the field." He pointed toward two tall, round cones, which appeared to be made out of tin. Dropping Laura's arm, his long strides carried him toward the new combine. He'd announced at breakfast that he intended to start the grain harvest that morning, and she'd been relieved that he wasn't going to let his stubborn pride stand in the way of doing what needed to be done.

"Mac! I can't drive." There was a note of panic in her voice as she ran to catch up with him.

"Look! I don't expect you to drive this beast." He patted the metal side of the monstrous piece of yellow farm equipment. A smile creased his austere features. "You might own this baby, but there's no way I'd turn you loose with it on my grain field. If you didn't kill yourself first, you'd probably mutilate every stalk of grain in the field."

"I don't mean the combine." Laura gritted her teeth to keep her temper in check. The real problem was harder to admit. "I can't drive the truck, because I don't know how to drive it."

"You won't need to shift gears." Mac sighed. "Just put it in first and go slow."

"Mac, you don't understand." Laura's face turned red as she tried to get her message through the man's thick head. "I have never driven a car, a truck, or any other kind of vehicle in my life. Aunt Alice wouldn't even allow me to have a bicycle. I don't have a driver's license, and I never learned how to drive!" There! She'd admitted her shortcomings. She closed her eyes and slightly ducked her head, waiting for his laughter.

When all was silent, she risked a peek. The look on his face said he didn't quite believe her.

"Aunt Alice never owned a car, and she didn't want me to learn to drive one either," she rushed to explain. "There's plenty of public transportation in San Francisco, so driving a car was never necessary." Laura defended herself, even as she recalled the many arguments she'd had with Aunt Alice over learning to drive.

"You're serious, aren't you?" Mac's face held a comic expression, as though waiting for the punch line. A slow grin spread across his face. "You really can't drive."

Laura folded her arms and glared as Mac whooped with laughter. Her impulses warred between smacking his smirking face and joining in the laughter ringing in the still, clear mountain air. Finally, one corner of her mouth turned up in a wry smile. Mac grabbed her arm to lead her toward the truck.

Her nervousness grew as she realized this wasn't just a pickup truck, but a big ten-wheeler with a vast cargo space for grain. "No, Mac! I told you I can't. Isn't there something else I can do?"

"Nope! You, lady, are about to get your first driving lesson."

Opening the door with one hand, he boosted Laura onto the seat before she could argue. Briefly, he explained the various instruments. Then, with a quick brush of his hip, he pushed her partway across the seat so that he could sit beside her. His proximity heightened her nervousness. Taking her hand in his, he placed it over the gear shift knob. She struggled not to snatch it back. Maybe if she went along, he'd soon see she really couldn't drive the truck, and she could escape back to the house. But with surprising patience, he repeated the starting, shifting, and stopping procedures over and over again until it started to make sense to her.

She drew back against the seat as far as she could, hoping distance would help her to concentrate on Mac's instructions. Her mouth felt dry, and it took all of her willpower to control the hand he held pressed beneath his own. It had a tendency to shake.

When Mac appeared satisfied with her abilities, he swung his legs to the ground and stood, bracing one hand against the open door as he coaxed her to slide behind the wheel.

"Okay, start 'er up," he ordered.

She wanted to scream, but she was determined not to humiliate herself that way. Instead, she reached for the starter. The engine roared to life the moment Laura twisted the key. *I did it!* Her moment of elation disappeared the second she realized she had no idea what to do next. When Mac told her to shift into first gear then head across the yard, she froze. *He's out of his mind! I'll run into something. I won't be able to stop.* A trickle of perspiration ran down her neck.

With an exaggerated sigh, Mac moved around the truck to climb in the passenger side. Looking as relaxed as if he were sprawled in his favorite easy chair, he nudged her arm.

"Go on, shift."

Sucking in her breath and closing her eyes, she squeezed the grip clutched in her right hand. Slowly, she pulled it toward her and slid it into place as Mac had instructed. She stifled a yelp and opened her eyes as the truck suddenly lurched forward. It made two lunges before the engine stalled. Mac reached out to turn the key to the off position.

"Right," he drawled. "Next time keep your eyes open, but for now, press the gas pedal a little bit."

After several jerky starts and stops, she managed to steer the truck across the yard. Following a second jaunt around the yard, Mac told her to turn the engine off. He opened his door once more, then turned back to issue more instructions.

"It will take me twenty minutes to reach the field with the combine and thirty or forty minutes to fill the hopper. In about half an hour bring the truck to the field. Wait where the grain has already been cut. When the combine stops, drive across the cut stubble until you reach me. Then I'll show you how to position the truck." Mac flashed a jaunty grin in her direction and walked away.

"Mac, why can't one of the hands drive the truck?" she called after him.

"Chance went with Bruce to drive his car back. Andy and Bill served notice on this type of thing a long time ago; they're cowboys, not farmers. They took horses up on the ridge to check the herd. Doc said no field work for Dad. You're all I've got, so drive that truck, *partner.*" Laughter trailed behind him as he gripped the narrow rail beside the steps leading to the combine cab and swung into the glass-enclosed cab.

Laura's knuckles tightened around the steering wheel. She felt like banging her head against it as she listened to the sudden roar of a powerful engine, then watched as the bright yellow machine lumbered across the yard and began its slow progress down the lane. She ran the damp palms of her hands down her jeans-clad legs. Mac had to be crazy! How could he possibly expect her to drive a huge truck?

While she sat fuming and steeling herself to follow him down the lane, she heard a light tap on the door beside her. She looked out the open window to see Hal smiling at her. He held a large insulated jug and a small cooler in his hands.

"It's going to be hot out there today. You'll need these."

"Hal, I can't drive this truck." Laura tried to enlist the older man's sympathy. "I'll probably wreck it and kill myself. I don't even have a driver's license."

"You'll do fine. And you don't need a license to drive farm equipment on your own property." He didn't appear concerned. "I've got to go back inside now. I'm expecting a long-distance conference call. When I first ran for office, I never imagined how much time I would spend on the phone. Can you imagine committee meetings by phone? But this is a mighty big state—bigger than Texas, if you ironed out all the mountains." He chuckled as he turned back toward the house.

Laura leaned her head against the back of the seat. *What am I going to do?* She couldn't just climb out of the truck and return to the house. She wasn't a quitter. She'd never run from a challenge. Taking a deep breath, she squared her shoulders and reached for the ignition key. The engine responded, and with meticulous care, she eased the truck into motion.

Her sweat-dampened hair clung to the sides of her face, and her fingernails left small indentations in the side of the steering wheel as the truck crept down the incline leading away from the house. The large vehicle seemed to have a mind of its own as it wobbled from one side of the narrow lane to the other. Each time she tried to correct its tendency to wander, she found herself nearly leaving the road on the other side. She seemed to be recklessly flying down the road out of control. Every rock and rut in the road made its presence known. Her foot hovered over the brake until the lane became more level.

She looked around for the gate Mac had mentioned, then breathed a sigh of relief. She could see where the combine had entered the field. However, the space looked too small to accommodate the truck. She'd never be able to turn it through that narrow opening.

She stopped to survey the situation. Her heart was pounding as she eyed the narrow gap between the gate posts. She suspected Mac was expecting her to quit. Then he could claim that he tried but she was the one who gave up. She squared her shoulders. She'd gotten this far; she'd get through that gate if it killed her. Mac wouldn't be able to accuse her of being a quitter! If she turned too sharply, she risked over-turning the truck, but a wide swing could take out a fence post or two.

Grasping the steering wheel in both hands, she turned it as she pressed her foot against the gas pedal. The truck lurched forward a few feet. She hit the brake, then repeated the process. By the time she got the truck into the field, her arms ached, her damp clothes were plastered to her skin, and a throbbing pressure was making itself known in her temples. She hadn't taken out any fence posts, though, only scraped one a bit. Pressing her foot against the brake, the truck quivered to a halt, and she shut off the engine.

As the roar of the engine ceased, a clamoring stillness took its place. Laura's arms continued to tremble, and she breathed a sigh of relief. Suddenly, a sense of elation crowded out her earlier fears. She'd done it! She'd actually driven a huge truck! It was hard to believe. She wanted to sing and shout. She even felt charitable toward Mac; he'd been a good teacher, in spite of laughing at her.

Brushing her hand across her damp face, Laura felt stifled by the heat. Perhaps if she turned on the air conditioning, the truck would feel more comfortable. She found knobs marked heater and fan, but none of the labeled buttons said anything about air conditioning. Pushing and turning knobs indiscriminately was too risky. As a matter of self-preservation, she rolled down the other cab window, which provided only minor relief.

Folding her arms across the open window, Laura rested her chin on them. Far in the distance she could see the combine moving steadily through the ripe wheat. In its wake appeared a wide swath of stubble, golden stalks shorn of their red-gold heads—not only shrunken in size but dimmed in color. The huge machine dipped behind a hill until it almost disappeared from sight, then with slow determination began its assault on the next hill.

Several minutes later, the combine stopped, and Laura took a deep shuddering breath. Panic assailed her senses. It was time to start the truck again. She congratulated herself when the engine roared to life with her first attempt. Once more, she found herself lurching slowly ahead with the back end of the truck seemingly set on departing sideways while she tried to force it forward. Each rut felt like it was the Grand Canyon as she jolted along in terror of bouncing away from the cut grain to trample the uncut wheat.

The truck picked up speed as it started down the last slope. Lifting her foot away from the gas pedal did nothing to slow it down. She pushed against the brake just as she had before, but the truck rumbled on. Her knuckles turned white where she gripped the steering wheel. Suddenly, the combine loomed in front of the truck. She couldn't stop! She couldn't turn! She closed her eyes and pressed all her weight on both pedals. Motion ceased. Then she heard it, the grinding sound of metal against metal. Her mind was flooded with visions of Mac lying unconscious, bleeding. What if he were dead!

"You can open your eyes now."

Slowly, Laura lifted her head. She peeped through her fingers. Mac was standing beside her, bracing himself in the open doorway. A wave of relief washed over her, but she couldn't meet his eyes. Nervously, she glanced toward the combine. No jumble of twisted metal met her eyes. It was dusty, but there wasn't a scratch on it. It safely stood a good ten or fifteen feet away. Was she so far gone that the sound of the truck door opening sounded like a crash? Glad Mac couldn't read her thoughts, she shut off the engine.

"What took you so long? It'll take a month to harvest this grain if you don't move a little faster than that." A broad grin softened his words. He edged Laura over so he could slide behind the steering wheel. She quickly scrambled to the far side of the bench seat. A series of deft motions by Mac positioned the truck beside the combine; then he returned to the big harvester to start a cascade of golden wheat streaming from the combine's massive hopper to the bed of the truck. When the last kernel of grain fell, Mac disengaged the two vehicles. With a flippant wave and instructions for Laura to hurry a little faster the next time, he leaped back to the combine cab.

Watching the machine creep away, Laura was struck by how much it resembled a dinosaur, with its huge cumbersome body and the grain auger appearing like a small head atop a long skinny neck. *How appropriate for a Neanderthal man!* She giggled.

The morning wore on with Laura sweltering in the heat, then racing to position the truck where Mac wanted it. She took long gulps from the jug of ice water Hal had given her and found herself envying Mac the air-conditioned comfort of the combine cab. By noon, she was no longer afraid of driving to meet Mac and felt confident she wouldn't run into the combine, but the more sweaty and disheveled she felt, the more obnoxiously cheerful Mac became.

"Okay, this is the last hopper the truck will hold," Mac shouted as Laura pulled the truck into place beside him. "You'll have to climb on top and use the shovel to level the load. Otherwise, the grain will spill over."

"I can't climb up there!" Laura protested.

"Sure you can." The breath whooshed out of her lungs as Mac suddenly swooped her up in his arms. "Let go of my hair." He laughed as he swung her over his head. "See that ladder on the side of the truck? Grab hold of it, and up you go." He tossed her toward the metal rungs.

Laura clutched at them, then scrambled to the top before she lost her nerve.

As she stepped over the side of the truck, her feet settled in the shifting grain, filling her shoes with the small, hard kernels. Walking on the wheat was an odd sensation, and she winced as the grain pressed against the soles of her feet.

"Wheat is like sand," Mac called. "Take your shoes off, and you'll find the going more comfortable. The scoop shovel is at the front of the load. When you reach it, just set your shoes on top of the cab. You can retrieve them when you're through leveling the grain."

Clutching the truck side with one hand, Laura stood first on one foot, then the other, to pull off her shoes, then picked her way to the front, still holding to the side. The grain beneath her feet shifted with each step, feeling surprisingly cool to her bare skin. It really was much like walking on loose sand. Sometimes her steps sank deeply, burying her feet to her ankles. She stumbled once as her foot plunged knee-deep.

Like a child playing in a gigantic sandbox, Laura laughed as the wheat began to rain from the auger's spout. Thrusting the unwieldy shovel into the flow sent the grain flying in all directions. Aiming the shovel lower, it became too heavy for her to lift. When she saw the golden grain rising rapidly in a huge mound, she gave up on the shovel and attacked the pile with flying arms and legs. Throwing herself against the pile, she pushed and scooted with her entire body to keep it from spilling over the closest side. When the flow of grain finally slowed to a trickle, then stopped, she sat back, gasping for breath.

Hearing a rustling sound behind her, she turned to watch Mac swing over the side of the truck. A layer of dust coated his blue work shirt and extended down the length of his jeans. His hair was tousled and looked several shades lighter than usual, but he looked happy. Seeing his unexpected smile, she smiled back.

Mac was surprised but pleased to see Laura's smile. He had half expected to see his city-slicker bride in tears. He had worked her hard in the heat and dust and had given her little chance to back out of driving when she was obviously afraid of the size and power of the truck. His eyes raked the length of her where she sat sprawled in the grain. Her hair was matted and dirty. It poked out at unexpected angles, and her skin was grimy with a faint red glow on the backs of her arms and the tip of her nose. For just a moment, he caught a glimpse of the little tomboy who had once dogged his steps.

Long ago memories mixing with youthful dreams filled his mind. Only this was no little girl. He moved more rapidly toward her.

Laura's eyes widened as Mac slid down on the golden grain beside her. Something in his eyes beckoned her. If she didn't run now . . . She began to scoot away from him. The shifting grain made rapid movement impossible. Laura's efforts to move out of reach were foiled as the wheat shimmered and rippled, mocking her attempt to escape by rolling her toward, rather than away, from Mac. His arm slid around her waist. The grain became his ally, sending her tumbling against him. Her eyes met his, and he gave her plenty of time to protest. She remained silent, and Mac's head began closing the space between them. She met him halfway.

The kiss was all he had dreamed, sweet and tender, yet he drew back, setting her free. *What am I thinking, making a move like that? Am I crazy?* She looked as confused as he felt.

As he kissed her, he had wondered if it might be possible to make their marriage real. *Not likely.* He knew full well she wasn't thinking in permanent terms. His optimism about their newly formed partnership was overshadowed by the memory of a young girl with her legs twisted at odd angles and blood pumping from a gash on her head, who still struggled to please her dying father by repeating the words he asked of her. *My wife, but not by her choice.* The words seemed to drum inside his head. Even at twenty-one, he should have known a marriage begun the way theirs did could not last.

Closing his eyes, he could see her torn and bloody sundress, hear her gasping voice, and see the dazed look in her eyes. He'd known then the marriage was only a legal ruse. He'd been a fool to stake so many dreams on it. Jake wasn't the kind of man who would have dictated his daughter's future, taking away her right to choose her own husband. Jake had hit on the plan to protect her from being controlled by her aunt, not to transfer that control to a husband who wasn't even of her choosing. How could he have forgotten his pledge that if she lived, he would wait for her to grow up, then allow her to choose whether or not she wished to continue the marriage? In the days since her arrival at the ranch, she'd made her intentions quite clear—she hadn't come looking for a husband. It was the ranch she wanted.

Laura remained still, feeling dazed and confused both by the kiss and by Mac's silent withdrawal. She was beginning to suspect she was falling in love with Mac. But she couldn't. She wouldn't allow herself to love a man she couldn't trust and who had so much power to hurt her.

She jumped to her feet. Ignoring Mac's outstretched hand, she turned her back on him to retrieve her shoes. By the time she reached the ladder on the side of the truck, Mac had finished smoothing the grain and was pulling a tarp over the gleaming gold. He went over the side first, then reached to assist her. How she wanted to refuse his help, to pretend as casually as he did that the kiss meant nothing, but she was just afraid enough of heights that she didn't dare refuse his assistance on the climb down.

Once her feet were on solid ground, she stepped away from him and shook wheat kernels from her shoes before slipping them back on her feet. As she turned to step away, Mac reached for her arm.

"Wait." Mac spoke softly.

"I'm hungry." She shook off his arm. "Hal packed a lunch for us."

"We need to talk."

"I can't talk on an empty stomach." Laura kept her eyes lowered as she walked away.

Mac tied down the tarp before following her to the truck cab. He took the cooler from her hands.

"We can eat in the combine cab. The air-conditioning has kept it cooler there than it is in the truck." He started toward the grain harvester. Laura shrugged, then followed him. The glass-enclosed cab was small, and they had to share the narrow bench seat, but it was a great deal cooler than the truck. She found the cooler temperature a welcome relief. Twice Mac tried to speak to her, but she brushed his efforts aside. Her stomach cramped, swallowing was difficult, and she couldn't push words past the lump in her throat. She knew that if she tried to talk to him about their situation, she'd burst into tears and make a fool of herself.

What was happening to her? She knew a number of men just as good-looking as Mac—intelligent men with fun personalities—but none of them made her feel the way Mac did. Of course, she'd had little experience actually dating those men. Aunt Alice had objected to her spending time with anyone other than the son of the president of the symphony board. He was very attractive, and she'd tried to fall in love with him, but his conversation bored her, and she'd suspected he wasn't really as enamored by her as he claimed.

She wished she could remember more of when she and Mac were children together. It was disturbing to know that Mac held memories of her as a child and as a teenager, but he was a complete stranger to her.

"Here." Mac held out a soft drink can.

Reluctantly, Laura reached for it. Her fingers burned where his hand brushed hers. She pulled her hand away, resenting the fact that a simple touch of his hand could stir a response while he appeared to remain unaffected. As unobtrusively as possible, she shifted to the edge of the narrow bench to avoid brushing against him as they ate.

Mac's jaw tightened. It was obvious Laura could hardly wait to escape his presence. He shouldn't have kissed her. He should have taken advantage of their being alone together to have a real talk with her, to give her a chance to get to know him better. At every turn where Laura was concerned, it seemed he made the wrong choice. He took a breath, ready to try some conversation. "You know, Laura, it might help our partnership if we knew more about each other," he suggested. "Tell me what it was like growing up in San Francisco."

"It really wasn't too exciting. I didn't go to school as a child. Aunt Alice taught me at home, and I took music lessons from Mother until she became too weak to sit at the piano. Sometimes Mother dressed me up to accompany her to a concert."

"Are you a musician like your mother?"

"Definitely not! Mother and Aunt Alice gave it their best shot, but I constantly disappointed them. I've had violin lessons, flute lessons, voice lessons, dance lessons, ten years of piano lessons, and the only instrument I play well is the stereo."

Mac chuckled at her little joke, then got Laura laughing as well as he described his own miserable attempts to play the trumpet back in high school.

"Hey! Mac!"

Laura jumped. Looking around, she saw another truck, almost identical to the one she had driven all morning, parked behind theirs. Standing at the foot of the combine steps was an unfamiliar young woman, one dressed in skin-tight jeans, a brief halter top, and a black western hat. Laura watched as Mac leaped down the steps and the woman plastered herself against his broad chest, their heads disappearing behind the wide brim of her hat.

fifteen

STRANGE EMOTIONS HELD Laura motionless. She wasn't jealous. Good heavens! She barely knew the man.

It just went to show what a fool she'd made of herself by letting Mac kiss her. He claimed their marriage was valid, but he certainly wasn't acting like a married man, at least the way she thought a married man should act. One minute he was kissing her, and the next he was lip-locked with some bimbo in cowboy boots!

"Laura! Laura, come down here. There's someone I want you to meet."

Well, I don't want to meet her! Laura muttered to herself while running her fingers through her hair to straighten its messy appearance. She tried to brush away the straw clinging to her clothes and shake away the last kernels of wheat hiding beneath her blouse. She didn't want to leave the combine cab, but she couldn't stay in it all day. She turned around, straightened her shoulders, and tilted her head before placing her foot on the first rung of the ladder-like stairs. *As Bruce would say, It's showtime, babe!*

Mac's hands settled on her waist to lift her down the last few steps, and she struggled not to react in any way. She would not let him know his touch affected her. She resisted pulling away from him when his hand lingered at her waist to propel her toward his visitor. As she stepped toward the other woman, she held out her hand.

"Hello, I'm Laura Hendrickson." She was determined to smile, even if it killed her.

"Laura, this is Rhonda Davis." Mac completed the introduction. "Rhonda and her father own the Circle D a few miles down the road. We trade help with the grain and roundup every year. I called them this morning to let them know we'd need their truck shortly after noon."

"And a driver." Rhonda arched her eyebrows and moved closer to Mac. She was about the same height as Laura and probably a little younger. Her bright red hair suggested it had help from a bottle. Laura wondered if the girl might still be in her teens, though her level of self-confidence suggested otherwise.

Rhonda smiled artificially at Laura, accepted her outstretched hand with limp fingers, and returned her attention to Mac almost at once. Sliding her arm through his, her green eyes sparkled as she looked up at him. She smiled sweetly.

"We'll have a couple of hours to ourselves, maybe more, while Laura takes her truck into Tremonton. I'm looking forward to riding in that air-conditioned cab with you, honey." Her voice was a silky purr, and she gave Mac's chest a suggestive pat.

Honey? Drive that truck where? Laura's heart pounded. She didn't know which phrase upset her more. She couldn't do it! She'd kill herself! Maybe that was what Mac wanted. No, of course not. Mac was bullheaded and he wanted the ranch for himself, but she knew he would never go that far. She didn't question how she could be so sure, but she was.

"Sorry, Rhonda." Mac tugged on one of her red curls. "Laura doesn't have a CDL; she can't drive on the highway. She'll do the field driving, and you'll transport." With one arm draped around the girl's shoulder, he escorted her to the loaded truck. When he returned, he handed Laura the water jug before climbing back onto the combine.

"You'll need this. It'll get hotter before it starts to cool off."

"Thanks." Laura tried to match his nonchalant tone. Inside she was seething. It didn't bother Mac at all to have his girlfriend flirt with him in front of his wife! *Good grief! Am I beginning to believe I'm actually married to him?*

The sun was going down, and the air had turned chilly by the time Mac turned off the combine engine. When he walked toward the truck, Laura moved to the passenger side. He slid in and silently drove the truck back to the ranch buildings. Several times, she felt his eyes on her, and she got the feeling he was rehearsing some speech in his head he was hesitant to voice aloud. His attention made her feel uncomfortable, though she strived to appear unconcerned. He parked the truck beside the building she'd heard him refer to as the machinery shed and turned to her. "Laura, would you like to go for a ride? I could have a couple of horses saddled in five minutes."

She paused with her hand on the door handle. The question was unexpected. A part of her yearned toward the horses she'd seen in a pasture beyond the barn, but she was exhausted and still confused by the attraction she felt toward Mac. "No, I don't think so. I'm awfully tired." It may have been her imagination, but she thought her answer brought a hint of disappointment to his eyes.

"You probably haven't been on a horse since you left here as a little girl. How about walking up to the bluff? I'd like to explain . . ."

"No, I'm really too tired." She released the door catch and hurried into the house. She was beyond being hungry or caring how dirty she was; she just wanted to crawl into bed and sleep for a week. And she wasn't ready to listen to Mac explain anything.

She didn't make it to her room before Hal stopped her and insisted she eat something. After swallowing a few bites, she stumbled up the stairs to her little room. Her shower was fast and hot. She was asleep the moment she stumbled into bed.

Morning came too soon. She awoke to Mac pounding on her door, ordering her to get a move on. She was tempted to refuse. He needed to learn she wasn't the kind of woman who took kindly to orders! On the other hand, she wasn't about to let him think she was backing out of their partnership! She leaped out of bed, then groaned as sore muscles taunted her all the way to the bathroom.

Driving got easier as the week wore on. She learned to wear a T-shirt with a sweatshirt and jeans in the early morning when the temperature was cool, peel the heavy sweatshirt off as the day grew warmer, then don it again in the evening when Mac made one last round after the sun set. She learned the subtle differences between the two trucks and took pride in her ability to park where the trucks were needed instead of waiting for Mac to maneuver them into place. She awoke each morning to discover her muscles aching from wielding the shovel to level the loads the day before, but following a hot shower and a quick breakfast, she was ready to go. No matter how tired she became, she never complained. Making certain that Mac wouldn't be able to accuse her of reneging on their deal became a point of pride.

Whenever Mac joined her in the back of the truck, Laura handed him the shovel and made her way to the ground. They shared their lunch each day in the cooler combine cab. At first, conversation was stilted, and Laura only spoke as much as she deemed necessary. But when Mac took care to avoid personal comments related to their relationship or to ownership of the ranch, their conversation became less stiff. The following days saw an easing of the tension between them, and Laura began to look forward to their shared lunch break.

A couple of times she remained in the combine while Mac made a circular sweep of the field. Viewing the grain field and the surrounding mountains from that perspective was enjoyable, but she made certain Mac didn't get an opportunity to make a pass at her again. With Rhonda around so much, her efforts were mostly wasted since Mac didn't seem to have much reason to try. For some reason, that piqued her pride.

If the combine was on the other side of the field when Rhonda arrived, the girl never left immediately with the full truck. Instead, she'd hang around waiting for the combine to circle the field and pause beside the trucks so that she could spend a few minutes with Mac before pulling out. During those times, Laura tried to be friendly and, at the same time, ignore Rhonda's chatter about all the wonderful experiences she and Mac had shared. Laura found the younger woman increasingly irritating.

She was surprised when Sunday came and Mac didn't pound on her door at dawn. When she went downstairs, flustered because she had overslept, Hal assured her there was plenty of time, then invited her to attend church with them. She decided to accept the invitation. She was curious about the church that had been important to her father and to which her mother had taken her when she was a child.

Her memories of attending church as a little girl became clearer as she sat in the chapel between Hal and Mac. Hearing the music and the talks brought a hint of déjà vu, reminding her of feelings of peace and love she'd experienced long ago. A second meeting followed the first, but in a smaller room. When it ended, Mac leaned toward her to tell her he and Hal would be attending a meeting just for men while she should stay where she was in a meeting for adult women called Relief Society. She enjoyed this meeting the most and was encouraged by the friendly smiles of the women closest to her. Several stepped forward to introduce themselves after the meeting ended. As soon as she could, she hurried to the front of the building where Hal waited for her. Mac joined them not long after.

When they reached the ranch, Hal hurried into the kitchen to check the roast he'd left in a Crock-Pot, and she followed to set the table. While they ate, Hal and Mac continued a discussion concerning temples and family history they'd begun on the drive back to the ranch. Temples had figured into the lesson taught in Relief Society, too. She didn't understand much of it and wasn't comfortable asking questions, but it stirred her curiosity, and she decided that after dinner she would go to the office and see if any of the books there would answer her questions.

When they finished eating lunch, they each carried their own dishes to the dishwasher, and Hal shooed both Mac and Laura away, insisting that it would only take a minute to scrub the Crock-Pot and straighten the kitchen. Laura wasn't sure where Mac went. She hadn't seen Rhonda at church, so she wondered if he might have gone to spend the rest of his day off with her. She shrugged off her speculations in favor of making her way to the office, where she found several books about temples and a couple other volumes that looked interesting.

She spent the afternoon in her room glancing through the books, one of which was filled with pictures of beautiful buildings that were identified as various temples. She discovered Mormons went to temples to be married forever. She wondered if her parents had been married in a temple and, if so, which one. She found something comforting about the possibility that her parents might still be married and happy together. She knew that though they were separated and lived apart, they'd never divorced, and she'd suspected before her mother's death that April still cared about Jake.

Monday morning found Laura behind the wheel of the grain truck again. At noon, Mac carried their lunch to the combine cab, assuming they would eat together in its coolness as they had the previous week.

About halfway through her sandwich, Laura worked up the nerve to ask Mac if he knew where her parents had been married. The books concerning temples had interested her more than any of the other books she'd borrowed.

"They were married in San Francisco." Mac spoke around a thick ham sandwich. "You have their marriage certificate, and it's written right on it."

"I mean . . ." She paused, uncertain how to word her question. "My father was a Mormon, and my mother joined his church. Weren't they married in one of the Mormon temples?"

"Actually, they were, but later," Mac said. "They went to the Boise Temple with you to be sealed."

"Sealed? Does that mean they got married again?" She wasn't certain what the term meant.

"It's a word Church members use to describe a relationship that is given a special blessing in a temple so that the relationship will continue after the parties' deaths." She suspected he was simplifying his answer, but she appreciated the explanation. He also told her she was sealed to her parents. Knowing her parents had taken her to their temple to have her sealed to them was strangely comforting.

In the following days, Laura's lunches with Mac became the highlight of her day. She was amazed not only that they found things in common to talk about but also that they had so much fun as they discussed various topics. Laura and Mac soon discovered they had a shared interest in a number of topics. Laura's university had emphasized environmental issues in every department, but she was surprised by the extent of Mac's interest and concern for environmental issues. She was embarrassed to admit she had believed that ranchers had only a self-centered interest in nature and the planet. They discussed shared usage of government lands, the damage to fragile ecosystems caused by overgrazing, and the introduction of cheat grass to the sagebrush range. They argued over whether deer without natural predators should be allowed to proliferate freely and agreed coyotes kept the rabbit population under control for cattle ranchers but were a nuisance for sheep ranchers.

One day, they watched pheasants take to the air amid a whir of bright color. Mac explained he kept his fields posted to discourage both pheasant hunters and backpackers, who trampled his crops unless warned to keep their distance.

"There aren't enough pheasants left anymore to be worth hunting. If they were eating large amounts of grain, I might feel differently, but for now, I don't object to a few hens raising their little ones in my fields. Hunters are more dangerous than the birds they hunt. I don't want to risk having my stock and machinery shot up nor risk fires started by smokers who wander away from the state park."

Mac both saddened and entertained her with stories of a hunter who shot a saddled horse, thinking it was a moose, and of ranchers who defended their machinery by writing *COW* in big block letters on their tractors. He told her of cut fences and gates left open, of confronting a hunter carting off one of his steers with a deer tag dangling from a stubby horn, and of a couple of vacationing young men who set up their tent in his wheat field, thinking the young green plants were a vast meadow of grass.

"Not all hunters or tourists are careless nincompoops," Mac pointed out. "Responsible hunters pay for wildlife projects and thin out animals that would otherwise starve to death since the land can only support a certain number of animals."

"That might be true, but I don't see how anyone could shoot something as beautiful and gentle as a deer." She thought of the gentle creatures that thrilled her each time she caught a glimpse of one in the fields or on the hills above the ranch house.

As the days wore on, Laura began to think of Mac as a friend. She preferred not to think about being married to him or their conflict over ownership of the ranch. He seemed equally anxious to avoid those topics, and by silent agreement, they avoided controversy.

Every two or three hours, Rhonda showed up to switch trucks and flirt with Mac. Mostly Laura stayed in the background when the other woman was around, but Rhonda's noisy exuberance and obvious infatuation with Mac grated on her nerves. Once, the redhead climbed up the ladder to join Mac where he was leveling a load. Her giggling laughter floated back to Laura, who chided herself for her immature attitude. Why should she care what Mac and Rhonda did together? After all, she didn't want him. She should be glad Rhonda was around to distract Mac, to keep him from bothering her.

All the logic in the world didn't make Laura feel better. She didn't like the way Rhonda stood so close to Mac, bumping her hip against his to make a point or grabbing Mac's hand to clasp it as she laughed and whispered with him.

The last field was almost finished when Mac tossed the shovel to the ground and climbed down the side of the truck, leaving Rhonda to make her own way down. He appeared to be annoyed about something but smiled pleasantly enough at Laura when he looked her way.

"Come ride with me." Mac motioned with his hands for Laura to join him.

She hesitated. She didn't want Mac to use her to make his girlfriend jealous, but what would a trip or two around the big field matter? She could see they were almost finished. A couple more swathes were all that remained of the golden wheat field. It was the hardest work she had ever done, but she almost hated to see it end. And she'd imagined viewing the fields and mountains from a vantage point inside the big machine's cab. With her hat in her hand, she ran lightly across the cut stubble. It scratched at her pant legs, but she no longer noticed. Mac leaned forward to offer her a hand up, swinging her onto the seat beside him. He grinned as she gasped for breath, patted her denim-clad knee, and then reached for the gear shift.

The growl of changing gears from behind them suggested Rhonda wasn't happy with their arrangement. Laura noticed that the truck bumped across the field toward the gate at a much more rapid speed than usual. Mac appeared oblivious to his girlfriend's displeasure, and somehow that pleased Laura. From high above the whirling reel that thrust the stalks of grain toward the blades, she swept her eyes from one side of the valley to the other. The mountains were gray, streaked with silver and highlighted with stark black. The wheat stubble glimmered a pale golden blond.

Sniffing the air, she reveled in the clean scent of the freshly cut grain, the juniper trees, and sunshine. A faint whiff of gasoline fumes reminded her of the city. A frown wrinkled her brow. Bruce expected her to return to San Francisco in a few weeks, but she no longer looked forward to leaving the ranch. She suspected her work with the symphony would not be enough of a challenge for her now. She had planned to look for full-time employment when she returned anyway, but suddenly she wasn't sure she'd be willing to be cooped up in an office all day every day. She liked living on the ranch, especially since she and Mac had started working together instead of fighting.

She wondered if the truce between them would last beyond the grain harvest. Being honest with herself, she admitted she'd come to enjoy being around Mac more each day. She liked his easy relationship with the men who worked on the ranch, and they obviously respected him. She had come to admire the efficient way he managed every aspect of the ranch. More than once, she found herself thinking with regret how different her life would have been if she and her father had made it to the ranch eight years earlier. Perhaps she and Mac would have fallen in love after a few years if they'd been given the time to get to know each other back then. She knew without any doubts or reservations that she loved the ranch and that she was happy to have gotten to know Mac.

"Want to go to a party tonight?"

Was Mac asking her for a date? No, that wasn't possible if he and Rhonda had a thing going. But she had seen herself how annoyed he was a while ago. Maybe they broke up. Besides, if she and Mac remained partners, perhaps they should get to know each other better away from the ranch. And if this was really a date . . . Suppressing a shiver of excitement, Laura told herself not to read too much into it.

"Sounds fun." She forced her voice not to give away her rising enthusiasm. "Should I dress up?"

"Casual clothes are okay. No one dresses fancy for barbecues around here."

sixteen

MAC HAD SAID casual, but she dressed with care for the barbecue and took her time fussing with her hair. When she entered the kitchen, she found him already there with a juice carton held to his mouth. He was an impressive sight in a soft gray and black flannel shirt with a slender thread of red running through the pattern and the sleeves rolled up. Snug black jeans hugged his hips. Glancing away to hide her sudden blush, she felt like a schoolgirl with her first big crush.

"Want some?" Mac held out the carton. Before she could answer, Hal's voice cut in.

"Didn't I teach you to use a glass?" He opened the cupboard, set two glasses on the counter, then reached into the refrigerator for another carton of juice. Laura shook her head; she didn't want to risk messing up her lipstick.

Mac laughed before taking one more swallow and tossing the empty container into the trash. Settling a black hat with a snakeskin band on his head, he held out his arm to Laura.

"Let's go!" There was laughter in his voice and a look in his eyes that made Laura's breath catch in her throat. "Going with us?" He turned to Hal.

"No, I think I'll wait for Chance and the boys. You go ahead." He motioned Mac and Laura out the door.

Mac's long steps led them quickly to his old pickup truck. It looked more battered than ever now. She knew that Mac had worked on it in the evenings during the past two weeks while she collapsed exhausted in bed or read.

"There isn't much I can do about the dents and scrapes," he told her with a grin. "Hammered them out the best I could."

"Would you like to drive Bruce's car?" she offered. "I'm sure he wouldn't mind."

Mac's smile faded. He forced it back into place as he held the door for her. This was the first Laura had spoken of him since he left, and Mac wasn't going to let it spoil his hopes for the evening. He wasn't aware of any phone calls between them, so perhaps Laura wasn't so dependent on Bruce as Mac had worried.

He wondered if she might be embarrassed to ride in his old truck. Bruce's car was certainly more impressive, probably more comfortable, too, but pride wouldn't let him escort Laura in the other man's car.

He admired her slim form as he helped her into the truck. She wore a pale yellow silk shirt and tailored off-white pants. Fervently, he hoped Chance had cleaned out the interior of the pickup. No wonder she'd suggested taking Bruce's car. Well, if she was serious about this partner business, she'd have to learn this was a real working ranch, and ranch vehicles were picked for durability, not flashy style! They often weren't any too clean, either.

Mac didn't drive many miles before he swung off the road to pass beneath a lava rock and timber arch. He parked near an old silo beside several dozen pickup trucks and SUVs. He helped her out of the truck, and together they strolled toward an area beside a long, low ranch house where plank tables had been set up on sawhorses. A crowd of people was milling around a couple of metal horse troughs. As they got closer, Laura could see that the tubs were filled with beer and soft drink cans floating amid chunks of ice. A nearby table was heaped with salads and covered dishes. She caught the spicy odor of barbecue sauce and baked beans.

Several voices called to Mac with friendly hellos. Her pulse quickened, and she felt a surge of pride to walk into the party beside him. She recognized a few faces from church, but most of the people were strangers. The few she'd seen before nodded to her but continued on their way. She smiled, thinking how surprised everyone would be if she and Mac suddenly announced they were married. She blushed. Where did that idea come from? Instead of viewing their marriage as a colossal nightmare, she was beginning to think of it as a delicious secret.

"Want something to drink?" Mac leaned closer to ask. His smile was slow and just for her, making her feel warm and shivery. She almost forgot to answer.

"Uh, sure. Sprite."

He scooped two cans out of the icy slush, popped the tabs, and handed her one, keeping the other for himself.

"There you are!" Rhonda appeared at Mac's side. "I thought you would never get here. I really need your help setting up another table." She smiled up at him as she took his arm to lead him away.

"Laura . . ." Mac hesitated.

"I'll wait here. Go ahead." She could afford to be magnanimous. After all, he had invited her, not Rhonda, to the party.

She watched them disappear into the crowd with a twinge of regret. A frown flitted across her face. Rhonda needn't walk quite that close to Mac! She took a long swallow of the icy soda pop in her hand.

The can felt cold and damp. She wanted to set it down, but she didn't see any place to dispose of it. Switching it to her other hand, she glanced around noticing the crowd was growing larger. No one was seated yet. They stood around in little groups talking and laughing. She felt awkward. Should she introduce herself to a few people or wait for them to approach her? Several curious glances turned her way. Perhaps she should just stay where she was and wait for Mac to return.

She shivered. She wasn't sure she'd ever get used to how the hottest day could turn cold as soon as the sun went down. She wanted to move closer to the bonfire that burned at one end of the lighted area. Her eyes scanned the crowd to see if she could spot Mac returning. She rubbed the goose bumps on her arms. Why wasn't everyone huddling around the fire? By this time, she knew the men at the ranch didn't seem to feel the cold as much as she did, but there were other women here. Of course, most of the women seemed to be wearing sweat-shirts or denim jackets.

She looked at her silk blouse, her linen pants, and her high-heeled sandals. Across the dry, brittle grass, she looked for women dressed similarly and failed to find even one. Jeans! Boots or running shoes! Why hadn't Mac warned her! He'd said casual. She hadn't realized he meant this casual! One minute she was lonely, the next she felt conspicuous. No wonder no one came near her. They probably thought she was some kind of snob.

What was taking Mac so long? Her mind conjured up the red-headed Rhonda. She should have gone with them.

"Hi! Haven't seen you around these parts before." She hadn't noticed the man's approach.

Laura turned her head toward the deep voice rumbling near her ear. She found herself staring into the navy blue eyes of the tallest, most handsome cowboy east of Hollywood. His smile could eliminate electric bills. His clothes were western in style but had a Beverly Hills edge to them.

"Name's Ace Turner. I saw you walk in with Mac. Seems he's busy elsewhere, so I thought I'd come over and introduce myself."

"Hi! I'm Laura . . . Hendrickson." Good grief, she'd almost said Burgoyne!

"Mac and I go back to high school days," Ace let her know in that deep, warm voice. "We used to drive into Tremonton, Utah, together to go to school most days, and we boarded at the same house when the weather was too rough to drive."

"Isn't there a school closer than Tremonton?"

"No, most high school students out here either board in Tremonton or Burley during the worst months and drive an hour or more night and morning the rest of the year."

"That's awful!"

Ace laughed. "It's better than it used to be. There wasn't even an elementary school around here before the dry farmers started sinking wells into the aquifer so they could irrigate and raise hay. Now most of them are year-round residents, and ranch life isn't as isolated as it once was."

Near the house, Laura could see several couples dancing on the patio. She looked again for Mac but couldn't see him.

"Enough of this chitchat." Ace reached for her hand. "The music is starting, and it's calling our names."

"I don't know."

"I do." His smile was enough to melt the coldest heart. "A beautiful woman, a beautiful night, tolerable music, and me! What more could a lovely lady ask for?" Laughter sparkled in his eyes as he tugged Laura toward the music.

Laura liked to dance, and Ace was good. Dancing was the one area her musically talented mother's genes had spilled over to her daughter. The music was different from the music she was accustomed to, but Ace led her faultlessly through two fast numbers. The next song was slow, and he gradually pulled her closer.

She felt uncomfortable being held so close. Ace flirted outrageously, and his more blatant innuendos made her uneasy. Like it or not, there was a good possibility she was married, and she didn't think a married woman should be held so close by anyone other than her husband.

Peeking over Ace's shoulder, her heart gave a little lurch. There was Mac with his arms around Rhonda. Her head was on his shoulder, and they were swaying to the lilting country tune. Laura had a sinking feeling that this was far from the first time Mac and Rhonda had danced together. She found Rhonda looking straight at her. With a triumphant smile, the other woman ran one finger down the side of Mac's face, and then leaned up to whisper in his ear.

Laura glanced away. The joy had gone out of the night. Why had Mac invited her if he planned to spend all evening with Rhonda? Lifting her elegant little nose in the air, she laughed at some remark Ace made. Forcing herself to keep her eyes on Ace instead of watching Mac, she was relieved when the music stopped.

Grabbing her around the waist, Ace suddenly twirled her around in a full circle before clamping her to his side. Several people laughed and clapped. Laura could feel the red creeping up her cheeks. She wished she could run and hide. Bravely, she attempted a smile.

"The music is starting again," Ace whispered in her ear. "Let's show 'em what we can do.

"I believe the next dance is mine." Relief washed through her at the sound of Mac's voice. Eagerly, she reached for his hand only to be brought up short by Ace.

"Finders keepers, losers weepers!" Ace taunted as he twirled Laura out of Mac's reach.

Mac ground his teeth together. Nothing had gone right since they'd gotten to this fool party. Before he could even begin to introduce Laura around, Rhonda had needed his help setting up extra tables, and then there had been a short in the speakers she'd asked him to fix.

He'd meant to turn Rhonda down when she asked him to dance, but then he'd seen Ace move in on Laura. Ace always did zero in on the prettiest girl at every party. Mac groaned, thinking of all the girls he'd lost to his so-called friend back in high school. But Laura was his wife. That should make things different. Even Ace wouldn't cut in on a friend's wife! Of course, Ace didn't know Laura was Mac's wife.

He ought to march right out there and tell the clown, only he didn't want to announce their marriage that way. He didn't know whether he'd ever announce it. In spite of their newfound friendship, Mac assumed Laura would still want an annulment or divorce. And even if by some miracle Laura decided she wanted to give their marriage a go, no one could know about their marital status until Laura was ready to tell them. He found himself dancing halfheartedly around the floor with Rhonda in his arms while his gloomy stare followed the gleam of white slacks and yellow silk.

"Daddy wants you to help slice the barbecued beef." He half heard Rhonda while his real concentration was on the couple in front of him. They were doing some kind of fancy step, and everyone had cleared a circle around them. Laura's cheeks were flushed, and Ace's smile lit up the night like a neon sign.

Rhonda began to massage his shoulder as the music turned to a slow number again. He shrugged her hand away, his eyes following Laura's every move. He watched Ace dip his partner low, then raise her hand to his mouth to kiss the tip of each finger.

He'd kill him! His fingers closed around Rhonda's arm. He quickly two-stepped her across the floor, then practically shoved her into Ace's arms as his own closed around Laura.

"Changing partners," he growled as he swept Laura away.

"What are you trying to do getting all cozy with Ace like that?" He hadn't meant to snarl at Laura. The words just came out that way.

"Cozy! That's rich coming from you!" Laura snapped. "With Rhonda wrapped around you like a second skin, I'm surprised you could even breathe, let alone remember I exist."

"Oh, don't be ridiculous." Mac rolled his eyes, then gave her a puzzled look as his arm brushed against her, and he felt her involuntarily shiver. "How can you be cold after all that dancing?"

"I got pretty warm during the fast dances, but during slow ones like . . ." Her voice trailed off as Mac drew her closer. She wanted to protest. She would in just a minute. She was confused by his sudden concern for her, but right now she felt so warm and right in his arms. They danced silently, slowly losing their stiffness, melting into the rhythm. When the music ended, Mac seemed reluctant to remove his arms. One hand slid down her arm to catch her hand. His smile lit a candle in the back of his eyes as he looked down at her.

"Darling, Daddy is waiting for you." Rhonda was suddenly beside them tugging on Mac's arm.

"Laura . . ." Mac started. He should have been prepared for all Rhonda's little chores. Her father never fixed anything and didn't have the foggiest idea how to carve beef. Rhonda had gotten into the habit of counting on Mac. Most of the time, he didn't mind, but tonight was different.

"Don't worry. I'll look after her." Ace's arm circled Laura's waist as he steered her away from Mac.

"Forget him, honey." Ace said. "Rhonda's had him roped and all but branded for a long time."

"But . . ."

"No buts about it! She's the only woman I ever met who can sit a horse, brand calves, or drive a tractor as long and well as he can. He's a workaholic, and she comes pretty close. Ranching is in their blood. Her daddy's already boasting that when Mac and Rhonda join their spreads, this'll be the biggest ranch in southeastern Idaho."

"Is this ranch Rhonda's?" Laura's voice betrayed her surprise.

"Well, it's her old man's, but he's just waiting for her and Mac to marry to turn it over to the two of them. Most of this crowd was expecting an announcement tonight until they saw Mac walk in with you. Seeing you arrive with Mac stirred up quite a few questions."

No wonder everyone avoided me, Laura thought sadly. *Rhonda is their hostess, and they've known her all their lives while I'm an outsider. They'll really hate me if they find out Mac and I are married.*

Laura moved like a sleepwalker as Ace helped her fill her plate and found a place for them at a crowded table. From the corner of her eye, she watched Mac with a huge white apron wrapped around his waist slice and lift the hot meat onto the plates filing past him. Once, Rhonda, also wearing an apron, leaned her head against his shoulder; then, laughing, she picked up a strip of meat with her fingers to pop into his mouth.

Laura lowered her eyes. Misery cramped her stomach. She'd been a fool to come. Mac had planned the whole evening to prove a point. He could have told her she was dressed inappropriately before they left the ranch while there was still time to change. Abandoning her in a crowd of strangers was cruel. Tears misted her eyes. She blinked, refusing to let them fall. She didn't fit in here, but she would never forgive Mac for the way he had chosen to make that clear to her.

Pride slowly came to her rescue once more. If he thought he could make her give up her claim by forcing her to see she didn't fit in, he was dead wrong! She could learn. And now that the ranch was in her blood, she would never give it up. She turned a dazzling smile toward Ace.

Mac muttered between his teeth. Nothing had gone right this whole evening. Rhonda had stuck to him like a burr to a saddle blanket, and Ace was doing his best to cut him out with Laura. He'd like to get Ace alone and clue him in to the real situation. To make matters worse, old man Davis had been hinting all evening that Mac and Rhonda wouldn't have a better opportunity to make an announcement. That irked him. He'd never so much as hinted he might marry the girl. They'd never even been on a date. He'd felt sorry for her, running her dad's big spread for several years now without much help from her father, and he had helped her out when he could. She was a cute girl, but they were friends and friends only!

There was only one announcement he'd like to stand up and make. He'd like to shout to this whole crowd, *Laura is my wife!*

Balancing his plate in one hand and a drink in the other, he worked his way through the crowd toward Laura. He'd finally managed to shake Rhonda; now all he had to do was get rid of Ace. Ace used to be a pretty good friend, but they'd chosen different paths after high school, and Mac certainly didn't trust him around a pretty woman, especially Laura. He kept his eyes on the back of Laura's head as he dodged elbows and sidestepped conversations with friendly neighboring ranchers. A few feet from his objective, he stopped. Rhonda stood beside Laura with one hand braced on the table. She was earnestly speaking to Laura and Ace.

"You go ahead with Ace, Laura. I'll explain to Mac for you. By the time we get everything cleaned up here, it'll be pretty late, anyway. If he doesn't have to worry about driving you back to his ranch, he'll probably just stay the night."

"No, I came with Mac; I'll go home with him."

He breathed a sigh of relief at Laura's response. He wasn't sure what Rhonda was trying to pull, but why should he stay to help clean up? She had plenty of hands to do that. And stay all night! He'd never even consider such a thing. Was she trying to make Laura think . . . So all that silly flirting she did with him . . . Dang it! He'd always assumed that Rhonda thought her father's idea of "a merger" was as ridiculous as he did. He started forward again but was waylaid by a serious-looking young cowboy from a neighboring ranch.

"Hey, Mac, I'm glad I found you!"

"Hi, Tom. What's going on?"

"My dad sent me to tell you that he saw some smoke coming from your north range. I've got my truck here—if you want to take off, I can find your dad and tell him what's happening, then give him a ride home later."

Mac had seen the effects of fire on the ranch before. He'd have to check it out. He couldn't see his father anywhere nearby, and Laura appeared to be deep in conversation with Rhonda. As much as he wanted to take care of matters here, he knew he couldn't waste another minute.

"Thanks, Tom. My dad's got his own truck with him, but if you could give him a heads-up, I'd appreciate it. Tell him to explain to Laura." Mac gave the boy a slap on the shoulder, then turned to run toward his truck

Unaware of the drama facing Mac, Laura was doing all she could to remain civil to Rhonda, who for some reason continued to linger at her table.

Rhonda's smile was also wearing thin when suddenly she smacked her palm on the table and said, "Look, Laura. If I have to spell this out in plain words, I will. Mac and I have had very little time together lately. Merging two large ranches into one is a huge task. The little bit of time we could have been together, you've always been underfoot. It was thoughtful of him to bring you tonight, but stop chasing him. You're only making a fool of yourself. He feels sorry for you being so far from home and not knowing anyone, but we would like some time together. Most engaged couples do appreciate a little time alone."

Laura's cheeks paled. Slowly, she stood. Her eyes were snapping fire.

"Thank you for the information, Rhonda. I suppose I'll be leaving with Hal then, not Mac." Though Laura kept her voice even, the crowd around her had fallen into one of those strangely random conversational lulls, so no one missed what she said next. "Just so you know, there will be no merger between the Circle D and the High Country as long as Mac and I are married. He claims he doesn't want a divorce, but perhaps you've convinced him otherwise. My husband can do as he pleases . . . although, you should know that if he makes one move to merge our ranch with yours, I'll bankrupt him and sell every rock and clump of sagebrush to an eastern developer who will turn it into a luxury game resort."

Anger had returned the color to her cheeks. Turning about, she slammed into a nearby cowboy, sending thick barbecue sauce streaming down his shirt front. Barely apologizing, she ran from the gathering to find Hal's SUV. Glad he hadn't locked it, she shut herself inside before she let the tears fall freely down her face.

seventeen

LAURA'S HAND SHADED her eyes. Spread below her was a panorama of silver and gold. The land she had first thought harsh and forbidding fascinated her in a way she couldn't explain. Some instinct told her that no matter how many wells were sunk, no matter how much of the wild, untamed land was brought under cultivation, there would still be something raw and free about this place. The harsh rocks, twisted trees, and the weather that dealt in extremes would endure for eternity.

How could she have threatened to sell the ranch the other night? It was true Mr. Sylvester had mentioned an eastern developer who was looking for a sizeable piece of property in southern Idaho to turn into an exclusive game preserve, but she hadn't considered the offer even briefly. Mac should know that. He knew how she felt about hunting.

As they always did, her thoughts returned to Mac. She hadn't seen him since the party. She'd thought they would at least meet at church, but she hadn't seen him there the day after Rhonda's party.

Hal had explained about the smoke sighted that night. Fortunately, it had been a false alarm, but Mac was now staying up at the cabin to continue his fire watch. Since the party, both Hal and Chance had taken pains to let her know Mac had never stayed overnight at the neighboring ranch, and he had never been interested in Rhonda. They claimed he'd only left the ranch long enough to attend priesthood meeting on Sunday and that he was keeping a close eye on fire conditions along the north range where the grass was long and dry. Neither man mentioned what Mac thought about her outburst at the barbecue, though she was certain he had heard all the details by now.

She hoped Hal and Chance were telling her the truth about Mac's reason for staying away. She knew enough now from the books she'd read and discussions with Hal that Mormons were opposed to physical relationships between two people who weren't married to each other, and she was pretty certain Mac's religion wasn't something he took lightly. She'd seen a better side of him while they were harvesting the grain, and it would bother her a great deal if she found he wasn't living his church's standards.

Bishop Eames had stopped her after church. He'd told her he'd known her father and that he'd admired him a great deal. He'd also said he was glad she'd come back and that he'd be happy to invite the ward missionaries to meet with her and answer her questions about the church if she would like. She'd told him she'd think about his offer and get back to him. Her life seemed to be in too much turmoil to give serious thought to his offer, but she was still reading her father's Book of Mormon and studying the books she found in Hal and Mac's library.

Her thoughts returned to Mac. She knew Chance saw him every day and that they were making preparations for the fall roundup. Chance had offered to take her to the cabin, but she'd turned him down, fearing she wouldn't be welcome. But welcome or not, she needed to apologize. She was wrong to have embarrassed Mac in front of his friends and neighbors. Rhonda's behavior was no excuse for her own poor behavior. Several women who had been at that unfortunate barbecue had seemed to avoid her when she noticed them at church.

Others had exhibited an uncomfortable amount of curiosity. She'd appreciated one young woman who was struggling with an infant and a toddler who had solicited her help with the children during Relief Society, thus rescuing her from uncomfortable questions.

Her fingers twined restlessly through the Appaloosa's mane. Hal had insisted she learn to ride again, and Chance had been happy to instruct her. It had been easier than she had expected. She and the mare had taken to each other at once, and sitting astride Apple produced a vague memory that she had once loved horses, and she'd experienced an almost instinctual recall of how to ride. Chance had reminded her that she had once ridden nearly every day in front of her father or Mac and later by herself on her own little pony. She found herself pitying the little girl she had once been for having to leave the ranch. The old cowboy had kept her near the corrals for the first day, but today she had ridden out alone, though not out of Chance's view.

"Why did I do it?" She spoke aloud, though there was no one to hear but her horse. She had been angry and embarrassed. She'd had such high hopes the night of the party. She'd been excited and thrilled to be with Mac. Daydreams had led her to hope there might be something romantic developing between the two of them. Her hands still shook when she recalled the way Mac had set her up and then left her to fend for herself in a crowd of strangers.

It was her own fault she had misconstrued his casual invitation to the party as a date, she lectured herself. No matter how much she disliked Rhonda, she'd had no right to embarrass her in front of her father and guests by publicly accusing her of carrying on an affair with a married man. She had known the minute she called Mac her husband that Rhonda didn't know. Mac would never forgive her for her thoughtless words, and she couldn't blame him.

For the past two days, she'd spent the better part of each day riding, which had given her ample time to do some soul searching. It hurt to admit there were a lot of things she couldn't go on blaming Mac for. If he really thought her dead all those years—and she had come to believe Mac and his father were telling the truth—how could she fault him for feeling possessive of the ranch? It was unreasonable to expect him to cheerfully hand it over to her. He'd married her to secure his claim to the property and because her dying father had asked it of him. Why shouldn't he resent her when she suddenly appeared, ruining his plans?

She patted her mount's neck. A wave of self-pity washed over her. Things couldn't go on like this much longer. She knew now, deep in her soul, that she hadn't left this land voluntarily as a child. Her mother had taken her away, and her father had let her go. Mother had been preoccupied with her music and disappointed in her talentless, noisy, tomboy daughter. Father had his ranch; he didn't need the bother of a small child. Aunt Alice had only tolerated her temper and impulsiveness to protect her own financial interests. Bruce was the one person who accepted her for herself, but someday he would marry and have less time for her, too.

She'd been a fool to start dreaming romantic dreams about Mac. Expecting more from people than they were able to give her seemed to be a failing of hers. She should have remembered that she and Mac were partners only. Believing they could be more had been the hope of a foolish child. It was time she started acting like a mature adult instead of the sheltered child she'd remained for far too long.

With a shake of her head, she leaned forward to gather up the reins. "What's gotten into me?" she asked Apple. "Why am I sitting around feeling sorry for myself? Mac can't make me leave the ranch, and I can learn to do my share. All this talk of marriage put a lot of romantic nonsense in my head. I should have learned something from my mother's experience. Rhonda isn't the problem. A woman can fight another woman, but how does a woman compete with dirt and sky? If he doesn't want me for a partner, I'll buy him out, divorce him, and he can go to Rhonda! He can build his empire on the Circle D."

It was almost roundup time, she reminded herself. Perhaps Mac thought he was being clever by running the ranch from his cabin, wherever it was, but he wouldn't be able to ignore her much longer. He was going to need money to hire more hands and trucks, and that meant he would have to talk to her. And when he did, he was in for a few surprises. She wouldn't be sitting around tamely waiting for him. Her birthday had come and gone, unnoticed by anyone other than Bruce, who had called to wish her well and see if she was ready to return to San Francisco. She'd called Mr. Sylvester that day, and he'd assured her that the bank had accepted her marriage license as satisfying the terms of her mother's will and that she now had complete access to the money she'd inherited no matter what she decided to do about the marriage. She was no longer anyone's helpless dependent. Purposefully, she slapped the reins against the Appaloosa's neck to urge her back to the barn.

Over the next couple weeks, Laura was a whirlwind of activity. Trucks and men came and went, unloading lumber and mysterious crates, extending wiring and pipes, and hammering until late in the day. When the hands arrived at the house for breakfast and dinner, they were met by hot meals but no explanations. She was sure they reported her activities to Mac, and she wondered if he might come in to see for himself. Hal had told her from the start that he was pleased with her plans for the house. His favorite modification was the new first floor bedroom suite for him so he wouldn't have to climb the stairs so often. She'd sworn him to secrecy, though it probably wasn't necessary. Hal hadn't seen any more of Mac than she had.

It was a Tuesday afternoon when the last workman finally packed up and left. Laura carried a frosty glass of lemonade onto the veranda. The moment she settled herself on the porch swing, Shep jumped up beside her. He licked her arm once then settled down with his head in her lap. At least Shep accepted her! He hadn't welcomed her that first day at the ranch, but they were pals now. With one hand she stroked the old dog's long coat as she sipped the cold drink. In the distance, a cloud of dust moved slowly toward the house.

Could it be Mac? A shiver of excitement ran down her spine. Mentally, she braced herself for an explosion. Laura was glad Bruce wasn't scheduled to arrive until tomorrow. The two men never seemed to get along, and she was already nervous about Mac's response to her latest activities. She assumed he was already upset with her for making a scene at the barbecue, but when he saw what she had done while he was away . . . Well, it was just too bad. She hadn't broken their bargain, and she hadn't touched any of the ranch's funds. If he could run the ranch from his cabin without consulting her, she could run the business end from the house without consulting him! For just a moment, she worried that she might have gone too far. She bit her lip nervously, never taking her eyes from the moving cloud of dust. She hoped Mac would like what she had done.

It was soon clear the approaching vehicle wasn't Mac returning. Coming up the lane was a white express delivery truck, not Mac's battered old pickup truck. Instead of feeling relief at the postponement of the confrontation she both looked forward to and dreaded, she experienced a kind of letdown. The vehicle stopped on the gravel parking strip. She watched as the delivery man made his way to her.

When she stood, Shep moved in front of her, teeth bared. A low growl rumbled from his throat.

"Shep!" Laura placed her hand on the dog's head to urge him to back off.

"Are you Laura Hendrickson Burgoyne?" the man asked.

"Yes." She cleared her throat and spoke a little louder. "Yes, I'm Laura Hendrickson."

"I have packages here for you and Paul MacPherson Burgoyne. You'll have to sign for them."

"Mac isn't here." Her voice came out in a whisper.

"I'll sign for Mac." Hal joined Laura.

"Sure, Senator. That'll be fine." The express driver handed Hal an electronic pad with a stylus.

Laura looked at the thick envelopes addressed to her and Mac. Hers was from Ms. Pederson, the Boise attorney Mr. Sylvester had arranged to represent her in the Idaho court. Mac's similarly sized envelope was from his new lawyer, Mr. Stewart. She ripped open her envelope and stared at the documents in her shaking hands with mixed emotions. This was what she'd come to the ranch for, to resolve the question of her inheritance and the legality of her marriage. Only she wasn't certain she wanted to resolve anything this way anymore. She and Mac had to appear in Judge Swazey's chambers in Boise on Friday. She'd known about the date for weeks, but suddenly it felt too soon.

A few minutes later, she stood before the wide window of the room that had become her own, staring sightlessly at the stark landscape before her.

Four days! What then? If Mac won, would she ever see the ranch again? Would she see Mac? And if she won, how much would Mac lose? Would he have to sell his share in the ranch to avoid bankruptcy? If they remained partners, would Mac divorce her? If that happened, would they be partners or enemies? She wasn't certain she could face being Mac's partner while another woman was his wife.

One thing was certain. Mac needed to see his own documents as soon as possible. With the range as dry as tinder and the roundup only a week away, Mac would need all the time he could get to look these over and prepare for court.

She stared at her own papers, regret in her heart. If only they had been able to sit down together and work out a solution on their own. They'd worked well together in the grain harvest; why couldn't they reconcile their differences over the ranch? She should have tried harder to make him see there didn't have to be a winner and a loser.

She slowly sank to her knees. She'd learned to pray as a child but had seldom bothered since her mother's death. Now she poured her heart out to a loving Father she'd come to know over the past month. After whispering amen, a fragile peace filled her heart. Perhaps it wasn't too late. If she delivered the packet to Mac herself, she could make one last offer to work out a compromise. He might not listen, but she had to try.

Hal seemed pleased when she informed him she intended to deliver Mac's envelope to him personally and asked him for directions to the cabin. He suggested she ride Apple rather than try to take either his car or Bruce's up the rough mountain road.

Two hours later, she pulled on Apple's reins to give the horse a breather. She glanced at her watch and groaned. She should have waited until morning. Hal hadn't said anything about how long the ride would take. Now if she didn't reach her destination in less than a half hour, she would have to ride back in the dark. She only hoped that after talking to Mac he wouldn't be too angry to drive her back to the house in his pickup.

There was the thick stand of cedars Hal had told her to watch for, so it couldn't be too much farther to the cabin. Hal had said that a narrow trail veered off to the left leading to a narrow canyon and that she should follow it. She urged Apple on and soon discovered the trail was much steeper than the dirt road had been. Twice she dismounted to lead the mare over a dry streambed. She was surprised to find pine trees above her on the slopes and shrubs, in addition to the junipers and sagebrush beside the trail. They looked dusty and tired where they drooped over the path she followed. Birds chattered and quarreled over dry specks of fruit clinging to their branches.

She caught her first glimpse of the cabin at last. Half a dozen scrawny pines cast long shadows beside the small log structure. To one side of the cabin was a lean-to and behind it, a pole corral with several horses inside it. A narrow lane disappeared behind the cabin in the opposite direction from which she had arrived. There was no sign of Mac's truck.

Had she ridden all this way for nothing? Perhaps Mac was working somewhere else on the ranch and would return later. *He might be visiting Rhonda,* a mean little voice in the back of her head reminded her. For more than two hours she had rehearsed what she would say to him. Now he wasn't even at the cabin!

The sun was setting, and she didn't dare ride a horse back down the trail in the dark. She would have to stay at the cabin overnight, she concluded. She wondered if a bit of matchmaking had been behind Hal's insistence that she ride Apple instead of driving Bruce's car. No, that couldn't be. The trail really was too rugged for Bruce's little sports car.

She led Apple to the corral, removed her saddle, and released the little mare inside the fence with the other horses and secured the gate. She felt tired and dejected as she trudged toward the cabin. With her luck, the door would be locked and she would have to spend the night in the shed. She didn't want to admit how much she had been looking forward to seeing Mac again.

With one hand she pressed against the wooden door. To her surprise, it swung inward. She took two steps. Her eyes opened wide, then quickly snapped shut. Slowly, she opened them again. Mac sat in a deep tin tub in the middle of the tiny room. Water streamed from his wet hair, plastering it flat against his head. Rivulets ran down his bare shoulders. His hands gripped a white china pitcher from which he had obviously just dumped the contents over his head to rinse his hair. The incredulous look on his face was surely a match for the one on her own.

Mac recovered first. Casually, he set the pitcher on the floor beside the tub.

"Come on in, *Mrs. Burgoyne.*" He waved a hand to indicate the tub. "Care to join me?"

Laura gasped and hastily turned her back, even though all but Mac's head and shoulders were hidden behind the high sides of the tub. She could feel heat rushing up her cheeks all the way to her hair. She heard a low chuckle behind her.

"You might close the door," he drawled. "It's getting a mite cool in here."

Laura slammed the door shut, then wondered why she hadn't walked through it first.

"I'm sorry I walked in on you. Please get dressed," she mumbled into the door.

"Has my little wife suddenly become shy? That surprises me. From what I hear, you didn't sound a bit shy when you were telling my neighbors all about my philandering ways." He sounded more teasing than angry.

"Mac, I'm sorry." She whirled around to face him. "I was so angry you'd taken me to that party and then left me alone. And then Rhonda told me you two were engaged. I guess I didn't stop to think. You know I wouldn't sell the ranch to hunters. Oh!" Seeing him reach for a towel, she hurriedly turned her back once more.

After a few moments of listening to splashes and the rustling of clothes, she heard him say, "You can turn around now." He touched her shoulders and slowly turned her toward him.

"Laura . . ."

"Mac . . ." They spoke at the same time, and this time there was no teasing, only a gentle probing. She rushed on to ask, "Do you think we could talk about our situation, the ranch, and what we each want without getting angry or making accusations?"

"I'd like to try," Mac answered in the same serious tone she had used. "But first, I'd like to empty my tub and build up the fire. This might take a while."

"All right," she agreed, noticing that the sun had set and the cabin felt chilly. She shivered, and Mac suggested she check to see if the pot of water on the stove was still warm enough for hot chocolate.

When Mac's self-appointed chores were finished, she carried two mugs she had found and filled with hot chocolate to a small sofa that faced the iron cookstove. Mac snagged a quilt off his bed and hung it around Laura's shoulders.

"You might need this until the cabin warms up a little more," he told her.

They sat side by side sipping the hot chocolate, each a little unsure how to begin. A flicker of golden light radiated from the small window in the firebox door. Mac savored the moment. He had imagined her there beside him in the cabin so many times. A moment's unease crept into his mind. Ignoring the niggling doubt, he assured himself everything would work out. She wouldn't have ridden so far so late in the day if she weren't sincere about working things out.

"I noticed the other night that you dance very well," he said, not sure how else to break the ice.

"Don't remind me of that night. I made a complete fool of myself."

"I doubt that, though I'll admit that wasn't quite the way I imagined announcing our marriage to our neighbors."

"I'm sorry." She ran a finger around the lip of her cup, then popped it in her mouth to lick off the residue of chocolate.

"Mac, are we really married?" He heard a note of uncertainty in her voice.

"Yes, we're really married."

"About what Rhonda said . . ."

"Forget Rhonda." He reached for her chocolate cup. After placing both cups safely on the floor, he closed his arms around her to draw her snugly to his side and drew the quilt around them both. A feeling of warmth and comfort overtook her, and she stifled a yawn. Her eyes felt heavy, and she found herself relaxing.

"Mac." She found speech difficult. "We have to talk about what happens next. The ranch . . ."

"Mm-m, later," he whispered. He couldn't bear to let anything intrude on the dream he finally held in his arms. They could talk tomorrow and all the tomorrows after that. She'd come to him, and that was all he needed to know.

Light was just beginning to creep into the cabin when Mac awoke. For a moment, he wondered if the previous night had been just a fantastic dream, but the warm, sleeping woman snuggled against his side assured him Laura was really beside him. She looked so innocent and vulnerable; his heart constricted. He wanted to touch her tilted little nose with the tip of his finger. He hesitated, reluctant to disturb her. Sleeping, she resembled the little girl he remembered from their childhood. There was no doubt in his mind that as much as he'd loved the child, he loved the woman more.

"Someday," he mouthed silently into her warm neck. "Someday, I hope we have a little girl with spiky braids and a snooty nose just like the little girl you once were."

A sliver of light crept across the room. Laura turned her head, and his eyes settled on her shining hair. He wondered if she'd ever grow it long again. He would never forget his first sight of her coming down the stairs in her aunt's house with that gleaming crop of mink-colored curls cascading almost to her waist.

He'd better get up and put another chunk of wood in the stove. He didn't want her to wake up to a cold room. Gently, he eased his way off the sofa, then turned back to look at her once more. She was so beautiful, and he loved her. He always had. When she awoke, he would tell her so. All the years he had fought to save the ranch were suddenly worth all the work and pain it had cost him. He'd saved it for Laura. Laura, his Laura, was home.

He straightened, hearing an unexpected sound. Coming from somewhere in the distance, Mac could hear the unmistakable sound of an engine growling as it came across the canyon road. Chance? No, it was too early. Chance and the boys never showed up until breakfast and chores were finished at the ranch house. From the window he spotted a familiar red Toyota truck.

Rhonda! What is she doing here? His eyes flew to the sofa. He was glad Laura was still sleeping. He'd better get out there and get rid of Rhonda fast. He closed the door quietly behind him and was waiting beside the corral when the vehicle halted beside him.

* * *

Laura awoke slowly. She was disappointed to find herself alone. She stretched and found she wasn't as stiff as she had expected to be from the long ride to the cabin. A smile curved her lips as she recalled falling asleep in Mac's arms.

They still needed to talk. She hadn't even told him yet about the envelope she'd brought. None of it mattered anymore. As soon as they returned to the house, she would call Mr. Sylvester to tell him to drop the case. She'd tell him she and Mac were making their own out-of-court settlement! With a feeling of contentment, she stretched and looked around for Mac.

Laura's curious gaze drifted around the one-room cabin. She'd hardly glanced at it the previous night. It was small and compact, boasting only a table, two chairs, built-in cupboards, a cookstove, a sofa, and a bed. Behind the stove a row of nails held a few clothes and a couple of towels. There was only one door and a couple of small-paned windows. The walls were polished logs. Obviously, there was no plumbing. A trip outside would be necessary. Perhaps that was where Mac had gone.

Laura was prepared to venture outside when she noticed a movement through one of the windows. Curiosity drew her for a closer look.

"No!" Her eyes widened in horror. Through the window she could see Mac leaning back against the corral poles. Rhonda stood before him, her red hair pressed against his chest, her arms circling his waist. His hands rested on her shoulders. Laura watched as Rhonda pulled away to run toward a red truck parked nearby. Mac followed her, and when she climbed inside, he jumped in beside her.

Laura's fingers curled into a tight fist that she carried to her mouth. She bit her knuckles to keep from screaming when the red truck began to move, carrying Mac and Rhonda away. She stood at the window with tears streaming down her face until the small truck was out of sight.

"How could he do this to me?" she stormed aloud. "What a sucker I am, always believing someone loves me when they're only using me. How could I forget he's like all the others? He'd do anything to keep this ranch! Even pretend he cares about me."

Laura's temper mounted as she stomped around the room, gathering up her jacket and placing Mac's envelope on the table. Noisy sobs shook her shoulders, and tears blurred her vision. She fled the cabin and called to Apple, who trotted to her when she called, despite her shaky voice. It didn't take long to saddle the docile mare. The horse didn't seem to mind the hasty pace Laura set on the ride back to the ranch house. They made better time than the night before.

She seethed. She'd teach him a lesson he wouldn't forget. Before she got through, he would be hurting as badly as she was right now. His skin was too thick to hurt him any way except through the ranch. She'd use every resource at her disposal to take it away from him.

Luck was on her side. When she arrived back at the house, she found Bruce lounging on the veranda. Thirty minutes later her bags were stowed in the trunk of his little car, and they were on their way. Hal made her feel guilty every time she caught his reproachful eyes following her, but he didn't try to stop her.

She couldn't help taking one last look across the valley before the ranch disappeared behind a hill. Three days from now it would either be all hers—or she would never see it again. She knew Mac didn't have enough money to buy her half, but if she won her suit, she would use the last dollar of her mother's inheritance if necessary to buy his half.

Across the valley she could see the narrow cut leading to the cabin. She felt a tightness constrict her chest. A weight of sadness settled in her heart, but her eyes were dry. A speck of movement on the road caused her heart to pound. Was Mac coming after her? She sat stiffly, staring straight ahead. Bruce pressed on the accelerator. The little car picked up speed, leaving the ranch behind.

eighteen

TAKING THE PORCH stairs two at a time, Mac raced past Hal. He knew before he opened the door that she was gone. From across the valley, he thought he'd seen Bruce's little red car carrying her away, but he'd hoped he was mistaken.

"She's gone." Hal stood in the doorway. "She said to tell you she'll see you in Boise."

"Oh, she'll see me in Boise all right! I thought we were going to figure something out today, but apparently, she just has to have her day in court."

"That must have been some fight you two had. She was in and out of here so fast poor old Bruce could hardly catch his breath." There was a note of curiosity in Hal's voice.

Mac gritted his teeth. So Bruce had been waiting here for her all the time. "Actually, we didn't have a fight," he said, beginning to wonder how he could have been so blind to read so much into what he could see now had just been a courtesy visit.

When Mac didn't volunteer any more information, Hal shrugged his shoulders and moved away. He stopped a few steps away, half turning, to say, "I figured you'd want to get an early start tomorrow, and it's time I got back to the capital too, so we might as well drive up together. It's doubtful your old truck would make it that far."

Mac sighed in exasperation as he sat down to pull off his boots. Dad could no longer run the ranch, but he still took far too much interest in trying to run his son's life. Of course, the

SUV would get him there faster, and Chance would need the pickup truck to get around in while Mac was gone. He had half a mind to tear off after Laura right now, but waiting a day was a good idea, too. It would give him time to check on fire conditions and outline several days' work for the men. Why was it that every time his gut told him to go after Laura, his head talked him out of it? Resolutely, he stripped off his shirt and headed upstairs for the shower.

He stood under a hot stream of water, but his mind returned to the cabin. Why did she have to be so beautiful? And smart and fun? Last night they had seemed to be as in tune with each other as a fine musical instrument. He groaned, remembering how elated he had felt thinking she'd come to him. Clearly, if Rhonda hadn't shown up this morning, Laura would have stayed only long enough to tell him that she was leaving with Bruce and that the next time he saw her would be in court.

Thinking of Rhonda brought a frown to his face. Leaping out of her truck, she'd told him she'd waited and waited for him to come explain things to her but that she couldn't wait any longer. She'd wrapped him in a stranglehold and promised to wait until he was free. He'd been worried that Laura would wake up and see Rhonda there, so he had decided it might be best to go where Laura wouldn't see them together while he made his intentions, or rather his lack of intentions, clear to her.

The pseudo-breakup took all the tact he could muster. It had not been a painless process. Rhonda had refused to believe he'd never been in love with her. She had looked puzzled and a little offended when he told her he'd never thought of her as anything but a cute neighbor kid. He'd carried Laura's image in his heart so long, he hadn't even noticed that Rhonda had grown up. He'd loved Laura at every stage but hadn't cared enough to notice the changes in Rhonda.

True, he hadn't dated any of the local women for years, and Rhonda had a habit of hanging on his arm every time they encountered each other. But giving her a ride into town a few times and dancing with her at parties wasn't the same as dating her! Was it? Ace had told him several years ago that he was out of touch with reality for spending all of his energy on the ranch and never taking any time to see more of the world. He could see now he'd certainly been naive where both Rhonda and Laura were concerned.

Rhonda had burst into tears and hugged him tighter, refusing to accept his explanations. She'd been a friend and neighbor for a long time, and he'd begun feeling not only irritated by her persistence but like a blind, stupid heel for hurting her, no matter how unintentionally. Growing up without any feminine influence in his life, he'd learned nothing about talking to women.

Once he'd finally convinced her in what he knew was a clumsy fashion that he didn't love her and that he had no intention of divorcing his wife, he'd hurried back to the cabin. He didn't want Laura to awaken and find herself alone. But instead of finding a warm, welcoming woman when he opened the door, he'd faced only an envelope full of legal papers lying on the table.

Of course, Laura had mentioned the ranch the night before, but he hadn't thought it important anymore. If they were together, what would it matter whether he owned the ranch or they were partners? The ranch would be their home. Fool that he was, he'd been thinking in terms of raising a couple of little buckaroos to eventually take over both their shares, while her sights were set only on the legal end of things. One thing was clear: he didn't know the first thing about women.

He groaned at the thought of the upcoming court appearance. He didn't like leaving the ranch with the roundup just days away and the range dry as tinder. He hadn't done anything about getting eight years of records together either. They were all there, but ferreting them out would take all day and half the night. He'd been tied in knots since he first spotted Laura at the service station and hadn't done one practical thing to protect the ranch.

Angry at himself, he stomped down the stairs. He knew he had a good case. He'd plowed nearly all of the ranch's profits back into it over the years, and several years he'd taken heavy losses as well. Dad's house in Boise should be safe. He could prove that was paid for with funds from the insurance payout after Dad's ranch house had burned down. Unfortunately, Mac had paid his taxes and fed the surviving stock that first year with the cash from Jake's life insurance. He might have to dig up the amount of Jake's insurance for Laura.

How could anyone determine how much of the stock Laura had a right to claim? As upset as he was, he still had no intention of cheating her out of one cent she was entitled to. Buying out her half of the ranch would be the hard part, especially in a drought year when land and stock prices were down, reducing his borrowing power.

He hurried into the office and came to a sudden halt. She'd changed everything. A wall had been knocked out to an adjoining storage room. New wood flooring stretched from one end of the enlarged room to the other. The new end had been converted into a modern U-shaped office module complete with computer, printer, fax, and copier.

In front of the fireplace, she had arranged a short sofa and a couple comfortably padded chairs around a low oval table. Turning to his familiar desk, now flanked by a computer stand sporting a machine he hadn't a clue how to operate, he spotted a neat stack of papers. He stared at them incredulously.

He couldn't believe her nerve. She must be awfully confident of winning. She'd taken advantage of his absence from the house to raid his files. She was so sure of her position, she'd left him a neat computer summary of all his financial records to taunt him. Suspiciously, he tore open desk and file drawers to see what documents she might have removed. Puzzled, he found everything in neatly labeled files. He leafed through the papers on his desk. They were clear and concise. Only one page made no sense. Following a complicated series of numbers, one amount was circled in red.

Why? What was she up to? A sneaking suspicion began to fill his mind. Like a sleepwalker he wandered through the house. The empty end of the big living room was filled by an imposing black grand piano, and new appliances gleamed in the kitchen. Laura's old playroom and the adjacent little bathroom had been converted to a first floor bedroom with an attached full-sized bath.

Upstairs, he opened the door to the nursery. Her boots and jeans lay where she had hastily discarded them. Her blouse had been tossed onto the bed. A pair of filmy stockings dangled from a not-quite-closed drawer. He caught a gleam of red silk through the open closet door.

She planned to return! An instant flash of joy gave way to anger. His suspicions had been confirmed. She knew his financial position, and she knew he couldn't buy out her share. It had probably never been her intention to sell her share to him. She was unmistakably claiming the house and everything else. She expected to win, and when she did, he would have no choice but to sell to her. The amount on that sheet of paper was the amount she intended to offer him. It was a fair amount, but he'd never sell.

He hadn't gotten where he was by being a quitter. He would fight her every step of the way. *A good lawyer could . . .* What had he said? A good lawyer! And he'd never even met the new attorney his dad had found for him. For all he knew, the attorney might be just as lousy as Cooper!

Sitting abruptly, he bowed his head against his clasped hands. He didn't stand a chance against Laura's lawyer. He'd be lucky if they didn't get laughed out of court, considering how little he'd given his new attorney to go on.

He wasn't sure how it got there, but he found Laura's blouse in his hands, the one she'd worn to the cabin. He ran his fingers across the smooth pearl buttons, thinking, remembering. A faint scent clung to the soft cotton. He breathed in deeply. It smelled of Laura. Angrily, he flung it across the room. He wasn't beaten yet. He'd use her fancy gadgets to send Mr. Stewart copies of all the papers she had thoughtfully left for him!

* * *

Laura toyed with the glass in her hand. She felt so tired. She'd spent all of Thursday afternoon in an attorney's office reviewing documents, checking affidavits, and going over tomorrow's testimony. Mr. Sylvester would not be representing her, but he would be present and would supervise the case. Since he wasn't licensed to practice in Idaho, it was necessary to have a local attorney serve as official counsel. Ms. Pedersen was acquainted with Hal, but Mr. Sylvester assured her she would represent Laura fairly.

She felt uncomfortable telling the new lawyer about the events that had occurred at the ranch. Of course, Laura hadn't told her everything. She didn't plan to let even Bruce find out she had fallen in love with Mac.

She'd known all along that the ranch came first with Mac and shouldn't have allowed herself to be misled by those times when he'd been companionable and charming. He couldn't afford to buy her out, so naturally he had tried to keep her from going to court to claim her share as her father's heir. Where anger and accusations had failed, sweetness and charm had nearly won. If she hadn't seen him with Rhonda on Wednesday morning, how long would she have stayed, falling more in love each day? She should be grateful to Rhonda for bringing her to her senses. But gratitude was far from her mind when she thought of Mac's red-haired neighbor.

Bruce returned to the table with his plate piled high from the dessert bar. His trip to the sweets counter had provided her with a brief respite from his grilling. She and Bruce were nearly the same age, but he'd long ago claimed the privilege of behaving like her big brother and had been overly protective ever since the accident that nearly took her life. She was grateful he'd bullied her into learning to walk again and kept her from surrendering completely to Aunt Alice's domineering tactics, but it was time he let go.

"Here, I brought you a piece of chocolate cake." He shoved a dainty plate in front of her. He watched her take a small bite then idly make fork tracks in the rich fudge icing. His exasperated sigh finally reached her ears.

"I'm sorry. I know I'm not very good company."

"If chocolate cake can't cheer you up, things are pretty bad. Don't you think it's time you told me all about it?"

"I've told you all I can."

"Something happened between you and that cowboy, and I'm getting a pretty good picture of what it was. You changed the subject and turned red when Sylvester asked about proceeding with the annulment. All tact and diplomacy aside, I'm asking you point blank, did you consummate the marriage?"

"Bruce!"

"Did you?" She recognized the stubborn glint in his eyes. He wouldn't drop the subject.

"No." She turned her head away. "Now can we please change the subject?"

Bruce reached across the table to take her face in his hands. "Oh, Laura . . ."

"Bruce, leave me alone." Tears spilled from her eyes. "I'm not a little girl anymore."

Bruce settled back in his seat. She could see the thoughtful expression on his face as he watched her closely.

"You love him, don't you?"

Blinking back her tears, she nodded almost imperceptibly. Bruce's big hand settled over hers on the table.

"Is there any chance you can make your marriage work?"

"No, Bruce. He's been seeing someone else, but even his girlfriend is less important to him than the ranch. It's his life. If he asked me to stay with him, it would only be to cement his claim to it. I could never expect him to truly love me. He married me to satisfy Daddy's determination to keep the ranch intact. He would stay married to me for the same reason. I can't accept what my life would be with him."

"Come on, I'll walk you back to your room." He helped her to her feet.

* * *

Mac sat on the opposite side of the room nursing a root beer that could have been mud for all he knew or cared. He'd spotted them the moment he'd entered the hotel restaurant. They seemed to be arguing about something, which gave him a small amount of perverse satisfaction.

Bruce left Laura for a few minutes, and Mac considered approaching her, but Bruce quickly returned, carrying a tray, before Mac could put his thoughts into action. The pair argued some more, then it looked like Laura was crying and Bruce was trying to comfort her. He watched them get to their feet and walk toward the elevator.

Taking the stairs two at a time, he reached Laura's floor almost as quickly as Bruce and Laura did. Sheltering in a doorway some distance down the long hall, he watched Bruce unlock her door and step inside with her.

Mac paced back and forth. He directed a black scowl toward the closed door. No amount of reasoning with himself could make him leave his post.

Mac had been with his new attorney all day, and his case didn't look anywhere near as promising as he'd thought. Mr. Stewart, with Dad's encouragement, urged him to put his differences with Laura aside. He argued that it wasn't too late to contact her to work out a compromise. Stewart had chewed him out royally for not seeking a compromise sooner. He made it clear he thought Mac's actions toward Laura had been immature and foolish, and he urged him to take her to dinner and have a serious discussion of their situation. Mac doubted Laura would accept such an invitation.

Stewart then suggested a counter move. File for divorce immediately. He could expect a better settlement in a divorce proceeding, and the delay would give him time to prepare a better case.

"No divorce. I won't be the one to initiate that." Mac was adamant but finally agreed to an attempt to reach an out-of-court settlement.

They'd drawn up the papers. He had them in his pocket, but his chances of catching Laura alone looked slim. A noise behind him sent him ducking into a doorway again. He didn't care to analyze why he felt such relief to see Bruce leaving Laura's room. He waited until another door closed down the hall before tapping on her door.

He breathed a sigh of relief when he heard the chain rattle loosely before she opened the door. Any other time, he would have chided her for opening her door without the security chain in place.

"Did you forget something, Br—You!" She tried to close the door, but already his shoulder widened the gap, and he stepped inside. She retreated across the room.

"Go away!" She glared at him.

"It seems I underestimated you." Mac smiled halfheartedly. "Kudos on your changes to the house. And on your financial analyses as well. I think I finally see that there isn't much you wouldn't do to make a success of the ranch, is there? That is, anything but give our marriage a chance," he added bitterly.

"Marriage! That word is a mockery coming from you." Laura stopped retreating and took a step toward him. "Your idea of marriage isn't mine. I've spoken to my attorney about a divorce. I won't stay married to a man who cheats."

"I haven't been cheating."

"Funny, I would have sworn it was you yesterday morning with a red-haired tramp plastered all over you!"

"You mean Rhonda?" His voice rose as he pronounced the name. She'd seen Rhonda, and she was jealous? Maybe jealousy was a good sign. Maybe that was the reason she'd left so suddenly. His spirits rose a fraction, then plummeted. It didn't make sense. Bruce had been waiting for her, and she'd done all that paperwork. No, she wasn't jealous. She was clutching at excuses to shift the blame onto him.

"Of course I mean Rhonda. Unless you have a second redhead you are carrying on with. Whoever it was, she's welcome to you. You can transfer your clothes and your truck to her house any day." Laura's eyes flashed, and her cheeks were brushed with vivid color. Forgetting her reluctance to confront him, she took several more steps in his direction.

"Look, Laura." He held his hands out toward her. He wasn't certain whether he was attempting to placate her or ward her off. "Can't we put our differences behind us? I'll admit you have a legitimate claim to a share in the ranch. I'm willing to buy out your half at today's market value."

"You don't have the money."

"Hear me out. Please, Laura." She couldn't believe her ears. Mac was actually pleading. She wouldn't have thought he would humble himself that far, even for the ranch.

He took her silence as assent. Pulling the papers from his jacket pocket, he handed them to her. "My attorney—not Coop, I have another one now—drew this up. Read it and give it to your attorney to read. If you're willing, I'll buy out your half of the ranch over ten years. You can keep the house, and I'll stay at the cabin until I can build a place of my own."

Laura walked toward the window with the papers in her hand. He watched her silently read them. Would she accept his offer? And if she did, could he bear it if she chose to make her home on the ranch, so close but so far out of his reach?

It took all of the control Laura could muster to keep her hands from shaking. Mac wanted to buy her out. He wanted to live separate lives in separate houses. She trembled with pain. He wasn't interested in a partnership. He wasn't even pretending he wanted her as his wife. He didn't care about her.

She began walking toward him. Her voice shook as she tapped the rolled papers against his chest. "I have a better plan. I'll hand you a check right now, today, for your share of the ranch. I'll give you forty-eight hours to clear out your personal property and get off the place. You can stay here in Boise with your father or move in with your girlfriend. It doesn't matter to me."

The papers fell from her fingers and rolled on the floor. She stepped back and ran her fingers through her hair. "You're just like my father. All you want is the ranch and to be rid of me."

"You're father was a good man. He cared about the ranch, but he cared about you, too."

"He didn't love me. All that mattered to him was his ranch. He and Aunt Alice fought over me because they hated each other. Aunt Alice wanted control of my mother's money to spend on her hateful cause, and my father wanted it, too, to pour into his ranch. Neither of them loved me for myself! A loving father would not send his daughter away and then ignore her for years on end."

"Jake didn't send you away. Letting you go with your mother nearly tore him apart. He thought a little girl needed her mother, and he was so much in love with April he couldn't hurt her by insisting you stay with him. He knew April was ill and that her decision to leave him had something to do with that, though she never told him the extent of her illness. He couldn't deny her the comfort of having you with her through whatever ordeal she faced, and until your meddling aunt refused to let him see either of you, he planned frequent trips to San Francisco. He always believed April would get better and then one day come back, and he would have you both again."

"You're lying!"

"No, it's the truth, Laura." *Poor woman, she really doesn't believe me.* Maybe he was beginning to understand what drove her. Jake and April had been so protective of their only child that they'd hidden too much from her. Laura didn't have any idea how much her parents loved her or why they'd separated. All these years she'd believed her parents had abandoned her. That bitter old lady who raised her had taught her to distrust her own feelings and the people who cared most about her. There had been so many secrets; she didn't trust anyone. And over the last month, he'd only made matters worse. He'd been as self-centered as her aunt, thinking only of how her return affected him and that she should simply go along with what he wanted. He'd let stupid pride get in the way of communicating with her.

He realized that tears were now coursing silently down her face.

"Don't, Laura. I'm sorry. Oh, honey, don't cry." He reached out to her, holding her against his chest. He stroked her hair until her sobs subsided. He'd hurt her again, not physically but far worse. He would sooner die than hurt this woman, yet he had hurt her over and over. He'd done little else but hurt her since the day she arrived at the ranch. Deciding he needed to be alone and assuming she did too, he kissed her forehead in a gentle gesture, then turned away to slip from the room.

* * *

Her tears fell faster after Mac left, though deep down, she hadn't expected he would stay. No one ever stayed for her, she told herself, and Mac was no different. She was too tired to be angry. She was only sad, terribly sad and lonely. She slid to her knees beside the bed, feeling an overwhelming need to communicate with the loving Father she'd come to know over the last month. A few halting words at a time, she began to pray. A tentative peace filled her heart. When she finished, she climbed into bed and lay on her back, watching the shadows on the ceiling, until she finally drifted to sleep.

* * *

Mac left the hotel. His steps led him to the river that ran through the city. As if remembering a path he'd walked before, he followed the winding trail beside the swiftly flowing water. As he walked, his mind filled with all the accusations and cruel words he'd flung at Laura since she arrived at his door innocently seeking a piece of her past. As Hal had tried to warn him that first day, he'd been way out of line.

He didn't understand why he'd been so quick to accuse her of plotting against him. The lack of a feminine influence in his life was no excuse for his behavior nor were his own insecurities. He'd attempted only once to arrange a discussion of their situation with her. His jealousy and arrogance had nearly gotten her killed. After that, he'd managed to derail the topic any time Laura had attempted to bring up the matter.

He stumbled into a bench placed along the path. Without conscious thought, he sank onto it, and his head drooped until he was cradling it in his hands. He'd been so sure she had ulterior motives to begin with, then equally certain that if she remained with him, he could take care of her, run the ranch, and she needn't worry about anything. He hadn't considered her insecurities, her dreams, or even what her real needs might be.

In his arrogance, he'd forgotten all of the lessons on marriage he'd heard and even taught at church but had never believed might someday pertain to him. He'd never even truly prayed about what he should do or what was best for Laura. Had he been afraid that he wouldn't like the Lord's answer?

He began to pray, and as he prayed, tears ran down his cheeks, reminding him of the boy who had run after April's car as it carried Laura away that long-ago day.

* * *

Laura awoke to watch the dark turn slowly to light. It seemed to take an eternity for night to become day. She thought about Mac. Deliberately, she tried to force away the memories of Mac throwing himself between her and a shattering windshield. She didn't want to remember the Mac who taught her to drive, who shared a hymnbook with her, who expected her to do her share of the harvest work and acknowledged her success without any coddling, who treated his father with gentle respect, who laughed with her and answered her questions about everything except her share of the ranch, and who annoyed her but made her feel more like a woman than she ever had before.

No! That Mac wasn't real. She forced herself to think of the man who would do anything to keep her land, who snarled at her, bossed her around, lied to her, and held another woman in his arms. Her fists tightened against her sides. Now she was angry! She pounded her fists against the mattress. Mac had too much power over her. Love made her weak, just as it had weakened her mother. Aunt Alice had ridiculed her mother for being weak, for letting her heart rule her head, and Laura was beginning to understand why her mother had given up a promising career to follow a man who was wrong for her. But she wasn't going to make the same foolish mistake.

She wasn't her mother. She wouldn't meekly step out of the way. Mac wasn't going to have it all his way.

nineteen

A LONG GLEAMING table ran down the center of the richly paneled room. Matching chairs with brocaded cushions surrounded the table and lined the walls. Judge Swazey sat at one end of the table with the two opposing parties facing each other down either side. Laura was glad they weren't in a regular courtroom. She could feel Mac's eyes on her from across the table, but she refused to look his way. If she didn't look at him, it would be easier to do what she had to do. Those intense gray eyes had a way of changing her mind, making her want what she couldn't have.

Her knuckles turned white where she fiercely gripped her hands together in her lap. She mustn't let him see how much she hurt. All he needed to see was that she could be as ruthless as he was.

". . . And so my client's claim to the ranch is far greater than his wife's. It is apparent she abandoned both the property and her marriage . . ." Mr. Stewart, attorney-at-law, droned on, painting a negative picture of Laura. "She is now set on destroying her husband, a man who has devoted his life to building a successful ranch from the ashes of misfortune and whose only crime was trusting his unscrupulous lawyer eight years ago."

She glanced past Mac to Hal. No emotion showed on his face.

Her eyes flew involuntarily to Mac's lounging form. His chair was pushed slightly back, and his long legs stretched beneath the table. His elbows rested on either arm of his chair. His face was partially hidden behind clasped hands. He made no indication he even heard the attorney's rambling diatribe.

When Mr. Stewart finally sat down, Mr. Sylvester conversed quietly for a moment with Ms. Pedersen before the tall, blond woman rose to her feet. Mr. Sylvester had chosen well. She was efficient, thorough, and even charming. Ms. Pedersen questioned Laura first, drawing out the facts she could remember from the accident eight years ago, her long convalescence, and her life in her aunt's home. She produced medical records verifying Laura's mental condition and memory loss following the accident. Bruce was asked to detail the circumstances surrounding the discovery of her father's will. His answers were brief but detailed and accurate.

When Ms. Pedersen called on Mr. Sylvester to testify, he lost no time producing letters from Aunt Alice and documents from his files showing Laura had no involvement in, and likely no knowledge of, either of her parent's estates.

"How long did you know Alice Wilson?" Ms. Pedersen asked.

"I first met her when her brother died, leaving his considerable fortune to his children: eighteen-year-old Alec and three-year-old April, Laura's mother," Mr. Sylvester began. "That was forty-three years ago."

"Alice's brother's estate was considerable. Did Miss Wilson ever indicate she was dissatisfied with his decision to leave it to his children?" Ms. Pedersen asked.

"She said she had been cheated for the second time. First her father bypassed her to leave everything to his son, then her brother overlooked her to give his fortune to his children. She petitioned the court to allow her to be April's guardian, and as her only available relative, Alice was duly appointed." Mr.

Sylvester paused, then added without being prompted, "Alice had expected that as April's guardian she would have absolute control of her money."

"And did she?"

"No, the money was tied up in a trust so April wouldn't be able to touch it until she married or turned twenty-five. Alice received a quarterly check for the child's support. Alice said it wasn't enough, and as her attorney at that time, I had to go to court to get permission to sell the family home to increase her stipend."

"Did that satisfy her?"

"No, she came back month after month with a new scheme for breaking the trust. She couldn't do anything about it until April married Jacob Hendrickson. She tried to get her niece to turn over administration of the money to her before April left California, but Jake interfered, suggesting April take only her furniture, leave the trust intact, and arrange for an allowance for Alice. There was a dispute over ownership of a grand piano."

"This is a waste of time." Mr. Stewart attempted to cut in. "This is about Laura Hendrickson, not April—"

"Your honor, it's important to my case to establish Laura's background and her relationship to her aunt. I intend to show that Alice kept Laura from learning about her father's property."

"Objection overruled. You may continue." The judge, who was acting more as an arbiter than a judge waved his hand for Laura's attorneys to continue.

Laura watched Mac huddle with his attorney for a few minutes. Stewart didn't appear pleased by whatever Mac said to him.

"Can you tell us why April left her husband and returned to San Francisco?" Ms. Pedersen continued questioning Mr. Sylvester. Laura leaned closer. She'd never understood the breakup of her parents' marriage. Until the previous night when Mac told her that it had been April's decision to leave against her husband's wishes, she'd assumed her father was somehow at fault.

"April came to see me a couple of months after she left Jake. She told me she was ill and didn't know how long she'd be able to handle her own affairs. She hadn't told Jake the extent of her illnesses, both multiple sclerosis and a slow-growing, inoperable brain tumor, because she feared he'd give up his ranch to be with her. She wanted to set him free so he could get on with his life. She also believed she had a much shorter amount of time to live than the slightly more than eleven years she actually survived."

"What arrangements did she make for her daughter at that time?"

"She specified that Laura should return to her father following her death. She also set up a trust for Laura similar to the one her own father had arranged for her care."

"Did she make any provision for Miss Wilson?"

"Yes. Alice was to continue to draw an allowance from the estate until Laura turned twenty-five or married. Then she was to receive a modest lump sum settlement."

"How old was Laura when her mother died?"

"Fifteen, almost sixteen."

Ms. Pedersen glanced at Laura before directing her next question to the attorney who had known Laura all her life. "Did Laura express a preference for remaining with her aunt rather than going with her father after her mother's death?"

"By the time April died, Laura was no longer the girl I had known earlier. She had become quiet and seldom expressed an opinion. She stared out the window and made no response when I explained she had inherited all of her mother's estate and that she would be going to live with her father."

Laura tried to remember events from that summer when her mother had died and her father had come to get her, but it was no use. She hadn't even known her mother was ill until the last few years before her death. It seemed her mother had always been distant and aloof, retiring to her bedroom for long periods of time. She had a few memories of accompanying her mother to concert performances and to church but not of laughing or playing together. Most of her early memories were of a mother who became more withdrawn with each passing day, who lay in a darkened room with cold compresses on her head, who walked with a cane and then sat in a wheelchair, and of an aunt who insisted Laura keep quiet and practice her music. She did remember the crushing pain of finally accepting Aunt Alice's often-repeated pronouncement that her daddy would never come for her.

"Was Alice aware of the terms of April's will?" Ms. Pedersen questioned. Laura turned her attention once again to the proceedings in the judge's chambers.

"No. Not until after April's death."

"So what was Alice's reaction to seeing the family fortune bypass her once again? Did she make any attempt to have April's will set aside?"

"Yes, Alice was upset. When I refused to petition the court to have her named Laura's guardian instead of Jake, she became hysterical, argued, and threw things. She fired me and hired another attorney, but then Jake was killed and Laura was hospitalized. Her new attorney sued the trucking company and received a sizeable settlement that Miss Wilson controlled. In the commotion, an accurate accounting of the extent of Laura's inheritance was never made, and no accounting of the insurance settlement was given to Laura by Miss Wilson's attorney."

Voices seemed to go on forever. Bewildering, disjointed thoughts streamed through Laura's mind. *Why didn't someone explain to me about mother's illness? I never connected her illness with my parents' separation. Did Daddy ever find out Mother was ill before her death? Aunt Alice should have called him so he could have been with her at the end.*

Guilt assailed her. She should have asked questions, demanded answers. She shuddered, remembering that Aunt Alice didn't like questions. She sent little girls who asked questions to bed without any supper or made them practice scales hour after hour. Later Aunt Alice had obviously discouraged questions about her father because the answers would have led to Mac and to her discovery of her mother's fortune. She couldn't prevent the bitterness that stung at her heart.

Laura forced herself to pay attention again. She glanced surreptitiously at Mac several times when she thought he wouldn't notice. What was he planning? Why didn't his attorney seem to be doing anything?

With a start, Laura realized the judge was leaving the room. Her mind had been so busy trying to make sense of all she heard, she'd become lost to her surroundings and the proceedings of the hearing. Could it be over? She glanced at Mr. Sylvester with a question in her eyes.

"It won't be long now." He patted her hand. "You go with Bruce, have some lunch, and we'll meet you back here in two hours."

The two hours dragged. She couldn't eat. Every time she moved her eyes, she saw Mac or someone who looked like Mac. She didn't trust his lack of action, his calmness. How could he be so certain he would win? Mr. Stewart had presented the barest of cases, relying almost entirely on the figures she had compiled showing how much Mac had contributed to the ranch and the reasonable salary he should have been able to draw all those years. Mac had kept quiet when Ms. Pedersen showed the judge the substitute document his attorney, Cooper, had given Laura to sign. It was almost like Mac didn't care. But she knew better. He'd do anything to keep that ranch.

At long last, they were ushered into the paneled chamber to await Judge Swazey. Mac lounged once more in the chair opposite her. His eyes were closed. He appeared to be sleeping. She couldn't prevent the sad little smile that appeared on her lips. He looked so tired. *Why couldn't you love me? Me, not the ranch.* She wanted to cry like a disappointed child. Instead, she turned her head to watch the judge enter the room and to give herself a chance to erase any emotions that might show on her face.

Bruce gripped her hand as Judge Swazey began to speak. She avoided looking at Mac. Instead, she kept her eyes on the judge. Little by little, his words penetrated her mind.

"This is an unusual case. Mr. and Mrs. Burgoyne, this has been a difficult decision to make. You are legally married—that issue is not in dispute. In this state, a wife is entitled to hold property in her own name; therefore, Mrs. Burgoyne is entitled to one half of the High Country Ranch and the entirety of the house her father bequeathed to her in his will. The court appreciates the work Mr. Burgoyne has put into the ranch, but it doesn't appear an acceptable effort was made to confirm his wife's death or to contact her closest relatives. I find that Mrs. Burgoyne did not intentionally abandon her claim and is therefore entitled to compensation for the years she was deprived of her inheritance . . . all monies in said bank account. . . the house . . . retain his truck, two saddle horses, one half of land and stock to be determined by market value . . . no punitive damages . . . each responsible for his or her own legal fees . . . division to be made by court appointed evaluator unless either party decides to sell his or her share within ninety days to the other party."

She won! She sat still, stunned. It was over. Bruce hugged her briefly, and both of her attorneys shook her hand. She couldn't take it in. Between the bodies gathered around her, her eyes met Mac's. They seemed to bore into her soul. He sent her a wry smile, a mocking salute, then turned to walk away.

This was her triumph. She should be celebrating, not fighting tears. A cold sickness gripped her stomach as Mac closed the door behind him. He would have to sell or mortgage his share of the ranch to pay his legal fees and the compensation the judge had ordered him to pay. He had no place to live other than the crude mountain cabin. If he left the ranch, where would he go? What would he do? Why hadn't he fought harder? She shouldn't care, but deep down she did. She would always care because she loved him! No matter what he had done, she loved him.

Bruce accompanied her back to the hotel. She moved in a daze. Her stomach ached. Her head hurt, and she wanted to be alone. At her most optimistic, she hadn't expected such a total victory. But it didn't feel like a victory.

If either she or Mac chose to sell their share, the other must be given first right of refusal and the share must be sold at fair market value. Laura went over the judge's words in her head. Mac would have to sell. She would own it all. She didn't feel the satisfaction she had promised herself. *What good is the ranch to me without Mac?* Slowly, one thought lodged in her heart. She'd destroyed the man she loved.

A knock interrupted her thoughts.

Mac! Her heart leaped as she hurried to the door. She couldn't hide her disappointment when, instead of Mac, she found herself facing Hal. Behind him stood Mr. Sylvester and Mr. Stewart.

"May we come in?" Hal asked. Laura opened the door wider and stepped back. It was hard to face Hal. It occurred to her that she had given no thought to how taking over the ranch would affect him. He was the elected senator from that district. If he could no longer claim to live there for at least part of the year, he would have to step down.

"I'm sorry, Hal." Her voice wobbled dangerously.

"Don't be." He patted her shoulder. "You only asked for what is rightfully yours. Mac was wrong to try to make staying with him a condition for claiming your inheritance."

"Mac wasn't trying to make me stay. Not really." She wiped her cheek with the back of her hand. "He never wanted me to stay."

"Listen to me, dear. Mac wanted you to stay in the worst way. He just never believed you would. According to his way of thinking, you'd already left him twice, so he didn't dare get his hopes up."

Stubbornly, she shook her head. If only it were true. She was going to miss Hal, even if he was a little too quick to meddle. In the past weeks, he'd become a surrogate father to her, and she'd come to value the time they spent together.

"Mrs. Burgoyne."

She jumped when Mr. Stewart addressed her by the name she wouldn't be able to claim much longer, and in fact never really had.

"Your husband asked me to see you and your attorney to offer to sell you his share of the ranch and stock except for ten acres on Cherry Creek including a small, one-room cabin. His offer includes continuing as foreman until after the roundup is complete this fall or until you find a replacement for him. He also specified that if you file for divorce in California, he will not claim any share of your property or assets in that state." He placed a lengthy document on the table.

The cabin! It would never do for Mac to live in, especially during the winter . . . Of course, he would be with Rhonda by then.

"Take your time. Read it over carefully. Mr. Sylvester can return it to me in the morning." The attorney started for the door. Hal followed him, then turned back briefly. Laura saw moisture shining brightly in Hal's eyes. She had a feeling she was losing the father figure she'd wanted most of her life. He made no effort to hide his sadness when he kissed her cheek.

"It's a fair offer," Mr. Sylvester said as he picked up the papers to bring them closer to her. "The price he's asking is reasonable, and as soon as this drought breaks, you'll have a valuable piece of property."

She stood at the window, staring at the dull scene before her long after the three men left her room. Boise was an oasis in the middle of a bleak desert, but today a pall of smoke hung in the air from a forest fire raging a hundred miles to the north. Across the treetops she could just pick out the spires of the Boise Temple. They seemed to remind her that in winning she had lost something precious. She hadn't won anything, she realized—not really. She'd lost Mac. He didn't love her, and without love, she couldn't stay with him. She'd promised herself long ago that she would not spend her life as her mother had, loving a man who placed his own obsession above being together. But had her father really done that? She didn't know what to think anymore.

She only knew she didn't feel like a winner. Her heart went out to the young man, little more than a boy, who had fought fire and drought, staved off creditors, and even married a dying child to hold on to the land he loved. He'd grown up with little softness in his life, not even the love of a mother. His mother had died before his second birthday. Mac had loved her as a child, and she had gone away, only to return years later to take from him all that was dear and familiar to him.

She blinked back tears. Though he didn't love her, she did love him, and there was one last thing she could do for him. She could give him back what he did love.

In less than two minutes, she was standing at Mr. Sylvester's hotel room door. Without even expressing a greeting, she thrust the papers she held at him.

"Mr. Sylvester, I'm not going to sign that paper. I'd like you to draw up a counteroffer."

* * *

Mac glanced at the clock. Nine o'clock. He wished he were back at the ranch—with Laura. No, he wouldn't think about Laura. Thoughts of Laura brought heartache and pain. More pain than he could handle now, even though he knew he'd done the right thing. When the phone rang, he welcomed the interruption. Chance's voice came over the line. The range above Cherry Creek Canyon on the north edge of the ranch was on fire. If the fire continued in its present direction, the stock and ranch buildings would be in danger.

Mac didn't take time to pack. Ending the call with Chance, he punched in another number. He pulled on his jeans and stepped into his boots while cradling the phone against one shoulder. Not bothering to change shirts, he grabbed his sheep-lined jacket with one hand and shouted into the phone with the other.

"Yes . . . That's perfect . . . Thank you! I'll be there in twenty minutes."

He slammed down the receiver and was halfway down the walk when he crashed into a figure coming up the walk. Frank Stewart staggered before regaining his balance.

Mac gripped the man's shoulders. "She signed it?" He scowled at the man as though the whole mess were his fault.

The lawyer placed a thick envelope in Mac's hand. "It's not—"

"Tell Dad I've hired a chopper to take me back to the ranch." Mac cut him off. "The north range is on fire. I'll call as soon as I'm able." He was in a hurry, but most of all he couldn't bear to hear the words. He'd not only lost Laura but also the ranch. He thrust the envelope inside his jacket pocket.

An hour later, he picked out the freeway and the small cluster of lights below that made up Snowville and wondered why he was rushing to save land that wasn't his anymore. He thought of his promise to Jake. Jake hadn't wanted the ranch broken up, but Mac suspected he hadn't meant for Laura to run it by herself and to own it all any more than he'd wanted Mac to have sole responsibility for it. He'd wanted to give her choices in life. His hand went to his pocket where he could feel the crackle of paper. At least he could help her for a while. He couldn't bring himself to pull out the paper and read it.

Mac asked the pilot to set him down near the narrow ribbon of orange staggering drunkenly five miles above Cherry Creek. Bureau of Land Management crews with heavy equipment were tearing up a strip of ground they hoped would be too wide for the fire to jump, and his own men and many of his neighbors fought the blaze with picks and shovels. Chance had driven his pickup truck to the edge of the fire strip. Mac tossed his jacket behind the seat of the truck, then reached for a shovel from the back and headed into the fray.

He shoveled dirt, lit back fires, and took turns spotting for the bulldozer operators through the long night and into the early morning. He prayed with each swing of his shovel. His face turned black with grime, and his muscles screamed for rest, but he fought on. Scrapes and bruises were ignored, as was the heat. The cabin was spared as the wind shifted, carrying the flames in a direct line toward the ranch house. He fought on. He'd let Laura down each time she had needed him. This time he would not.

It became a mantra over and over in his head. *For Laura! For Laura!* She wanted the ranch, and it was the only thing he could give her. He would not let it be destroyed by fire.

Chance and the other cowboys had already cleared the north range of cattle before Mac arrived, and he was grateful for their efforts to save the stock. The cowboys stood by to push the stock farther back if necessary. Finally, Mac made a dash for the machine shed for his biggest tractor. He attached a disc and began clearing a wide swath between the stubble and the approaching fire. If the fire could be stopped before it reached the grain stubble, the house and barns would be safe.

Smoke traveled toward him and dust mingled with the thick black cloud, causing his eyes to run and his throat to burn. He fumbled to tie a bandana across his face and struggled on.

Gradually, he became aware of a lessening of sound and a thinning of the cloud of smoke. One of the large Caterpillars drew near. He couldn't hear over the roar of the two engines, but the operator pointed back behind him and offered a weak smile. Mac lifted his eyes to see only a few smoldering spots of flame. He continued to widen the fire break.

With the dawn came a certainty that the fire was under control. It wasn't as bad as the fire eight years earlier had been. BLM crews had arrived much more quickly, and he'd worked faster and driven his crew harder. Their efforts had paid off. At last, he stood on a blackened hill, breathing the acrid air, and knowing he had won. The fire was stopped. By late afternoon, it was out.

After the BLM crew and Mac's neighbors left, he remained behind to watch for hot spots. He alternated between scanning the blackened acres with field glasses and thanking God for getting him through another fire. When Chance relieved him at about four o'clock the next morning, he stumbled through a few chores before falling into an exhausted slumber in the bunkhouse. His last thought was of Laura.

When he awoke late in the afternoon, his first thought was also of Laura. He wondered when she would arrive to claim the ranch. He should go up to the house and clear out all of his and Dad's things. He got as far as the kitchen.

"Flip those pancakes, boss," Chance called as Mac walked through the door. "You ought to hire yourself a real cook."

Chance always complained when Hal wasn't at the ranch to do the cooking. "Connie'll be here any minute, and she'll have my hide if breakfast ain't over and dishes done afore she gits here."

Connie? Mac shook his head. Of course, Connie Flowers, who worked part-time at the café in Snowville. She always showed up to take over his kitchen and keep his men fed during roundup. Roundup started today. It had completely slipped his mind. The cattle from the north range had already been brought into the lower ranges ahead of the fire by Chance and his men. That would save time and shorten the roundup, but there was still plenty to do.

He glanced out the window to see neighboring ranchers and the extra hands he had hired pouring into the yard with horse trailers. There wasn't time to clear out his things. He hoped that if Laura showed up, she'd understand.

Mac had always enjoyed roundups. He liked riding out over the open rangeland, scouring the brush and hidden draws for the cattle and watching the herd grow as small groups were united with the main herd. It gave him a feeling of continuity with the land and the rugged cowboys who trailed herds from Texas to Idaho during the nineteenth century. He used to dream of someday teaching his sons to ride, to search the gullies for strays, and to enjoy the hot sun on their backs and the cool breezes blowing down from higher peaks. Somehow, he'd always pictured a young girl with spiky brown braids and a wide grin riding along with those sons. Now there was a particular poignancy to each task he performed, knowing it was the last time he would survey this range and "boss" the roundup.

This year, Mac's thoughts were bleak. He didn't suppose he would ever have a son or the little girl with stiff braids he'd often imagined riding a pony across this land. He tried not to think about Laura, but she haunted him night and day.

Rhonda rode out with the men the first few days of the roundup, but she avoided speaking to Mac after he growled at her the first time she attempted to touch his arm. After that, she kept her distance. The cowboys kept their distance, too.

Each evening, he wondered if Laura would be there at the house when the men returned, but a week passed and she never came. The nights were long and lonely, filled with dreams of Laura. In the mornings, he couldn't face himself in the mirror, so he stopped shaving. His temper grew short, and the men knew better than to try to satisfy their curiosity by asking questions about Laura.

Once the cattle were gathered, the men began the process of separating the cattle to be sold from the breeding stock Mac planned to keep. He avoided as long as possible making arrangements for their sale. He wasn't certain he still had the authority to act for the ranch.

Finally, braving the office where Laura had so firmly left her mark, he was impressed to discover she had left checks awaiting his signature to pay the cowboys he'd hired. He only needed to dial a telephone number and trucks would begin arriving to haul away the cattle to be sold. He whistled when he saw the price she had negotiated for the cattle. She might know nothing about ranching, but she certainly wasn't a novice to business.

She still hadn't arrived by the time roundup was over. He suspected she was allowing him plenty of time to move out. With a heavy heart, he began gathering his clothing and personal items from his bedroom, packing them in boxes.

He felt like a ghost moved with him everywhere he stepped in the house. He saw her in the kitchen teetering on a bar stool while she ate her breakfast, he could see her pale and weak in the bedroom after the accident, and he stood staring at the piano imagining her bending her sleek hair over the keyboard. He saw her curled in the porch swing with Shep's head in her lap. He watched her long legs cover the ground between the house and barn or run across the golden grain stubble.

When he got to the cabin, it was worse. He imagined her scent still hung in the air. The quilt he'd wrapped around her was unbearable to touch. He couldn't look at the chocolate-stained mugs still resting beside the tin washbasin. Surely, he was going mad! After hauling the boxes from his truck to the cabin, he couldn't bring himself to unpack. He sat at the table with his head in his hands for hours until long after the sun dipped behind the western peaks.

He had been so wrong about her. She hadn't been spoiled and pampered. That old dragon of an aunt had punished and threatened until all the spunkiness had gone out of her. He grew angry thinking of his impetuous little tomboy being forced into lacy dresses and patent leather shoes to sit for hours listening to concerts when her heart cried out for jeans and boots and wide open skies.

She hadn't known her mother was dying and that it was her illness that had made her increasingly remote. He'd read that in her face when that attorney friend of hers was talking. He wished he could have another chance to explain to her how much her father loved her and that the marriage he had pushed on her was to protect her more than the ranch. Jake had known Alice was a bitter, twisted woman, and he had trusted Mac and his old friend Hal to take Laura home and give her the chance at a life he knew Alice would deny her. Jake had a deep faith in God, and that had been part of his concern. He'd wanted his daughter to grow up in the Church, to have an opportunity to learn the gospel free of her aunt's hate and bitterness. Why hadn't Mac been able to see the hurt, lonely little girl inside the grown-up Laura?

He sat on the lumpy, old sofa with his bowed head in his hands. He'd tried his way and lost. Not only had he lost what he held most dear, but he'd let Jake down. He began to pray.

Father, I failed her. The first time she left, I was too young to do anything about it. The second time, I accepted lies without question. I lost my final chance through fear. I mistrusted her and refused to listen. I chased her away. If only I'd sought Thy help instead of reacting out of fear. I don't suppose a man gets more than three chances, so I'm just asking Thee to please help her find happiness. As he prayed a slow peace filled him. He felt comforted that he had saved the ranch for her, just as Jake had wished. He was glad about that, though he hated not being part of her future. Knowing he'd lost her again brought back the searing pain of the time when he believed her dead. He prayed harder and felt a small measure of peace again.

If she didn't find another foreman right away, perhaps he'd still be able to see her. Knowing that she was alive and would be living in the ranch house pleased him. He wouldn't be her husband, but at least he could watch out for her, look after her interests. It wasn't the life he had dreamed of, but it was better than believing there was no hope of meeting her again in this life. Perhaps he could do one more thing for her. He'd talk to Bishop Eames and see if he would approach her about having the missionaries teach her. She'd confided in him once, as they rode that fancy combine, that her mother had taken her to be baptized but that she really knew nothing about the Church. As long as she was alive and he was alive, he would hope and pray for her happiness.

"Guess I'd better bring the rest of my things in," he said to Shep, who had accompanied him to the cabin. When the last box had been taken inside, Mac picked up his fleece-lined jacket, dirty and stained from its long sojourn behind the seat of the truck. He had forgotten about tossing it there the night of the fire, but suddenly he remembered the papers he had placed in its pocket. He drew the envelope out and looked at it where it lay limp and lifeless in his hand. The time had come; he had to look at the papers.

They didn't look the same. His signature wasn't at the bottom. There was no check, no instructions for the ranch. Slowly, the letters formed words, and the words formed sentences. It was a transfer of deed! She was giving him back the ranch—every acre, every cow, the house, the piano, and even that monstrous yellow combine. It was all his. She wasn't coming back!

His fingers crushed the paper. He leaned against the side of his truck for support. *Why would she do such a thing? She'd rather give it all up than live near me or have anything to do with me! She hates me that much! I'll refuse the ranch! No, she'll just sell it to someone else. But if I accept, I'll never see her again!* Mac stared bleakly down a long corridor of years filled with regrets.

At last, he decided he would accept her gift. He would keep the ranch because it was his only link to his old dreams, but the years ahead would be lonely and joyless. He'd never know whether she married or if she was happy. He'd never know if somewhere a little girl with brown, spiky braids galloped a pony across a green meadow.

twenty

LAURA CLOSED THE last box with a sigh. Bruce would be here any minute to help her move her belongings from his mother's house. The apartment she'd found was small but in a beautiful neighborhood overlooking the bay. Bruce was wild about the view and highly vocal about the parties she could hold on her fourth floor deck, but she would have preferred sagebrush and wheat stubble in exchange for a view.

A few months earlier, she wouldn't have dared lease an apartment in such an expensive neighborhood nor contemplated living alone. Now money seemed unimportant, and being physically alone seemed nowhere close to the difficulty of facing the rest of her life without Mac.

"Do you need any help?" Aunt Amy paused in the doorway. She had urged Laura to stay longer and told her repeatedly that there was no reason to rush into finding an apartment. In the weeks since her return to San Francisco, she'd grown close to Bruce's mother and regretted that Aunt Alice had kept their association severely limited during the years she was growing up, particularly after the accident. Resisting the urge to yield to the anger and bitterness that thoughts of Aunt Alice generally brought to her mind was becoming easier. She had Aunt Amy and the bishop of the ward she'd been attending to thank for that.

"I'm all finished." She crossed the room to give her aunt a hug. Aunt Amy, Uncle Alec, and Bruce were the only family she could claim now.

"Laura, I wish you'd reconsider. This has been too much for you. You've lost so much weight, and the dark circles under your eyes tell me you're not sleeping at night. You remind me of your mother after she left Jake. She couldn't sleep and was so sad back then." Amy kept an arm around her.

"Do you know why she left?" All she'd learned the past few months seemed to contradict her long-held belief that her mother was unhappy and unwanted on the ranch. Aunt Alice had told her so many lies; she no longer knew what to think about her parents' relationship.

"I don't think she meant to leave him when she came back here," Amy answered thoughtfully, drawing Laura to sit beside her. "April had fallen a few times and was having vision problems. She came to see a doctor and was diagnosed as being in the early stages of multiple sclerosis. With Aunt Alice's encouragement, she became convinced she couldn't return to her life on the ranch so far from medical assistance. Alice encouraged her to believe she would be a burden to Jake if she returned. It was much later that her doctor found the tumor, and by then, it was inoperable."

"What about Daddy? Why didn't he give up the ranch and come with us if Mother needed to be near a doctor?"

"He never knew. April didn't want him to give up the life he loved, so she never told him. For years, only she and Alice knew. He came to see you both and tried to change her mind, but Alice told him to stay away and that his visits were too upsetting for you. April couldn't bear saying good-bye over and over, and she couldn't handle the scenes Alice created each time he came. April loved Jake too much to keep him tied to an invalid, yet her sacrifice and all the misery they both went through was wasted. Jake never stopped loving April and refused to divorce her. Alice finally convinced him to stop coming."

"He upset me?"

"You staged terrible tantrums for almost a year after April brought you to San Francisco. Each time Jake came, you demanded to be allowed to go home with him. When he'd leave, you'd scream for your daddy, your horse, and your friend. Alice would lock you in your room to keep you from running away to find them. From what you and Bruce have told me, your friend must have been Jake's partner's son, Mac."

Mac! The man who had stepped so briefly into her life and back out. She was learning she was more like her father than she had supposed. He'd loved only once and had refused the freedom April had offered him, and Laura suspected she too would love only once.

Pasting a determined smile on her face, she refused to allow Mac and dreams of the life they might have had together lessen her resolve to get on with her life. She'd attended a nearby ward since her return to San Francisco a couple of weeks earlier, and the bishop had arranged for her to take the missionary lessons. He'd also taken the time to speak with her and offer counsel. Her growing faith was the only joy in her life.

"If you don't want to stay here with us, you could go down the coast for a week or two to lie in the sun, or you could take a cruise." Laura's attention was drawn back to Aunt Amy. "It might be that a rest is all you need. From all you and Bruce have told me, your stay in Idaho was not very restful."

"It's not that I don't want to stay here. I just need to get out on my own. I need to find a job."

"A job! If you never work day in your life, you'll still have plenty of money!"

"It's not the money. Besides, I'm not certain I want to keep the money my great-grandfather had a dubious right to in the first place. I'm thinking of donating a portion of my trust fund back to the Church. Besides, I need to do something; I can't spend my life doing nothing."

"Of course. And I'm sure you'll find something wonderful." Aunt Amy shook her head. "I'm sorry, but I just can't get over April having all that money. I knew Alec had inherited from his father and that Alice resented that he had received her father's money when she was the one who had stood by him and assisted him in his cause. We thought Alec was his father's only heir. He always felt guilty that his little sister had nothing and was dependent on Alice. He even tried to get custody of April, but he was only eighteen when their parents died, and the judge felt she would be better cared for by a woman. Later, April refused to accept money from him, and when she inherited her share, she never mentioned it to Alec."

"I suspect she never really wanted the money, especially after she joined the Church and learned where the money had come from."

Amy laughed and shook her head. "I can't take in how Alice schemed to keep that money from you and your mother. If she were extravagant and wanted a lot of fancy things, I could understand better, but you know how she was. She never spent a dime, if she could help it, on anything except supporting some hate group that opposes everything the Mormons do. She never even had a telephone or a car."

"I don't think it was only misplaced hatred," Laura defended her aunt. "It wasn't right for her father to never acknowledge her loyalty or sacrifices. He ruined her chance of marrying, then unfairly left her with no means of support. She had so little; she learned early to hang on to the little bit she had. When Bruce and I cleared out her house, we counted thirty-seven boxes of papers she had accumulated in her lifetime. I doubt she ever discarded anything. To her, I was one more thing she had to fight to hang on to."

"Oh, honey, I'm sure she loved you. It wasn't just the money. She was harder on you than she was on April because she was older by the time you came. Your early stubbornness and temper made her uncertain she could control you, and when Mac informed her you had married him, she must have been frightened of losing both you and her income."

"The hardest part for me to forgive is that she knew I was married and that I had no memory of it. She withheld that information from me and encouraged me to commit bigamy. She was determined that I should marry that grandson of her friend who is president of the symphony board." Tears began to fall.

Amy held the sobbing girl in her arms. "She was old, Laura, and she never had been able to accept that things were any way other than the way she wanted them to be."

Laura turned away, reaching for a box of tissues. "I'm sorry, Aunt Amy. I didn't mean to turn into a watering pot. Someday, I hope I can forgive her completely, but I'm not there yet. Bruce will be here any minute, and I want to get most of this downstairs before he arrives." She picked up a box and started down the stairs just as the doorbell rang.

"I guess he forgot his key again," Amy said.

"No, he gave it to me. I plan to give it back to him today," she called back to her aunt as she flung open the door to see the man who was never far from her thoughts standing before her.

Mac! No! It couldn't be. She closed her eyes tightly. She'd seen his face everywhere she looked for weeks. He haunted her night and day until she wondered if she were losing her mind. For just a moment, she'd thought he stood on Aunt Amy's front step.

"Laura." Now she was hearing his voice. Her eyes slowly opened. Brown eyes stared into steel gray.

"Mac!" Her voice came out in a strangled whisper. She took an involuntary step backward.

"Don't close the door." He reached past her to place his hand on the door. "There are a few things I have to say before you kick me out of your life for good. Is there someplace we can talk?"

"You must be Mac." Laura hadn't heard her aunt's approach. "Come in. Laura, why don't you take Mac into the family room and get him something to drink." She chattered amiably as she ushered them to the large sunny room at the back of the house. Blindly, they let her. In moments they found themselves facing each other across a low table loaded with a tall pitcher of juice and two glasses filled with ice.

Laura's hand trembled as she reached for the pitcher. Mac's hand stopped her.

"I didn't come for a drink or small talk, Laura. I came because I had to see you."

"No, Mac, you didn't have to come. I meant it. The ranch is yours. I should never have interfered in your life." She had to think of some way to get him out of here. If he didn't leave quickly, she'd lose the slim hold she had on her self-control. She'd throw pride out the window and make a total fool of herself. She'd be telling him she loved him and beg him to take her back to the ranch with him.

"I have to say this, and then I'll go," he promised. His long legs carried him to the window where he stood for long minutes with his back to her. At last, he turned to face her. "Laura, I wasn't honest with you. I was never even honest with myself. When your mother took you away, I cried and carried on for weeks. Once, I ran away. I was on my way to find you and bring you back when Dad caught up to me halfway to Snowville. It took no small effort to convince myself I didn't need some little kid tagging me around before I could face the fact that you were gone."

She felt the urge to go to him. His face was contorted with remembered pain. "It was so long ago, Mac. We were children."

Mac turned to face her, his voice harsh. "But not the second time. You were, but I was a man when I lost you again. You were so beautiful, and I was embarrassed by how much I was attracted to you. You married me because your father was dying and he begged you to, but I married you because I wanted to be your husband. I wanted to hitch a ride and follow that helicopter to the hospital, but Dad insisted we return to the ranch and arrange for Jake's burial first. When we got there, we found the place was an inferno with wildfire bearing down on the ranch buildings. Stock was dying, and I couldn't leave. I thought I would die, too, when I got that letter telling me you were dead. For the next eight years, I lived for that ranch because it was all I had left of you. The ranch wasn't for me, it was for you. It was always for you."

"Mac! Why didn't you ever tell me all this?" She stood up and reached for him. His hands closed around her upper arms, holding her away.

"Don't stop me now, Laura. I have to say it all." His eyes looked shadowed, and his hair was mussed where his fingers repeatedly ran through it.

"The third time is supposed to be the charm," Mac continued with a note of bitterness in his voice. "When you first arrived at the ranch, I couldn't believe you were really my Laura. I think I knew in my heart long before my head finally got the message." He cast a quick, oblique glance Laura's way. "Once I realized who you were, I let fear—fear you would leave again, fear that I'd lose the ranch—goad me into trying to force you to stay or to relinquish your inheritance. I'm sorry. It was wrong of me. And now you've given it all up. It's just not right."

"Thank you, Mac, for your apology. But it's best this way." She struggled to hold back her emotions. "I can't run the ranch by myself, and I came to see that I wouldn't be comfortable working so closely with you if you decided to pursue

Rhonda after all. I do love the ranch, and I will miss it, but it will be easier for me knowing someone who loves it is there." What did it matter if she made a fool of herself? In a few minutes he'd walk out of her life. She couldn't look him in the eye, but she had to say the words, just once.

"Mac." Her voice was whisper soft. "I know you don't want to hear this, but there's something else I have to say. I grew up feeling unloved and unwanted . . ." He moved toward her, and she held up one hand. "No, I have to tell you. I have since discovered that much of what I believed before is untrue, but a couple of months ago, I went to the High Country believing my father had abandoned my mother and me because of that ranch. I expected to hate it, but I didn't. It felt like home to me. I wanted to hate you for what I thought you had taken from me—not just my property but also my father. Instead, I fell in love with you. When I saw you with Rhonda, I realized that our own relationship couldn't work out."

Mac took her by the hand. She looked up at him, not sure what to expect.

He looked dazed. "I'm sorry," he said. "Our relationship was all in her mind. By not taking her seriously and putting a stop to her fantasy, I hurt her. I regret that and have apologized to her. She understands now that there will never be anything between her and me. She knows, too, that if you had really been dead, no other woman would have ever taken your place. There has never been anyone but you."

Laura's mind seemed to move at a snail's pace as she struggled to reconcile his words with the assumptions and pain of the past couple of months.

"Answer one question for me please, Laura." Mac's voice held leashed excitement. "Do you still love me, or did I manage to make you hate me?"

"I love you." The words barely carried past her lips as she buried her face against his chest.

"Laura, are we still married? You haven't . . . ?"

"No, I couldn't . . ."

"Good." His arms closed around her. "I don't care whether the ranch is yours or mine, but I do care about being married to you." He held her away from him so he could look into her eyes. "But I want more than the hasty words you don't even remember. I love you. I always have, and I always will. Will you be my wife for eternity?"

Laura's smile reached her damp eyes. "Yes, I will."

Mac leaned toward her for a kiss, and she closed the distance. It was a moment of tenderness infused with the excitement they felt for their future together.

"You know, it may be months before I can get a recommend from my bishop. I'm taking the missionary lessons, and I already know the gospel is true, but in spite of my childhood baptism, in most ways I'm a new convert." She no longer doubted that the papers Bruce found told the truth: she was a Mormon, and she was married to Mac. But she was glad Mac understood her need to repeat the vows. This time, she knew nothing would make her forget the promises they would make. Heavenly Father would be a part of their lives, and this time, their vows would last forever.

"I've waited eight years for this. I think I can wait a few more months." Mac grinned broadly. "Besides, it might not be a bad idea for us to go out on a date or two before we have the wedding."

She laughed and agreed. "You may have a point there."

"So, Mrs. Burgoyne, which temple would you like to be sealed in? Oakland? Salt Lake? Twin Falls? It's the closest one to *our* ranch." He squeezed her hand, leaving the choice to her.

"I like the Twin Falls idea," Laura murmured. "We'll be able to go there often, and it will be a reminder that we love each other enough to be married twice—for now and forever."

About the Author

JENNIE HANSEN GRADUATED from Ricks College in Idaho, then Westminster College in Utah. She has been a freelance magazine writer, newspaper reporter, editor, and librarian.

Her published novels fall in several genre categories including romantic suspense, historical, and westerns.

She was born in Idaho Falls, Idaho, and has lived in Idaho, Montana, and Utah. She has received numerous first and second place writing awards from the Utah and National Federation of Press Women and was the 1997 third place winner of the URWA Heart of the West Writers Contest. She was awarded the 2007 Whitney's Lifetime Achievement Award.

Jennie has been active in community affairs and currently serves in the Jordan River Temple. In addition to ward and stake responsibilities in the LDS Church, she served a term on the Kearns Town Council, two terms on the Salt Palace Advisory Board, and was a delegate to the White House Conference on Libraries and Information Services.

Jennie and her husband, Boyd, live in Salt Lake County. Their five children are all married and have provided them with ten grandchildren. When she's not reading or writing, she enjoys spending time with her grandchildren, gardening, and camping.

Jennie Hansen loves to hear from her readers. She can be contacted through her blog: www.notesfromjenniesdesk.blogspot.com